3 Ways to Wear Red
A Jennifer Cloud Novel

XO
Janet Leigh

JANET LEIGH

ISBN-13: 9781545381991
ISBN-10: 1545381992
Library of Congress Control Number: 2017906199
CreateSpace Independent Publishing Platform
North Charleston, South Carolina

For my two favorite fashionistas, who love the color pink:
Joanna Adrian and Karla Perry.

Joanna: thank you for giving me Ian.

Karla: thank you for sharing your story of Toecheese.

Prologue

*L*egs dangling, the little girl sat at the antique dressing table, admiring a display of delicate perfume bottles. The large, round mirror attached to the back of the dressing table reflected each elegant piece of décor and her cherubic face. She twisted a strand of her long blond hair as she glanced over her shoulder at the door. Seeing no one, she reached out with a chubby hand and squeezed the pink bulb of the atomizer, causing a fine mist of White Shoulders perfume to cascade across her chest. Inhaling deeply, she replaced the bottle carefully on the table.

Hooking her feet around the chair legs for balance, she leaned back and pulled open a long drawer that held an array of lipsticks, eye shadows, and blushers. She would try on just the lipstick. The pink tube revealed a creamy hot-pink color that she had trouble keeping in the lines of her lips.

She examined her face in the mirror. Her eyes looked pale in comparison to her lips. She opened the peacock-blue eye shadow and was surprised to find a tiny brush inside. The blue would just match the color of her eyes. She used the brush and stroked the blue powder across her eyelid, as she saw her mother do each morning while she dressed for work. Her mother's eye shadows were not as glamorous, however. They were browns and grays, not like the rainbow of colors the little girl had found in the drawer.

She admired herself in the mirror. The part of her eyes above her eyelids looked naked in comparison to her new blue lids. She chose a shimmering neon green and loved the way it sparkled next to the blue as she covered every inch from her eyelid to her brow.

The girl was delighted to find a pair of false eyelashes in a clear box hidden under a blusher. She opened the eyelashes and tried to dab them with a bit of the special glue to make them stick. The glue wouldn't work. The eyelashes peeled up and fell off. The girl decided her own long eyelashes had prevented their attachment. Jumping down from the chair, she knew exactly where to find the solution.

In the next room, a little boy was dressed in the official Native American headdress of a warrior chief and was stepping on the long train of feathers it trailed as he danced around the room. He wore the headdress proudly and pretended to shoot arrows at his plastic cowboys.

The girl interrupted him. She wanted to borrow his scissors. He knew he wasn't supposed to let her have them—she was too little—but she made him a bargain he couldn't refuse. She would use the makeup to draw real warrior paint on his face and chest. He agreed, but only if she would allow him to borrow her Barbie dolls to use as settlers. The agreement was made, and a few minutes later, he looked like the warrior chief he was meant to be.

The boy climbed up on the wrought-iron bed to retrieve the supply box from his backpack and removed the scissors. The box had Darth Vader on the top and was tattered from the school year.

The girl watched the boy toss his supply box back on the bed. She took better care of her things—her Little Mermaid box looked brand-new. A wooden trunk with intricately carved wolves on its sides sat on the floor next to the bed. The girl peeked inside.

"Why aren't you wearing the necklace?" the girl asked, lifting a medallion on a silver chain from the box.

"Necklaces are for girls," he said and handed her the scissors.

"I think it's a charm...you know, like to keep the bad spirits away."

The boy stopped and stared at the medallion. "Put it on me," he demanded.

The girl did as she was told and used the lipsticks to draw a few more lines on the boy's face. When he was satisfied, she returned to the dressing table. Sitting on her knees in the chair, she leaned in close to the mirror and carefully snipped the first eyelash. It made a little click and tickled as it hit her cheek and fell to the glass-topped table. For the next few minutes, it was click...tickle...click...tickle... click...tickle...until her left eye was free of the lashes in the way of her full and luscious falsies. As she reached for the set of false eyelashes to glue it to the now-smooth ridge on her eyelid, she heard a commotion in the other room.

The boy was in trouble. She knew the tone of the woman's voice. The girl slid off the chair and peeked into the next room. The woman was tall and smelled of the same perfume the girl had sprayed earlier. Her bottle blond hair, pinned up in a twist, matched the angry twist of her lips. The woman was kind, and the girl loved staying at her house after preschool, but she was angry about something the boy had done.

Hands placed firmly on her hips, the woman asked, "Land sakes, where'd you git that?"

"Aint Elma gave it to me," he said.

"She shouldn't of done that," the woman scolded. "And where'd you git that paint on your face?"

"She did it." The boy pointed at the girl.

The woman turned to see the little girl at the same moment the little girl noticed her Barbies scalped and hanging by tiny nooses from the wrought-iron bed frame.

The little girl screamed, and a second woman came running. She was slender, shorter than the first woman, and had bright-blue eyes. The little girl had met her only a few times but enjoyed her funny stories about faraway places.

"Why did you give him those?" The tall woman pointed at the newly arrived woman.

"He should have them," the short woman said, dropping to her knees and wrapping her thin arms around the boy. "He might need them one day."

"Not as long as I draw breath," said the first woman. "Take them off," she commanded. The boy's lips started to tremble, and tears began to wet his cheeks.

"Did you have to make them cry?" the second woman asked, drawing the little girl into a hug.

"This one is missing her eyelashes, and this one scalped all the Barbies," the tall woman said, pointing at each child in turn. The little girl cried harder, clutching one of the hairless Barbies to her chest. "What are we going to tell the parents?"

Chapter 1

I woke to a loud banging against my wall. My bed vibrated from the force of each thrust. They were at it again. I pulled my pillow over my head, trying to drown out the noise and get another hour of sleep, but it was no use. I knew from past experience this would go on for another fifteen to twenty minutes. Brodie has stamina—I'll give him that.

From the time my cousin Gertie and my coworker Brodie began hooking up, my nights had been interrupted. Still, I knew I shouldn't complain, because I'd never seen Gertie so happy.

A shiver of excitement ran through my body as I thought about the day ahead. I, Jennifer Cloud, am a transporter for the WTF, otherwise known as the World Travel Federation. I inherited a genetic gift from my great-aunt Elma Jean Cloud, lovingly referred to as Aint Elma. She was a kind old woman with a deep dark secret: she, and now I, can travel in time. Not to the future, where I could possibly get a glimpse of my future self or find out the winning lottery numbers and live blissfully rich for the rest of my life. No, I am able to travel only to the past.

When I accidentally discovered I also had this gift, my whole world changed. Not many people can say they met the guy they are dating in the year 1568. I've heard it's not a good idea to date someone you work with, but so far, we have managed to keep our love affair in check. Caiyan taught me how to use my gift, along with the other two pieces

1

that allow me to time travel: my vessel and my key. *I* taught *him* what a blonde with long legs can do in the bedroom. I reached up and ran my fingers across my empty décolleté. The place just below my neck in the hollow of my throat was cold and vacant. Smiling to myself, I hoped my key would be there very soon.

I threw off the cozy blankets and pulled on a robe. Bending over, I scooped my hair up on top of my head and wound it into a messy bun. After I secured it with a hair elastic, I checked my face in the mirror. Having a man in the house so early in the morning put a kink in my habit of wandering downstairs in my nightshirt and crazy hair.

I examined my face in the mirror over my antique dressing table. Was that a pimple on my chin? I moved in a little closer for a better look. My mantra began to play in my head, and I immediately jerked the record from its invisible turntable. Not today. A little pimple threat was not going to scare me. I gave myself the stamp of approval to go downstairs and make coffee.

When I walked out into the hall, Gertie's attack cat was sitting guard outside her bedroom door. Brodie had kicked him out of his normal sleeping spot in Gertie's bed.

"Rough night, huh, Smoke?" I asked the cat as I reached down to scratch him behind the ears. He gave me a gentle swat with his paw. I considered this his way of high-fiving me. He followed me downstairs in a kindred bond against the sleep wreckers.

Gertie and I lived in my childhood home, a two-story, four-bedroom town house in the small town of Sunnyside, Texas. My parents had bought it because it reminded my mom of her brownstone in New York. After my parents moved to a community for adults over fifty, they rented the town house to me. I couldn't afford my shoe fetish and the town house by myself, so Gertie moved in while she finished her studies at SMU.

A steaming pot of coffee was waiting for me in the kitchen, and I silently thanked the inventor of the programmable coffeemaker—and Gertie—for planning ahead. Smoke rubbed against my leg, demanding a cat treat. I complied and then poured myself a cup of coffee. He gobbled it up and licked his paw with satisfaction. I stirred sugar in my coffee and walked over to the sliding glass door. Brushing aside the sheer curtain,

I looked out at the small fenced-in backyard. This was the big day. If the WTF gave its stamp of approval, I should get my key back today.

My vessel sat in the backyard, surrounded by a haunted aura of depression. The outhouse was tall and made of solid wood with remnants of green paint streaked through its planks. The emblem of my key was carved above the door—a crescent moon with tiny stars dancing around it. I often wondered how these ordinary objects became vessels, but no one really knows the secret. I was told the gods had given this gift originally to a tribe of Ancalites, an ancient Celtic people, but the history of the gift is all speculation. I took a sip of my coffee and surveyed the small space.

Normally, my backyard was bursting with glorious plants and flowers, thanks to my vessel's green thumb. When my outhouse was in the same spot for more than twenty-four hours, the landscape became the Garden of Eden, but since I've been grounded, the flowers looked wilted, and a spot of crabgrass threatened to take over the area. My outhouse liked to travel, and my inability to do so was reflected by the surroundings.

A walking path led from the back gate to the covered patio, where a wrought-iron table and chairs were centered next to a rusty barbecue grill. I opened the door to let the cat out for his morning stroll. A cool April breeze swept inside, along with the whooping of a whip-poor-will alerting the other birds that Attack Cat was in the vicinity.

I closed the door and sat down at the kitchen table, pulling my feet up under me. My legs were lean and muscular from my training. The WTF's main job is to chase bad guys, also known as brigands. These brigands relentlessly travel back in time to pillage, plunder, despoil, and fleece the poor, unsuspecting residents of whatever time they choose. We are sent back by the WTF to stop them.

Time travel is somewhat finicky, and there are a lot of rules. Some of these rules are inherent with our genetic gift, and some of them are meant to be broken, mainly the rules enforced on us by the WTF. Our travel is concurrent with the day and time of the present, but thank God we can travel only during the full-moon cycle, or I could be living my life without indoor plumbing.

The defenders do the stopping. Since they normally can't carry two people in their vessels, if they are lucky enough to catch the brigand, they summon the transporters. We escort the brigand back to the WTF. Except I haven't traveled in a while. I was grounded for disobeying my commanding officer. The WTF frowned on my inability to follow orders and locked up my key. In the short time I have been a time traveler, I've broken the code and taken Gertie back in time, accidentally, of course. I prevented a murder, which somehow managed to screw up the past, which meant I screwed up the future; I also caused Caiyan to lose his key. I don't consider the last one my fault. We travelers have only about three to five days to get our mission accomplished and return home. If we don't return, the time portal closes, and we are stuck in the past until the next month, when it opens again. When the portal snaps shut, it's very painful for the traveler and not something I ever plan to experience.

On his last travel, Caiyan stayed to help an old friend, and I went back to save him. Somehow things went awry, Caiyan had to cut a deal with a nasty little brigand and trade his key to save me. Caiyan is the WTF's best defender, and the head honchos were pretty pissed when he showed up without a key.

I was looking forward to getting my key back. The lateral travel was the main reason I hadn't run away from this job screaming with fear—I can travel to any part of the world, anytime I want, as long as I fly under the radar. This means I don't get into trouble, and I don't allow anyone to see my outhouse. If I travel at night, I can usually do this without being detected.

In order to see each other, Caiyan and I relied on the help of Ace, a fellow transporter, to haul our butts around. Only a transporter can carry one or two extra riders. Occasionally, if Ace was unavailable, Caiyan would use his company's jet and come see me. Lately, his visits had been few and far between. He has a business in New York dealing mostly in art and antiquities. Go figure. He has an apartment in the city that overlooks Central Park, a flat in London, and a country house in Scotland. I've visited only the New York address. It had been three months since the last time we'd been together. He frequently traveled out of the country on business, and this trip was the longest one yet. He had agreed we should meet as soon as I received my key.

My inner voice pulled out her planner, and I mentally perused my day. Keeping up with the pretenses of my normal life, I would go to work at my brother Eli's chiropractic office, located in the quaint town of Coffee Creek. After I returned home from work, Ace would pick me up and whisk me away to headquarters, where my boss would convince the military commander in charge of the WTF I am ready to resume my duties as a transporter. If everything went as planned, I would meet Caiyan in New York City. He would—I hoped—have dinner reservations at Marea, one of my favorite restaurants, and we'd engage in a much-anticipated night of romance. I was pretty pleased the former playboy had settled down and become the man of my dreams.

Brodie stumbled into the small kitchen, wearing a big grin on his face and sweatpants that hung loosely on his wiry frame. He was average height, and Gertie swore he resembled Keith Urban, the smokin' hot country singer, but I was leaning toward Shaggy from *Scooby-Doo*. He did have a nice set of abs, and if his sweats dropped any lower, I was going to see what else he had that was nice.

"G'day to ya," he said as he helped himself to the coffee.

"Good morning…sleep well?" I asked with a hint of sarcasm.

He flashed his megawatt smile at me. "I did. I take it ya didn't."

"Very funny. You two fornicate like rabbits. I don't know how you go to work every day."

"I'm like Thor. It gives me energy." He popped an English muffin in the toaster and took a sip of his coffee as he waited for the muffin. His goatee was perfectly groomed to the angles of his face, and his shoulder-length, brown hair was pulled back in one of Gertie's pink hair elastics.

"Well, Thor, you don't have to worry about keeping me awake tonight, because I'm getting my key back today."

"That's great—'ow is Caiyan handling that news?"

"What do you mean?"

"The fact that ya will be able to travel, and he will be left at home, sitting on his duff?" Brodie slathered butter on his muffin and joined me at the table.

I hesitated. I hadn't thought about how Caiyan would feel when I traveled without him. Would it be similar to a scenario where the husband lost his job, and the wife had to be the breadwinner? I knew money was not the issue with Caiyan, but would his ego stand the fact that I was going to travel again?

Gertie yawned as she came into the kitchen. "Good morning," she said, and I gave her the stink eye.

She smiled sheepishly, and I couldn't help but be happy for her. She had dated one loser after another until she finally connected with Brodie. It was a connection he had been blackmailed into; however, it turned out they had a lot more in common than he had anticipated, including equality in the sack. It was good she and I were both in relationships now. At least I *thought* I was. Caiyan used the term very loosely.

"The moon cycle opens tonight at midnight," Brodie said, taking a bite out of his breakfast. "Who are ya goin' to travel with?" His Australian accent hacked off pieces of each word, and I felt as if I was having a conversation with Crocodile Dundee.

"I don't know for sure if I'm getting my key back, or if I'm going to be allowed to travel."

"You're goin'," Brodie said. "That little fucker Mitchell Mafuso has been flyin' under the radar. You are the only one young enough to track him."

"What do you mean?" asked Gertie.

"He's been going back to the late nineteen eighties and early nineties. We can't get to him, because the rest of us were already alive then, and ya know we can't travel to a time when we're already born."

That was true. I'd thought I was going to lose Caiyan in a previous travel, when the dummy had given his key to a beautiful rock star and hadn't been able to get it back to make the travel home. The fact that he was being born in a week had never crossed his mind as he handed over his key.

"At least I'll have indoor plumbing," I said, taking another sip of my coffee. "I doubt my boss will let me go anywhere alone."

"I dunno; he's getting pretty desperate to get Caiyan's key back."

"That's just crap. Mitchell is using Caiyan's key," Gertie said. She made her way around the table, refilling everyone's coffee and setting a plate of English muffins on the table.

"Sure, it's a slap in the face," Brodie said. "The WTF even tried to trade Mitchell's key back for Caiyan's key, but the Mafusos refused."

"Why would they refuse?" I asked. This was news to me. I hadn't realized they'd tried to make an exchange. "Wouldn't Mitchell be happier with his own key?"

"You forget—they have Caiyan's vessel. We don't know what Mitchell's vessel looks like, and they know Caiyan can't travel without a vessel."

It was true. We had captured Mitchell, the youngest member of the Mafuso family, on a previous travel. The Mafusos were deep in the Mafia and had a number of travelers running through their bloodline. They were the biggest brigand threat and were continuously trying to recruit new members, including Caiyan's nephew, Campy, but we'd interceded, and now he was the youngest defender to work for the WTF.

Currently, Campy was training and approved only for lateral travel. Occasionally, he would pop over, and we would have a *Star Wars* marathon together. He had his uncle Caiyan's good looks and was already breaking hearts at his school in London.

I offered Gertie a muffin, and she shook her head and frowned at me. I'd forgotten she was on a no-bread diet. I sent her an apologetic shrug and took one for myself.

"Do you know where you are going this cycle?" I asked Brodie as I spread strawberry jam on my muffin.

"Ace and I've been trying to find the vessel for the Thunder key we found in Ireland." Brodie finished off another muffin and pulled Gertie into his lap. "We've been back to Ireland the past seven travels but can't seem to find any trace of the vessel."

Gertie giggled as Brodie kissed her hard on the mouth.

"You took it off a girl, right?" I asked and took a bite out of my muffin, the strawberry jam dropping to the plate.

This made Gertie frown, because Brodie and Caiyan seemed to sacrifice their bodies to get keys and information in the past. I was actually comforted that Caiyan wasn't time traveling, but there were still plenty of women right here in this time to be wary of.

"We did. She was a pretty gal, looked a little like my Gertie." The way he said "my Gertie" made her face turn a light shade of red.

"But she didn't have the gift, right?" I felt so disconnected from my team. During my suspension, I hadn't been allowed even to attend any meetings.

"No, she was a NAT," Brodie said, finishing his coffee. "We don't know where she got it. We had been back months and years prior to taking the key, and she never wore it until the night I snatched it from her pretty little neck."

"What's a NAT?" Gertie asked.

"You're a NAT," Brodie said, tapping Gertie on the tip of her nose. "Not-a-traveler."

"It's a term usually reserved for people who have family connections to a traveler but don't have the gift," I added. I thought about the girl and the Thunder key. It didn't really make sense that she had just given the key away.

Gertie giggled, and they rubbed noses. *Ick*, my inner voice sighed, but the outer me tried to stay focused on the problem with the Thunder key. I was either going to follow Mitchell or go to Ireland with Brodie and Ace. I was hoping to follow Mitchell. Bathrooms and junk food were high on my priority list; however, if Mitchell was flying back to the '90s, even I was too old.

"Maybe you should go back after you take the key to see what happens," I said, chewing on my muffin. "Whoever gave the girl the key surely would not be happy if she just gave it away to the first lusty Lawrence to come along."

"That's not a bad idea." He thought about this for a moment. Then he ran his hand up Gertie's leg, and they went back upstairs for round two.

Chapter 2

*A*fter a shower and an attempt at hair and makeup, I stood looking in the full-length mirror attached to the back of my bedroom door. Yellow smiley faces randomly sprinkled over bright-blue fabric stared back at me. I was constantly trying to get Mary, the office manager, to rethink the array of ridiculous scrubs we wore at the office. Eli thought they looked cute, but I felt like a poster child for an emoticon foundation. I headed downstairs to grab a cup of coffee for the road. Gertie was in the kitchen making an omelet.

"Mmm…smells good," I said to her.

"Thanks," she said, folding the egg over in a way that would make Paula Deen proud. "Ever since I started dating Brodie, I have been eating healthier. This omelet is egg whites, bell peppers, and onion. All organically grown, of course."

"Of course," I echoed as I poured coffee into my to-go mug. "Where's Brodie?"

"He had to leave, something about a cow issue back home." Brodie worked on his family ranch in Aussieland with his three brothers. He was the only one who had inherited the gene for time travel. Having a girlfriend in America was his excuse for the extended absences from home, and it worked out well for him.

Gertie watched as I took a spoon from the drawer and stirred three scoops of sugar into my coffee.

"I've also lost about ten pounds." She beamed.

"That's terrific," I said. I had noticed she was slimmer, and I made a mental note to cut back on the amount of sugar I added to my coffee.

"I can't believe all those fad diets I was on, and the trick was eating smarter."

I thought maybe the weight Gertie had lost was more from all her midnight activities with Brodie rather than the smarter eating choices.

"Do you want part of my omelet?" She gently maneuvered it from the pan to a plate.

"No, I'm late." I took my North Face jacket from the hook next to the door and waved to her as she sat down to enjoy her breakfast. "See you tonight."

I was so happy Gertie and Brodie were dating. It was fun to see them together. I had been a little skeptical, because he was a defender and with that came the misery of worrying about him when he traveled. I guess it was no different than dating a police officer. At least she only had to worry about him during the full moon.

I motored down the highway in my white Mustang, singing along with Adele. Her songs hit home, and I could relate to the pain in her voice. Men. I don't know why they cause so much heartache. I hoped Caiyan would be happy for me if I got my key back. I arrived at work five minutes late—pretty good for me. I parked and entered through the back door, as I normally do. There was a ruckus going on in the front office. I heard Mary say, "Dr. Cloud is never late. I'm going to call the police."

I speed walked to join them. "What do you mean by 'late'?" I asked.

Mary and the two other office girls, Elvira and Paulina, stopped talking and rushed toward me.

"Dr. Cloud is late," they chimed in unison.

"Thank God you are here, Jennifer," Paulina said, hugging me. I rolled my eyes at the excessive drama.

My brother is no saint, so I wasn't worried that he was late. "Maybe he overslept," I said.

"He has *never* been late," Mary said.

"Did anyone go upstairs to see if he's at home?" I asked. My brother lived above the chiropractic office, so he wasn't exactly stuck in traffic.

They looked at me like I was asking the inconceivable.

"We didn't want to disturb him if he was...you know, occupied," Elvira said, running her index finger through the circle made by her opposite fingers.

Ewww. Eli had been focused on his work, and I knew he wasn't dating anyone at the moment.

"Can you go check on him?" Mary asked.

I sighed and walked out the front door. The stairs were on the side of the building and reminded me more of a classy fire escape. They rattled as I took them two at a time, and I was proud I wasn't huffing when I reached the top. I knocked on the door. No answer.

I dug in my handbag for the spare key Eli had given me in case of an emergency. In my mind, an emergency was running out of lunch money and needing a sandwich. I hoped this was that kind of emergency.

I unlocked the door and slowly pushed it open. "Halloo?" I hollered as I entered his space. Eli's apartment was characteristic of the old buildings that surrounded the square. The vaulted ceiling was open to the rafters with exposed ductwork. His love of sailing was evident throughout the apartment. Nautical prints of sailboats and the ocean hung on the walls. I had a straight view past the small dining nook, through the galley kitchen, and on to the bedroom that lined the front of the apartment and overlooked the cobblestone streets and antiquated square of the picturesque town. His bedroom door was closed.

To the right was a small den that had a navy sectional sofa with navy-and white-striped throw pillows scattered about. An old trunk that looked like salvage from the Titanic sat in front of the sofa and held a white lantern, health magazines, and the TV remote. I caught the toe of my shoe on the jute rug that stuck out from under the sofa. The rug was new. My mom had definitely been here, adding her touch to Eli's decorating.

"Eli?" I called again as I moved past the round maple dining table toward the kitchen.

He came barreling out of his bedroom and shut the door behind him quickly. "Hey, sis. I'm running a little late today."

I raised an eyebrow in the direction of the bedroom. "Yes, the girls were worried and sent me to check on you."

He sort of laugh hiccupped. He was hiding something. Reaching for his white medical jacket, he grabbed my arm and escorted me out of his apartment. He started toward the stairs.

"Don't you want to lock the door?" I asked.

"Oh, yeah," he said. He adjusted his glasses and turned to put his key in the lock. He secured the door, and we started down to the clinic. I was surprised the staff wasn't waiting at the bottom like a group of cult worshippers.

"OK, what's going on?" I asked as we made the rest of the stairs.

He smiled. "I met the most amazing woman last night."

"And you have her held captive in your bedroom," I said, envisioning some poor girl strapped to the headboard with Eli's neckties.

"No," he said, grinning ear to ear. "She's in the shower."

Eli wasn't a stranger to dating. He was tall and had an athletic build combined with our father's good looks. I stood back and got a good glimpse of him. His jet-black hair, normally shellacked with a super-strength gel, was tousled. His eyes were bright blue but a little on the bloodshot side. He normally wore scrubs to the office, unless he had a meeting or a special event that required a shirt and tie. Today he must have had a meeting, because he wore a deep-purple dress shirt with the Ermenegildo silk tie I had given him for Christmas. This girl must be special for my brother to go full lab coat. I couldn't wait to meet her.

Eli and I entered the office through the back door. He was pulling on his lab coat when he was surrounded by the group of inquisitive women. The girls made a big fuss over Eli's tardiness. He assured them he had overslept.

"What?" he asked the curious faces.

"Dr. Cloud, have you been doing some *laundry?*" Elvira asked as she started to move her left index finger toward the OK sign formed by her right hand.

I shook my head no, and she halted midgesture.

My brother's face flushed slightly, and he did his best impersonation of looking confused. "Elvira, I haven't done *laundry* all week. In fact, I have a huge pile of *laundry* if you aren't busy on your lunch break."

Paulina giggled. "Dr. Cloud, I do my *laundry* every night."

"*Every* night?" Eli wiggled his eyebrows at her, and his glasses moved in sequence.

The three other women looked at her, shaking their heads. "Paulina," Mary said. "You are setting a bad example for the rest of us who only do *laundry* once a week."

Elvira nodded. "Yep, you do *laundry* every night, and the men expect it."

Paulina shrugged. "I like doing *laundry*. Sometimes I have to do it by myself, because my husband is watching football."

Eli held up his hands. "OK, ladies, you win this conversation. Yes, I met a nice girl, and I am taking her out to lunch today, so you can all get a good long look and get it out of your system."

The three of them looked at me as he retreated to his office for safety.

"When was the last time *you* did any *laundry*, Jennifer?" Paulina asked, concerned I might not be doing my *laundry* in a timely fashion.

I was saved by the first patient of the morning coming through the front door.

"Oh, gosh, there's Mr. McCreedy coming in for his treatment." I grabbed the chart and went to greet him.

I heard Elvira harrumph as I left the room. "I think that girl is doing *laundry* at more than one Laundromat."

Paulina added, "Do you think Mr. McCreedy can still do laundry?"

I escorted Mr. McCreedy back to the therapy room. I noticed something highlighted on the top of his chart: today was his seventy-third birthday.

"Happy birthday," I said as I prepared the decompression table.

"Thank you. I'm turning twenty-five today." He smiled as I helped him lie faceup on the table.

"That's too bad. Twenty-five is too young for me," I joked as I strapped the harness around his midsection, clipped the ring to it, and hooked him up to the machine.

"Well, I guess it's not too young for Doc Cloud. Saw him out last night with a real hottie."

"Yes, I heard he was dating a new girl," I said as I adjusted the settings on the machine. It started the slow, even pull that would give Mr. McCreedy relief from his lower-back disc problem.

"How is the weight today?" I asked.

"It's just fine. This machine has saved me from back surgery." I nodded, knowing many of our patients had good results with the machine. "In fact, the missus likes it too. I've been able to cut down on my Viagra. Those pills are twenty dollars each."

Well, that answered Paulina's question. I gave Mr. McCreedy the alert button to cut off the machine if he became uncomfortable. I charted what I had done and went to help the next patient.

The morning ran smoothly. Helga, the massage therapist, asked me if I wanted to grab lunch at the Italian place, and I agreed. A slice of pizza sounded great, and it would take my mind off the trip to headquarters and my key. When our acupuncturist had to leave the country on a family emergency, Helga had been her temporary replacement. Eli had an available room, and the patients had loved her. When the acupuncturist had returned, they had decided to share the space by alternating days.

We finished with the last patient, and Helga was cleaning her room. I was getting my handbag to walk around the square to the pizza place when the bell on the front door pinged. I went to see if a patient had forgotten something and stopped dead in my tracks. In the center of the waiting room stood my archenemy, Mahlia Mafuso.

Five foot ten inches of brigand occupied Eli's office. I didn't have a weapon except for my own fists, but I felt they would do a fine job. Her long brown hair hung like a perfectly ironed sheet down her back to her perfectly round butt. The dark skinny jeans and white button-down were accented with a Marc Jacobs fringed leather vest. She had on a pair of cute brown shorty boots that I had earmarked in *Vogue* just the week before. The bitch.

Here she was in my coveted shorty boots, looking amazing and coming at me in my workplace. I'd show her a thing or two. My inner voice popped open a switchblade as I marched out to the waiting room. My brother came out of the front office, cutting me off on my way to kick booty. He entered the reception room ahead of me.

"Jennifer, I'd like you to meet Mahlia." He took her hand, and she batted her fake eyelashes at him.

"Nice to meet you," she said, offering her other hand for me to shake and running her eyes over my smiley scrubs with a hint of laughter pulling at her Restylane-injected lips.

Oh, shit! Mahlia was Eli's special someone. My mind was racing. All the reasons why the bitch from hell would be dating Eli were being computed in my head like stats for the presidential election. I wanted to break every bone in her skinny body, but I felt myself pumping her hand up and down and saying, "Nice to meet you."

Her hand was hot to the touch, and I broke grip quickly. Mahlia gave me a half smile as Eli introduced her to the other girls. He announced they were going to eat at the barbecue restaurant and practically skipped out of the office behind her.

"I don't like her," Mary said after they left. "There is something fake about her."

Good vibes, Mary. Maybe she could talk some sense into Eli.

"I think she's pretty, and they have so much in common," Paulina gushed.

"Like what?" Mary asked.

Paulina thought about it for a second. "They're both tall."

Mary harrumphed at this, and they went to finish up in the office and close for lunch.

After they left, I turned to head out the back. My WTF boss needed to know about this. There was no way she'd accidentally met my brother. She was after something. I needed some privacy to make the call and my car was the closest, safest place. As I was fishing my cell phone out of my handbag, I bumped straight into Helga's chest. She was almost six feet tall and could have auditioned for WrestleMania.

"You not going to eat wit' me?" she asked in her strong German accent.

"Oh, Helga, so sorry—something's come up." I waved my cell at her as if I had an unexpected problem. Well, I did have a perfectly tanned and waxed problem that was humping my brother.

"No big deal. Helga has lunch with Paulina instead."

"OK, great. Have fun," I said as I fled out the back door.

The WTF is supervised by the CIA. My best friend and former lover, Jake McCoy, worked for the CIA. Initially, he hadn't known I was a traveler, and I hadn't known he'd been hired to oversee the WTF employees. The CIA always has its hands in the secrets of the world, and now Jake knew all my secrets.

As soon as I got to my car, I phoned Jake.

He answered on the second ring. "McCoy." His voice was touched with the sharp tone of an annoyed CIA agent.

"Jake, we have a problem. Mahlia is here in Coffee Creek, and she is with Eli." I practically yelled it into my cell.

"Jen, slow down," he said in his *Jen, get a grip* voice.

I repeated myself much slower this time, explaining the details of the situation. "Why would she be here?"

"I don't know," Jake said. "Are you sure Eli doesn't have the gift?"

"Well, I've never felt anything when I'm around him, and I've hugged him plenty over our lifetime—not even a tingle of energy." I tucked a loose strand of hair behind my ear and thought about Eli. Surely Aint Elma would have known if Eli had the gift.

"Maybe she's after your key." He paused. "After the Mafusos took Gertie captive and we invaded their space to rescue her, they've been resistant to keeping things civil in the present. We have an agreement, but I don't know if they can be trusted to honor it. Maybe you should ask Caiyan."

I could hear the smirk come across the line. Mahlia had once been Caiyan's informant and lover. Their relationship had been terminated before I came into the picture, but the informant agreement had ended much later.

"Caiyan doesn't talk to Mahlia anymore," I said, but my voice wavered with uncertainty, and Jake picked up on it.

"I can't say that's a good thing, because she did give us valuable intel on the Mafusos."

"Has she been traveling with Mitchell?" Mahlia was Mitchell's older sister. Maybe they were cooking up some way to steal my key.

"No, Mitchell has been flying solo back to 1990. I'm not sure why. I don't have anyone who can track him yet."

Yet was the key word. He was referring to Campy. I knew Caiyan did not want him to travel alone until he was a few years older and had many more travels under his belt. It was killing Caiyan not to be able to show him the ropes, and we did not have a transporter young enough to accompany him to 1990.

"I'm going to find out what she wants with my brother."

"How are you going to do that?"

"I'm going to ask her."

He let out a long, concerned breath. "Be careful and report back to me after you speak with her."

"Will do, Agent McCoy." I saluted the phone.

"And Jen—"

"Yeah?"

"Just talk to her. Try not to get in a hair-pulling, face-slapping fight."

"Jeez, you think so little of me. I have SuperJen training now. I can use my fists."

"I know; that's what I'm afraid of."

He disconnected, and I stared at my cell phone for a minute. Why was he so worried? I could handle an adult conversation with the woman I hated more than menstrual cramps. Besides, she couldn't have my boyfriend *and* my brother. I had to draw the line somewhere.

I drove through Mickey D's for a fry infusion and a large mocha coffee. I needed the fast food to fuel the energy I would need to make it through today. I thought about calling Caiyan as I sat in my car eating my fries, but I didn't want to ask him when he had last spoken to Mahlia. He either would be pissed I was asking, or he would give me an answer I wasn't prepared to hear. Maybe that conversation could wait until after our night of pure carnal pleasure. My inner voice agreed and packed her new VS cheeky lace panties.

When I returned from lunch, Eli was sitting at his desk. His face had that goofy smile a guy gets when his dick is doing all the thinking. My grandmother, Mamma Bea, told me the reason is because all the blood rushes to the guy's penis, and he can't concentrate.

"Hi," I said as I sat in the chair across from Eli. He perked up and flashed his perfect white, toothy smile at me.

"What did you think of Mahlia?" he asked. "She's hot, right?"

The wheels in my mind were turning, trying to think of something positive to say.

"She's definitely hot." I couldn't disagree with that. "Where is she?"

"She had to get back to work." He continued with the wide smile, and I frowned at him.

"Where did you meet her?"

"I was having dinner at the Burger Barn, next door to the Cut and Blow."

I raised an eyebrow in question. He rarely ate red meat and never a burger. He continued, "I had my hair cut, because I'm going with the parental units to Melissa Jo's wedding on Sunday. When was the last time you *saw* our parents?"

Crap. I'd forgotten I promised my mom I would go to my cousin Melissa Jo's wedding. "You were telling me about Mahlia."

"I was eating a chicken sandwich."

Only Eli would eat chicken at a burger joint. "And?" I asked, trying to steer him toward Mahlia and away from my lack of family values.

"And she walked over and asked if she could sit with me, because she was all by herself."

Bless her little heart. "Where's she from?" I took a sip out of my iced coffee and waited to see what kind of lie she was telling.

"Get this: she's from New York City, just like Mom." His voice escalated with his good fortune. Our mother would approve of a fellow New Yorker. "Except Mahlia's from Manhattan."

Our mom was from a different borough of New York City, but this didn't make a difference in the camaraderie of a New Yorker away from the motherland.

I rolled my eyes. OK, I would play along. "What does she do for a living?"

"She's a model." He sat back in his chair and interlocked his fingers behind his head, smiling.

"Wow, a model." My forced enthusiasm went unnoticed by my brother.

"I know, right?"

"Why is she in Coffee Creek?"

"She was doing a video shoot for some online company." He removed his hands and stood up as if he might jump up and down with happiness. "Do you know what the best part is?"

"Her legs are longer than a giraffe's?"

"No." He stopped and grinned. "They are long, aren't they?" He put his hands on the desk and leaned forward until he was in my face. "She drives a Harley."

Damn. She even let him see her vessel. "You didn't share any of our family secrets, did you?"

"Like what?" He looked confused. I was pretty sure Eli didn't know about the gift of time travel or the magic keys.

"I'm just kidding," I said. "Did she drive her Harley all the way from New York?"

"No, she is staying in Dallas for a while and had it transported here."

I nodded my head as if that was a cool thing, but I knew she'd just hopped on her Harley and motored here via lateral travel. My brain was still trying to comprehend why she would be here. Maybe she was trying to get my key. Well, over my dead body. Actually, that *was* the only way. What if she was going to have me killed? My inner voice pulled out her bucket list and teared up at the thought of all the things she wouldn't be checking off.

"Earth to Jen," Eli said, snapping his fingers in front of my face.

I pulled myself back to attention and away from my imminent demise.

"I was saying Mahlia isn't full of herself like other girls I've met who are models. And get this…she wants to meet the family."

I bet she does.

"In fact, I might bring her to Melissa Jo's wedding."

Oh, jeez. I had to put a stop to this before she became Eli's plus-one at our family function.

My inner voice was making a list of the places I might find Mahlia: the nail salon, the spa, getting an expensive blowout, Caiyan's bedroom. OK, that last one I was striking off the list. As far as I knew, Caiyan had stayed away from her. He didn't have a key, so she would have had to pop in on him. Maybe she was still at Eli's apartment. If she'd spent the night, I'm sure she would need time to pack her Louis Vuitton luggage with her magic mirror and evil spells.

Paulina poked her head in and let Eli know about the patient who was ready. He practically floated out the door, and I didn't have the heart to burst the lust bubble levitating him to danger.

I scooted upstairs and let myself into Eli's apartment. I heard someone in the bedroom, so I used my stealth mode to sneak up on her.

She was zipping her overnight bag (Louis Vuitton) and had her back to me. "If you are going to sneak up on me, you should probably be a lot quieter." She turned and came face-to-face with me.

Damn. She was four inches taller than me with the heels, which gave her the advantage.

"What are you doing here?" I asked.

"I'm packing my things to take to UPS," she said as she motioned toward her luggage. "I have to mail them. You know how difficult it is to travel with baggage."

"Why are you messing with my brother?"

"I like him; he's cute," she said as if she were talking about a new puppy.

"What are you after?" I crossed my arms over my chest and took a wide stance.

"Jennifer, I think we should call a truce." She moved away from me and picked up her purse—the new Kate Spade Lietta cross-body bag with the sparkly tassel—from the dresser. "I mean, your brother is a great guy. Any girl would be lucky to have his attention."

"You're not any girl, and I want you to stay away from him."

"Are you going to make me?" she asked with a challenging glint in her eye.

"Yes, I am," I said as I took a step forward.

"You're not wearing your key." She pointed to my empty neck. "Did it clash with your outfit?"

I touched the bare spot where my key usually lay.

"Or did you get in trouble, and the big boys took it away from you?" Her sarcastic tone bounced around the room. "What do they call that? Oh yes, *grounded*, like a misbehaving toddler." She stood in front of me, hands on hips. Her purse dangled by its strap from her shoulder.

I balled up my fists and took a swing, just as I'd learned in my training. She dodged me with an acrobatic lunge. I swung again and grabbed a handful of her hair. Pulling her around, I slapped at her face. Jake would not be happy about my fighting technique. She was holding me at arm's length by my head and fumbling with her shoulder bag.

I had a wad of her hair and was about to wrestle her to the ground when I heard a loud clicking noise and felt a sharp jolt under my ribcage. I fell to the floor in pain. The bitch had outsmarted me.

She stood over me holding her stun gun, watching me writhe and slobber on myself.

"That's a good look for you," she said as she snapped a selfie with me in the background and let herself out the door.

A few minutes later, I was able to drag myself to the bathroom and wash my face in Eli's sink. My plan to fake a nasty stomach bug and leave work early so I could make my travel to Gitmo was no longer necessary. My pasty complexion, nausea, and headache would be enough to convince Eli I wasn't feeling well and needed to go home.

Chapter 3

I recovered from my Mahlia encounter and was dressed and ready by four o'clock. A pink mohair cardigan layered over my favorite white tank, skinny jeans, and blush studio flats would be acceptable for my meeting with Major General Arthur C. Potts. He's the military personnel in charge of the WTF on the naval base at Guantanamo Bay, better known as GITMO. We are a covert operation in the basement of the most terrifying prison in the world, hidden from all eyes of the government except the president and his close advisers. I was informed we could be used as a weapon if the right people knew about us.

Travelers had to use extreme caution when traveling laterally. We valued our freedom, and that freedom would be revoked if we were caught spying on the enemy, so to speak.

Luckily, President Lyndon Johnson had used great foresight when developing the WTF and had made a special doctrine that no member of the WTF could be used to aid in the military functions of the world. I am sure he wrote this with a heavy heart, because sending a traveler back to stop the evils of Hitler, Saddam Hussein, or Osama Bin Laden—just to name a few—would have saved lives. But it also would have changed life as we know it, and that's a pretty big risk.

Brodie had returned from his family duties, and the pots and pans had been clanging against the pot rack since I had returned from work. It was quiet at the moment, and I sat at the kitchen table sipping a Coke while I waited on Ace.

The wind spun outside, and a flash of lightning stroked the window, announcing Ace's arrival. He knocked politely, and I pulled open the sliding glass door. His long brown hair was tucked back in a tight ponytail, and he wore white skinny jeans, a baby-blue Marc Jacobs button-down with black suspenders, and a black polka-dot bow tie. His five o'clock shadow gave him the Russell Brand appearance he was going for, and I loved the look on him. He often dressed in drag when he went to parties, but when he reported to the WTF, female attire was a big no-no.

"'Ello, love," he said as he entered my house. I gave him a side hug and admired his new canvas shoes.

"Are those Sperry?" I asked.

"No. These babies are the latest driving loafer by BOSS—you like?" He extended his foot so I could admire the new shoes.

"No," I said, and Ace's face fell. "I love them!" This got a smile and a swat on the arm.

My first job out of college had been as an assistant shoe buyer for Steve Stone shoes. I had loved purchasing the shoes for next season— and the great discount. Unfortunately, Steve Stone had been arrested for tax evasion and was serving time in the federal penitentiary. He was managing to run his business from jail, but it was online only. I guess he had plenty of time to buy his own inventory.

The banging from upstairs began again, and it rattled the canisters on the kitchen counter.

"What the 'ell's that noise?" Ace asked.

"Brodie and Gertie," I said, rolling my eyes.

"No kidding? I'm such a great matchmaker." He patted himself on the back.

"Didn't you blackmail Brodie by threatening to tell Jake about a certain trip to the past that involved stealing a valuable sapphire necklace from a certain royal jewelry collection that should have ended up in the Titanic at the bottom of the Atlantic Ocean?"

Ace flashed his Cheshire cat smile. "Sugar, I have lots of stored information on every traveler. Your man better be on his best behavior, because you never know when that information might surface."

Caiyan had confided in me about the blackmail on Brodie, and I didn't want to know what else Ace had in his memory banks. "I will be sure and keep my nose clean, just in case."

"Oh, hon, you wouldn't steal a thing. It's just not in your blood," Ace said, flicking his hand in the air.

Maybe stealing was not one of my strong points, but I hoped being a good transporter was in there somewhere. I wondered if the gods ever made a mistake—like maybe I was a mutation, and the gene for time travel should have passed to Gertie instead.

"Let's go, doll," Ace said, motioning toward the back door. "All that thinking has your hair starting to frizz."

I shouted good-bye up to the ceiling as we left the house.

The sun was shining, and the tiny buds of roses were showing themselves around my vessel. "It won't be long now," I said to my outhouse as we walked by, and I thought it stood up a little straighter.

Ace and I climbed into his vessel, a 1950s-style photo booth. The purple-velvet seat cushions and the piped-in music gave it all the comforts of home. Ace liked to travel in style but wouldn't reveal his secrets to anyone. I had tried to put a chenille cushion in my outhouse to make the ride a little less hard on my rear end, and the outhouse had vomited me and the cushion out the door.

Ace pulled the curtain, closing us off from the outside world; mumbled his travel password; and in three magic flashes, we were sitting at Gitmo.

"Was that a Taylor Swift song playing?" I asked while admiring the black-and-white photo strips he had plastered all over his vessel. Most of them were of the unconscious brigands he had transported back to Gitmo, but a few were pictures of Ace and me. I especially liked the one of us in front of the Eiffel tower. I would have to ask him for a copy.

Ace swallowed hard and nodded.

"Why, Ace, you're a Swifty."

"I like the way she sticks it to the guy who did 'er wrong by writing a song about him. In fact, I'm thinking about writing a song."

Ace was a playboy in the past and the present. He would have to write an entire compilation of songs to match up with the rejected lovers in his little black book. I laughed, and we exited his vessel into the landing area.

The WTF has a landing pad for its travelers at the secret headquarters. It consists of twelve landing blocks forming a four-by-three grid housed in a large underground space similar to an aircraft hangar. The vessels land on the blocks, and I knew that tomorrow, when the moon cycle opened, most of the blocks would be filled with vessels. I hoped mine would be one of them.

We were met at the door by a man in a black suit. CIA. When I'd first started to travel, the British secret service worked with the CIA and had an office at Gitmo. Somewhere along the way, they'd had budget cuts, and the CIA had been given total responsibility. Jake had become Caiyan's boss, and all hell had broken loose in the battle of who was the best man for Jennifer Cloud.

Jake and I have come to a friendly compromise. He is my boss. I try to follow the orders he gives, and in return, he doesn't give me a hard time about dating a man with criminal activity marking up his credit report. We were always better friends than lovers, but occasionally I wish for that uncomplicated life I had in college.

Ace wished me good luck and told me he would wait to make sure I didn't need a ride home. If I did, it would mean I hadn't gotten my key back. It was nice of Ace to hang around and provide the moral support I would need if I failed.

The black suit escorted me to the conference room. A long table sat in the center of what I call "the Blue Room" because it has dusty-blue wallpaper from the '90s running down to meet mahogany paneling in the middle at a chair rail.

I sat down, leaving the head of the table for General Potts. Jake entered, crossed the room, and gave me a hug. Usually, hugs are given only if there are no other WTF personnel in the vicinity; otherwise, I get a nod. His hair was spiked to perfection today, as if not a single hair had dared to move out of place. He had a file in his hand and a locked box tucked in the crook of his arm. I hoped it was my key.

"How did things go with Mahlia?" he asked, placing the box and the file on the table. "You were supposed to call me."

"Yeah, sorry. I was running late. She told me she liked my brother, and that was all." I left out the part about the hair pulling and the stun gun.

"Are you sure nothing more happened?" Jake raised a dark eyebrow at me.

"We might have had a few cross words," I said, absentmindedly removing a thread hanging from my cardigan.

Jake pulled his cell phone from his pocket and showed me the picture Mahlia had taken earlier at Eli's apartment. Damn, was *everyone* connected?

"How did you get that?" I snatched the phone and examined the photo of me with drool running down my chin. Mahlia's smiling face was in the foreground. She had captioned it *Better luck next time*. The bitch.

"Apparently she has my number." Jake reached out and plucked the phone from my fingers.

"We had a little disagreement," I said.

"I told you not to get in a fight with her. She's dangerous. You're lucky she only tased you."

I dropped my head in disgust with myself. "It was only a stun gun."

"I'm not going to report on this, because I need you."

"You do?"

"Yes, with Caiyan out of the picture and Campy not finished with training, I need all my travelers." Jake started to run a hand through his hair. It was a nervous habit from childhood. He stopped when his fingers met his shellacked masterpiece. It was cut military-style, very short by his standards, but it emphasized his big brown eyes. "I can't believe I actually just said that. Your grounding was the best thing that happened to me."

"Thanks a lot." My shoulders slumped. "I thought I was making improvements."

"You're doing great." Jake gave my hand a confident squeeze. "I meant that I knew you were safe. It was selfish on my part."

Our conversation came to an abrupt halt as General Potts made an entrance. His burly frame edged in through the doorway, and he proceeded to his place at the head of the table. I read somewhere owners resemble their dogs, and I am sure General Potts had a bulldog waiting for him at home. The WTF secretary, whom I referred to as Ms. Beotch, because she was riding Jake before we officially put our relationship out to pasture, followed closely behind the general. She was Jake's assistant when General Potts was off base, and that was quite often, according to the guys in the travel lab.

Jake and Ms. Beotch took their seats on either side of the general, and Jake handed the file to Ms. Beotch, who opened it and placed it neatly in front of the general. She threw a smirk my way as she settled back in front of her laptop. General Potts cleared his throat, and the meeting began. He reviewed my file, commending me on my training.

I *should* be commended. I had been at Gitmo every weekend doing combat training with one of the black suits. The guy looked like John Cena, and when he was training me, his 250-pound body wore fatigues and a permanent scowl. I was also experimenting with all types of weapons. I knew the difference between an AR-15 and an AK-47. I could load and fire a flintlock rifle and shoot a target in the heart, but I usually preferred to aim at an arm or a leg. The defenders may be able to shoot someone dead, but SuperJen would rather injure them and make a quick escape. I also spoke fluent Spanish and could mutter through conversational French.

My inner voice gave me a poke check, and I realized everyone was staring at me. Obviously, I had missed a question. I looked over at Jake, and he rolled his eyes.

"Jennifer," he said. "Don't you feel like you are ready to go back out in the field?"

"Oh, yes, sir," I said, sitting up straight and looking General Potts in the eye. "I am ready. I have been training here every weekend and three days a week at home."

My body was proof exercise works. My muscles had muscles. My arms, originally similar to the consistency of spaghetti, were toned and tan from the outside training at Gitmo. I could run up three flights of stairs without breaking a sweat, and I could carry double my own body weight in a fireman's carry back down the same stairs.

Jake was reporting all this good news to the general. He seemed pleased and gave Jake the official head nod to give me my key. Jake unlocked the metal box and lifted a small mahogany box from the container. He slid the box in my direction. The carvings on the top of the box reminded me of ancient Egyptian hieroglyphics. My fingers grazed across the carvings as I opened the lid.

My key sparkled up at me from its black-velvet bedding. The blue diamonds twinkled as they pirouetted around the crescent moon. I reached in and lifted my key from its prison. The weight of the titanium chain felt heavy in my hands, regardless of all my new muscles. I secured it around my neck, and the key glowed with an excitement that had been dormant for far too long.

General Potts did something I had never seen him do—he smiled. It was a nice smile that reminded me of George Clooney's. "That's the damnedest thing I've ever seen," he said, shaking his head. "Almost like that thing's alive."

I placed my hand over the key, and I felt a warmth trail through my fingertips and radiate throughout my entire body. The sensation made my inner voice do a tap dance. Any prior concerns about my abilities to be a good transporter vanished as she took a bow. I was ready to travel again.

Ms. Beotch clacked around on her laptop and stood to pull a sheet of paper off the nearby printer. She handed the paper to Jake, sending a complacent glance in my direction, and followed General Potts as he excused himself to go fight the greater evils of the world. As he left, he reminded Agent McCoy to go over the details of my probation.

"What details?" I asked. "What probation?"

"General Potts and I feel you should have a few rules in place before you travel alone. Since your defender is not traveling at the moment."

"What rules?" I frowned and gave Jake a questioning glare. "Don't I already have enough rules to follow?"

"These are specific only to you," Jake said, reading from the paper. "Number one, you cannot under any circumstances purposely *change* events in the past."

The added emphasis on *change* made me grimace. I might have done that a few times in my travels. "That applies to everyone."

"Yes, but you seem to have the most difficult time remembering it." Jake stared pointedly at me. "Number two, you may not travel laterally without permission."

"What the hell?" I asked, my voice increasing a few decibels. "Do you have to approve my every move?"

"Yes, if you want to keep your key."

Damn, now I would have to ask Jake permission to see Caiyan. My inner voice threw baggy sweatpants over her cheeky panties and pouted.

"Jake, I was planning on meeting Caiyan tonight to...um...celebrate."

His jaw clenched, and he clicked his pen a few times. He raised his eyes to mine, and I saw the regret he had over our lost relationship. "I'll allow a short trip, but remember the moon cycle opens, and I need you back here for the traveler meeting."

I refrained from throwing my arms around his neck. Jake frowned at my gleeful disposition and moved the paper he was reading in front of me.

"And number three, when you go on a mission, you must travel with a defender at all times." Jake handed me his pen and pointed at the paper in front of me to sign.

"Who doesn't have a transporter?" I asked, scribbling my name on the paper and taking a mental head count of my team members. Ace was Brodie's transporter. Gerald had Tina, and as far as I knew, all the other defenders on other teams had transporters—except Campy, and he was still in training.

"I don't," a voice from the doorway responded.

Marco.

Marco was tall, blond, and belonged on the cover of *Men's Fitness*. My aunt Elma and his grandfather had been involved in a secret love affair back in the day. Marco had watched both of them die and refused to travel or be part of the WTF. My last travel had been a little touchy, because I'd kidnapped Marco to help me save Caiyan. We'd completed the mission, but Marco had wanted me as payment.

I stood slowly. "I thought you were never going to join the WTF?"

"I had a change of heart." He sauntered over and stood facing me.

"This is going to be messy," I said, referring to the fact Caiyan was not going to like me traveling with Marco. I turned to Jake. "Is this a ploy to keep me away from Caiyan?"

"Caiyan's dangerous, Jen, even without his key."

I huffed. Marco stood there, his blue eyes cutting into me like a samurai at a sushi convention.

Jake moved from his chair and walked to where Marco and I were having a stare down. He explained they had been doing recon on Mitchell Mafuso and said we should report Saturday morning at 0600 hours to get our travel instructions. He looked at Marco and then at me. "It was the best I could do to keep you safe." He turned on his heel and left the room.

"I need to walk back to the hangar and tell Ace my good news," I said as I sidestepped Marco. He reached out and grabbed my forearm. A jolt shot through my elbow as if I'd been touched by a hot poker.

"Ouch." I jerked my arm away.

"We need to have a discussion about this relationship," he said.

"There is no relationship; it's business," I said and walked out of the room.

As I reached the hangar, I saw two vessels on the landing pads: Ace's photo booth and Marco's formula-one racecar. The shiny red body reflected the light from the overhead fixtures. Marco was a Ferrari, a family of time travelers from centuries past. The limbs of my family tree thinned out at my great-grandparents, but his traced back to the Knights of the Round Table.

Ace came bounding up to me. "I see you got your key back."

I caressed the key that lay in the hollow of my throat. "Yep, but I also got an unexpected new defender." I gestured toward Marco's vessel.

"I can't believe they got 'im to travel," Ace said, having a bit of a hissy fit. "Girl, you are so lucky to be close to that body. He's built like Superman."

"I'm not sure *lucky* is the right word. Caiyan's not going to like his replacement."

"Be strong, love. Caiyan can be a bad boy." Ace put one hand on his slender hip. "Marco might be just the thing to put a kink in that Scot's knickers."

Ace left, reminding me he would see me bright and early the next morning for our travel duties. Cuba was one hour ahead of Dallas time, so that meant I had to get up even earlier. As soon as Jake learned where the brigands landed, he could give our orders, but I didn't understand why we couldn't meet at nine instead.

I turned to go back into the building and have a word with Jake. This simply would not work. When Marco and I were in the same room together, things happened. He had an uncontrollable spark. He had been my first kiss when I was sixteen, and the sexual tension between us would never allow us to work together.

Marco was leaning against the doorjamb to the hangar. His long legs were encased in faded jeans that hugged all the right spots. A white T-shirt was covered with a navy button-down that I knew Marco would throw off as soon as he left Gitmo. It was common for the travelers to wear shirts they could button to hide their keys from the ungifted population. Marco's was already open at the neck. The moonstone pendant with blue diamonds sparkling along the oceans of mother earth lay gleaming against his suntanned skin.

"I can't travel with you," I stated plainly, but I was coming to the conclusion that if I didn't travel with Marco, I didn't travel.

"Jen, you have been after me to join the WTF, and now here I am." The dimple in his chin intensified as he spread his arms wide, indicating he was indeed at the WTF of his own free will.

I crossed my arms over my chest. "I am dating Caiyan. I can't repay my debt to you right now."

A slow smile crept across his face. "The time will come, Jennifer Cloud, and so will you." He laughed as he left me rooted to my spot with my mouth hanging open. He got in his vessel and with a loud engine roar was gone. Geesh. He was an overconfident asshole, but I was afraid he might be right.

I shook off the aftershocks of his machismo and called my vessel. I decided I didn't have the energy to go head-to-head with Jake. I was still suffering some fatigue from the stun gun, and the thought of seeing Caiyan again had me heading for home. A long, hot bath and time to transform myself into sexy Jen were my goals for tonight.

My outhouse appeared at once. I was glad to have it back, and I think it was happy to see me too. I climbed aboard, concentrated on my backyard at home, and said the magic word, "Hanhepi." In an instant, I was home. The ride was a smooth one, and I stroked the chipped wood of my vessel. I felt a small vibration run through my hand. If an inanimate object could purr, I'm sure that's the way it would feel. "I'm glad to have my key back too," I said as I climbed out of the outhouse.

Gertie greeted me as I entered through the sliding door. She was making a pasta salad and singing a song from the Disney movie *Frozen*.

She took her gaze from the pot of pasta and caught a glimpse of my key. "You got your key back. That's awesome."

"Yes, *that's* awesome, but my new defender is Marco." I sat down hard in the kitchen chair.

"Marco?" She walked over to me. "Is he traveling?"

"Not just traveling, but he signed up to work for the WTF."

"Holy cow!" Gertie sat down in the chair across from me. "I guess he can't get you off his mind."

"What do you mean?"

"Well, I saw a clip of him in *People* magazine, and he had a gorgeous model on his arm…oh, what's her name, the skinny one?"

"They're all skinny."

"Anyhow, I thought he was dating her."

Smoke jumped up in Gertie's lap and gave her a friendly nudge with his head.

I reached out to stroke him, and he hissed at me. Damn, this morning I'd thought we were bosom buddies.

"I can't help thinking there is more behind this than Marco wanting to collect on his debt." I took an apple from the fruit basket on the table and took a bite while I chewed over the reasons Marco would decide to travel.

"You better hope Caiyan doesn't find out about that debt," Gertie said as the timer went off on the stove, indicating her pasta was ready.

She was right. I didn't want Caiyan to find out, although after his escapades during the last time travel, I would have been more than justified. My inner voice nodded in agreement.

"You want some pasta?" Gertie asked as she mixed chopped, grilled chicken into the pasta.

"No thanks. I'm having dinner with Caiyan, and I want to be hungry." My cell phone pinged, and I fished it out of my pocket.

I read the message from Caiyan: *Can't wait to see you. Wear something sexy. We are dining out tonight.* I pocketed the phone and went upstairs to change and get ready to dine with the dangerous Scot.

Chapter 4

The red Valentino dress clung to my body like a second skin. It would be considered a crime to wear undergarments with this dress, and the thought of having dinner with Caiyan commando sent a tingle down to my boy howdy. There wasn't a secret hiding place for my cell phone, so I would have to carry a small purse. I could keep the purse in my coat pocket for the trip to New York, but if we were going somewhere, I didn't need a full-length leather coat that might be a problem.

The picture of Caiyan and me lying on an isolated beach in the Caymans formed a hope bubble in my mind, and my inner voice changed into her string bikini. I pulled myself away from the daydream. Jake had told me a short trip was allowed. Maybe a quick trip to Italy for a gelato would be OK, as long as I reported to headquarters at 6:00 a.m.

I shuddered at the early hour and focused on the problem at hand. If I took a wristlet and strapped it to my arm, it should be fine; otherwise, it might end up in pieces. Lateral travel works if I have small objects in my pockets, but purses and bigger items tend to end up shredded and ready for the bottom of a rabbit's cage.

The Chanel watch Caiyan had given me for my birthday would be fine, and so would the diamond drops in my ears.

Completing the ensemble, I added a pair of black FMPs that made my legs look a mile long. They were Manolo knockoffs, but the high platform-stiletto heel complemented the dress and would hopefully give me the results I desired without falling on my ass and twisting an ankle.

Caiyan was acting so mysterious. He wouldn't tell me where we were going after dinner. He simply left me instructions to meet him at his house in Manhattan.

I glanced in the mirror for a final check of my perfectly straightened hair. The process had taken an hour, but it was worth it. I added a swipe of Eminence cinnamon lip gloss, which promised big, luscious lips, to the red lipstick I had previously applied. I dropped the lip gloss, my cell phone, a debit card, and MAC lipstick in Brave Red into my vintage black, beaded wristlet and secured it to my arm. That would do.

Gertie met me at the top of the stairs. "Wow, you look amaaazing."

"Thanks, I'm heading out, and I probably won't be home tonight." An uncontrolled blush sent heat to my face, and Gertie laughed at me.

"You probably won't be home until next month when Caiyan sees you in that dress."

"No can do. I have to be at headquarters early tomorrow morning. The moon cycle is beginning at midnight tonight. After the WTF gets the read on the brigands, I might have an assignment."

"Don't drag me into this one," Gertie huffed. "The last time you almost got strangled, and traveling back in time gives me the heebie-jeebies."

"I thought you had fun in 1985?" I crossed my arms and brought my index finger to my chin. Gertie had met a gorgeous drummer on our last travel together.

"If you are referring to the drummer, when I returned to present day, I Facebook stalked him. He was old and had five kids by four different women. No thank you!"

"You never told me you found him on Facebook."

"I started dating Brodie and forgot all about the little drummer boy." She flipped one of her braids behind her shoulder and started off in the direction of her room. "Besides, I would rather watch old movies and drink wine with Itty."

Itty was Caiyan's great-aunt. Too old to time travel safely but young at heart. She and Gertie had bonded during my last time travel, but I hadn't realized they were hanging out.

"Aunt Itty's coming over?" I felt a pang of jealousy. When was the last time Gertie and I had spent any time together? I made a mental note to plan a girls' night out when I returned from my mission.

"Yeah, I get a little depressed when Brodie time travels. I'm afraid something bad might happen to him, so Itty comes over and keeps me company."

"Gertie, I'm sorry. I didn't know."

"It's OK. You were always at training during the moon cycle. I think Jake was afraid you'd hitch a ride with someone and end up at the Spanish Inquisition."

"You're probably right. His lack of faith in me is starting to grate on my nerves."

"He's worried about you, and now Itty and I can worry about you too." She started toward her room and then paused and looked over her shoulder at me. "Have fun, and Jen, be careful."

"You know me—safety first." I smiled and headed downstairs, but I had a big uncomfortable knot in the pit of my stomach. I blamed it on the excitement of getting my key back and my night out with Caiyan.

I searched the coat closet for my full-length black-leather Roberto Cavalli coat. Last year, Ace and I had scoured the leather shops in Florence, Italy, to find great bargains. I'd bought the coat, which he'd said I wouldn't get enough use out of, because I live in Texas. April in New York tended to be brisk, and the weather forecast called for temperatures in the low fifties and a chance of rain. I was landing in a secluded spot in Central Park. It was surrounded by a dense clump of trees, and other than a few drug addicts partaking in their daily score, the secret spot was usually empty. If any of the druggies saw me land, they would assume they were hallucinating.

I pulled on the coat. It hung loosely on my shoulders, thanks to all the self-defense training and exercise Jake had been demanding. I had lost twenty pounds of fat and gained five pounds of lean muscle. I felt good, but I was a little sad the coat now swallowed me. Wrapping a black faux-fur warmer around my neck, I double-checked my wristlet. Fastening the buttons of my coat, I exited to my vessel.

The final sliver of sunlight was disappearing over the horizon as I closed my eyes and focused on the spot in Central Park. Hopefully, all the derelicts would be seeking refuge from the cool weather at one of the local soup kitchens.

My vessel made a smooth landing, and I was grateful I didn't tear my dress in an unexpected dismount. I dropped my wristlet into my pocket for safekeeping. As I stepped out of my vessel, a cold wind whipped madly at my hair. I cussed the air like a sailor under siege.

"My, my, such a pretty lass with a veery foul mouth." Caiyan was leaning against a large tree trunk, smiling at me. His dark hair was covered with a black watch cap, and he wore head-to-toe black. If I hadn't known any better, I would have thought he was a mugger.

"I didn't know you were going to meet me," I said, trying to secure my flyaway hair. "I spent an hour straightening my hair, and now I probably look like Barbie on acid."

He walked over to me and brushed a kiss across my red lips. "I hope your dress is that same color of red."

"Why?" I raised a curious eyebrow in his direction as I encircled his neck with my arms.

"Ye look good in red," he said, taking another nip at my lips. "And yer veery tasty too."

My inner voice gave me a high five. I knew Caiyan chewed cinnamon-flavored gum, so I was counting on the cinnamon lip gloss leading to more taste testing.

He pulled my arms from around his neck and interlocked his fingers with mine, and we began walking away from my vessel.

The outhouse disappeared with a flip of my free hand and a fleeting thought of *see you later*. I walked, tucked into the warmth of Caiyan's arms, through Central Park toward his apartment. We passed a few couples taking a walk through the park and a woman pushing a baby stroller who was clearly trying to get her kid to sleep. She looked at Caiyan with that longing that comes from too many dirty diapers and not enough "me time."

The busy sounds of the city drew closer as we made our way to the exit. Caiyan's co-op apartment was located on the upper west side of Central Park. The white-brick facade of the building came into view, and he picked up the pace. We crossed Central Park West and walked a few blocks to Caiyan's building, where we were greeted by his doorman, a short butterball of a man with silver hair and blue eyes that were almost lost under gray, bushy eyebrows. The man gave Caiyan a nod of recognition and held the door open for us.

The lobby always took my breath away. A high rotunda ceiling, stacked with layers of intricately carved crown molding, dressed the extravagant entrance hall of the expensive Central Park address.

As we entered the foyer, a small seating area with a massive stone fireplace provided a welcome warmth. The clicking of my stilettos against the Italian marble floors echoed as we crossed the lobby to wait for the elevator.

I tilted my head back as he pulled the scarf from my neck and drew me in close. He kissed the inside of my neck and nibbled on my earlobe.

"If you keep doing that, we won't make it to dinner, and I'm starving," I said, taking a step back out of his reach.

"Maybe I can do something to distract ye from yer hunger pains, aye?" The elevator doors opened, and he pushed the button for the penthouse. About halfway up, he stopped the elevator and began kissing my neck.

"Caiyan, dinner?" I asked as I reached over and set the elevator in motion.

"Yer not much fun tonight," he said, pouting. He removed his gloves and exchanged them for the apartment key in his pocket.

"I'll be fun after we eat." I wanted a date. A real date with dinner and conversation. One that held all the excitement of a first date. It seemed Caiyan and I had made a habit of too much sex and ordering takeout in our stolen moments together.

He reached over and tucked a stray hair behind my ear. His gaze held mine, and my desire for first-date excitement was forgotten. As he moved in closer, our lips parted for a deep, lingering kiss. My hunger pains for food were replaced with a craving for Caiyan. Leaving traces of red lipstick on his neck, I reluctantly exited the elevator as it opened on his floor.

By the time we reached his apartment, dinner was an afterthought. He took off his cap, spilling glorious waves of dark hair across his brow. His eyes stayed on mine as he removed his coat. I started to unbutton my coat, but he stopped me and continued the task himself. As we stood in his entry hall, I did a small spin so he could admire my dress, and he whistled.

"You like it?"

"I like *you*. The dress I like on the floor." He brushed his lips against mine, and in one swipe, he sent my dress into a heap at my ankles. I stood naked, with the exception of my stilettos, on his marble floor.

"Even better," he said and scooped me up in his arms.

Caiyan's apartment was decorated in early medieval. The furniture was solid and strong but comfortable. His extensive art collection decorated the walls, and ancient artifacts were placed on the tables. Indiana Jones would have loved the place. Caiyan's bed was a large sixteenth-century four-poster. He'd told me it had been redesigned to fit his height and reinforced for other things. A zebra-skin rug covered the hand-scraped wood floors.

He laid me gently down on the soft, down-filled comforter. Leaving my stilettos in place, he ran his lips up the inside of my thigh and kept going until he reached my hard nipples, kissing me in all the right places along the way. I reached down and brought his lips to mine and lingered in his sensual kisses. He proceeded to make his way down south and do that thing with his tongue that took me to my limit. I cried out in uncontrolled ecstasy as he rolled his tongue around and brought me to climax. My inner voice reminded me I had only been here five minutes. *Shut up!*

Caiyan was fully dressed, and I was completely naked. I lay panting on his bed as he removed his clothes.

"Why, kind sir, what about my dinner?" I asked, fluttering my eyelashes and doing my best Scarlett O'Hara impression.

"Frankly, my dear, I don't give a damn," he quoted playfully as he moved on top of me and entered me. The ride started slow and smooth and became more turbulent with every thrust. His muscular chest contracted as I ran my hands across his nipples. We moved in sync until I was begging to reach the peak and cascade down the vertical drop. We went over the edge together, falling to a blissful release. Afterward, we lay spent in each other's arms.

"Ye are beautiful, Jennifer Cloud," he said, running a hand down my side in a way that caused my nipples to stand up again. "And now I think we should eat."

"Eat? Oh, yes." I had forgotten how hungry I'd been earlier, but my grumbling stomach reminded me. "OK if I borrow your shower?" I asked, gently skimming my fingers over his abs. The WTF wanted all its defenders in combat condition, and so far, I hadn't seen one who had an ounce of fat on his body.

"Yer training is paying off," Caiyan said as he watched me walk toward his bathroom.

"Why do you say that?" I asked, feeling a little awkward standing naked in front of him again.

"I can tell Agent McCoy has had his hands on you."

I frowned. Was he referring to my physique, or did he think I was still having sex with Jake? Caiyan and I hadn't been specific about our relationship. He'd told me he loved me, once, maybe twice. I, on the other hand, hadn't said those three little words out loud, but I thought Caiyan knew how I felt. The fact we had never identified our relationship had me second-guessing myself. I'd assumed we were a monogamous thing, but maybe Caiyan wasn't ready. *Or maybe you're not ready,* my inner voice chided.

"No," I said, ignoring my inner voice and pulling my hair to the front so it spilled over my right breast. "Jake is doing weapons training. The big guy, Max, is the one who has been physically training me."

Caiyan smiled, came over, and kissed my shoulder. "Veery nice—firm. Get dressed. We've dinner reservations."

"I need to shower and redo my makeup. Which is a problem, because I don't have any makeup here."

He kissed me gently and stared into my eyes. "Ye look lovely just as ye are."

I told my inner voice to fuck off. *I'm ready.*

⌒

I took a quick shower in the guest bathroom and fiddled with my hair. My makeup wasn't too bad, so I added the red lipstick to my lips and compact powder to my face.

As I walked into the living area, a slow, sexy whistle greeted me. Caiyan was leaning against the counter of his fully stocked bar, wearing a black Armani suit and tie. He looked incredible, and I felt my nipples harden. *No,* I told my inner slut. I wanted to go on our mystery dinner date, not spend the night—like so many others—in bed. Thankfully, he finished the scotch he was drinking, and we left for our night on the town.

Caiyan hailed a cab for the short ride to Marea. As soon as we walked in the door, Caiyan was greeted by the staff like a member of the family and escorted to a private table with a view of Central Park. He ordered a bottle of wine and some Russian caviar. I wasn't a big fan of caviar, but this stuff was the bomb. I went over the details of my probation, leaving out the part about Marco joining the WTF and becoming my new defender. Why ruin a perfect evening? Throughout dinner, Caiyan seemed a little preoccupied. He hardly touched his tagliata as I hoovered through a beautifully prepared capesante. It was almost too pretty to eat, but I was starving.

"Aren't you hungry?" I asked.

He pushed his plate away and asked if I wanted dessert.

I smiled, and he signaled the waiter for a tiramisu. He took a few bites that I spoon-fed him and continued to play with his fork.

"OK, what's up?" I asked.

"Do ye want to go to Scotland?"

"Scotland?" I asked. "What for?"

"I want to show ye my family home."

My inner voice did a fist pump. Yes, I wanted to see the family home.

"When?" I asked, mentally planning to ask Eli for some time off work.

"Tonight."

"Right now?"

"Yes."

"I guess I'm driving."

"Aye, lassie, ye get the reins today. But it won't be long before I'm back in the saddle."

I raised an eyebrow at him. "Should I ask what you mean by that?" My inner voice pulled out her magnifying glass and her Sherlock Holmes *Guide to Sleuthing*.

He paused briefly, as if debating what he should tell me. Finally, the corners of his mouth drew up in a sexy smile. "I'm sure Mitchell Mafuso will screw up, and I will get my key back soon."

He paid the bill, and we walked into Central Park to a cluster of trees so I could easily access my vessel.

"How will I know where to go?"

He pulled out his iPhone and showed me a picture of a beautiful stone estate. He scrolled down a few pictures to a meadow a short distance away.

"Land here," he said, pointing to a spot in the meadow. He Google mapped it for precision while I called my outhouse.

We climbed aboard my vessel. "I'm surprised you don't have a special landing pad inside your Scottish fortress."

"Aye, I do, but 'tis a tight squeeze, and I'm afraid ye'd end up in the moat."

I rolled my eyes at him. *Wait, did he say moat?* Geesh. These men and their lack of confidence in my traveling skills. What was the point of going through all that training if I was going to be treated like a toddler? My inner voice nodded in agreement and snapped on her leather driving gloves. I focused on the meadow and the map location as we disappeared into the night.

Chapter 5

We landed in the exact spot in the small meadow from the picture. I gave Caiyan a smirk. *Not enough skill, my ass.* A misty rain was sprinkling on us as we exited my vessel. The dark sky, illuminated by brief glimpses of a cloud-shrouded moon, threw shadows on the landscape. I squinted into the distance and thought I could make out rolling hills dotting the horizon.

I was surprised to see a black BMW sedan waited with the engine running at the bottom of the lane. A driver held the door for me as I settled myself against the soft leather seat. Caiyan greeted the driver and slid in next to me. The smell of dewy grass and fresh country air reminded me of the first time Caiyan and I had met in Scotland. A cold shiver ran down my spine, and I shuddered in response.

"Are ye cold?" Caiyan asked. He leaned forward and asked the driver to adjust the thermostat in the car.

"No," I said, keeping my voice low. "Just having a déjà vu about the first time I was in Scotland. I was eighteen, and you seduced me and took my virginity."

"If I had known who ye were, lass, I would never 'ave been so rude." He smiled faintly.

"You mean you would not have tried to seduce me?"

"No, I didnae say that. I couldnae have helped myself, because ye were so beautiful—loud, but veery beautiful." He chuckled at the memory as the car eased its way up a steep incline. "If I remember correctly, ye seduced me, because ye were freezing and used my body for warmth."

"I seduced you because I was freezing?" I asked a little skeptically.

"Aye, I had secured a place in the barn, ye kin?"

I nodded. I did remember finding a dry place to wait until the sun came up. It was a cold, rainy night. I hadn't known where I was or how I had traveled back in time.

"And yer teeth were chattering so loud I thought ye would wake up the owners of the barn and get us kicked out into the rain. I put my arms around ye for warmth; then ye kissed me."

"I kissed you?" That wasn't right at all.

"Aye, ye did. It was a fine kiss too, and because I'm a gentleman, I kissed ye back."

"A gentleman?"

"Sure, I didnae want ye to feel rejected."

"Rejected?" I questioned his story.

"All the lassies get mad if ye don't show affection when they come at ye with their lips puckered and ready to be kissed."

I narrowed my eyes at him. He laughed and slipped an arm around my shoulders. "Best roll in the hay I ever had. I wish I had known ye were a traveler. I would have hunted ye down and had another roll instead of waiting so long."

The car angled upward as we maneuvered the curves of a narrow, steep hill. Darkness and a dense tree line blinded my view of any other living beings within miles. If I were a kidnapper, this was where I would bring my victims. At the top of the hill, our driver pulled through a stone archway and into the circular drive of a large stone castle. A valet opened the door for me and welcomed Caiyan home.

Home? So this was the grand estate Caiyan owned in Scotland. His family home.

"Caiyan, this is a freakin' castle," I said as we entered the grand foyer.

"Not really. It was my grandfather's estate in the highlands." He bowed to me with a sweeping arm. "Now it's mine."

"It looks like a castle," I said, taking in the entry. "I'm pretty sure I saw Rapunzel lowering down a rope made of hair from the tower thingy as we entered." My coat dripped on the expensive Oriental rug that covered the stone floor. We handed our coats to the valet and proceeded through two immense stone archways to the main room. A roaring fire was crackling in a fireplace so large I could have stood inside it, and an oil painting Caiyan told me later was of his great-grandmother hung above.

"Are you sure this isn't a castle?" I asked.

"No. It's considered a country estate. One of my ancestors built it in the fourteenth century. It was seized by the English during the Scottish rebellion but returned when my great-great-grandmother married an Englishman." He led me to a large window that overlooked a courtyard lit by half a dozen antique park fixtures. I was surprised Sherlock Holmes wasn't leaning against one, smoking his pipe.

"See? No moat." Caiyan pointed out the window.

"So you were joking about the moat?"

"Weel, there was a moat, but my ma had it filled in, because she couldnae keep me oot of it and was afraid I might drown."

He usually didn't talk about his parents. I knew they had died in a car accident, but he hadn't shared the details of his past with me. Any information I had came from the WTF.

We sat on the velvet sofa, and an older man with a gray beard and blue eyes that twinkled when he spoke brought us each a snifter of brandy. The man seemed to dote on Caiyan like a long-lost son who had just come home from the war. He had an air of ownership about him and kept calling me *miss.*

As the man left the room, I turned to Caiyan and joked, "If you tell me his name is Alfred, I'm going to demand to see the Batcave."

"I'm sorry. I should have introduced ye." He raked a hand through his hair, and I noticed it was longer than normal. His work must have kept him from getting his monthly trim. "I've never brought a woman here, and I've forgotten my manners."

"Never?" I asked.

"No. Ye know ye are veery special to me. The man was Nials. He will give me some grief aboot not being properly introduced to my lady friend." Caiyan explained Nials had been with his family for years. He and his wife had practically raised Caiyan after his parents' death. Nials's wife had passed some time ago, and now Nials ran the house.

After we finished the drinks, Caiyan gave me a tour of the home and its many rooms. We ended up in the study, a cozy room with a desk and bookshelves lining three walls. A palisade of windows with a view of the heated swimming pool made up the fourth. As I watched the steam roll off the pool, I could feel the tension in Caiyan.

"Why did you bring me here?" I asked.

"I wanted ye to see more of me."

I laughed. "I think I've seen all there is."

He smiled and took both of my hands in his. "What I mean is ye are an important part of my life, Jennifer Cloud, and I want to share more of it with ye."

Was he about to propose? Was this my moment? I felt the excitement start at my toes and run up my body. My inner voice was searching venues and bookmarking wedding dresses in *Brides* magazine. *Stop!* I ordered my inner voice to chill. I didn't know if I was ready. Did I want to be married? Did I want to be married to Caiyan? I had lost my train of thought, and as I refocused, I heard him saying he needed a favor.

Wait, where was the proposal? Damn. He needed a favor. I should have known better, but somewhere down deep, I was relieved I didn't have to make a major life-changing decision today.

"What?" I asked him. "What kind of favor?"

"I need you to take me on a little trip," he said as he ran his fingers up my arm, generating a heat that only a person with the gift can create.

"Where are we going?" I asked, withdrawing my arm from his touch.

"Germany," he said. His gaze drifted away so he wasn't looking me square in the eye.

"What year?" I had a feeling he wasn't referring to a lateral travel.

He pulled a map from his pocket and spread it out on the massive desk for me to see. It was old, and some of the detail was faded.

"Here." He pointed to a section of Berlin called Friedrichshain.

"What's so important in Friedrich-whatever?" I asked, trying to decide if I should give in and take him there, risking my neck and my travel license if Jake found out.

"There is a veery special painting I would like to save from a particularly nasty fire."

That sounded legit. Caiyan was, after all, an art collector. He owned an extensive collection of rare art that he had acquired through non-traditional means. Most of it he'd stolen before it perished by some natural disaster.

"Are we stealing the art?"

"Not exactly. Ye know I would never steal unless the reason was important." He looked hurt that I would even suggest such a thing. "If we don't save the painting, it will perish in the fire."

"OK," I said.

He looked surprised that I had agreed so easily, and that made me wary. I was all about saving the art, and it was my fault he didn't have his key. I was considering this an even-steven sort of trade. I would take him to get a painting that was going to burn up in a fire, and the guilt I felt over him giving away his key to save me would be less. *Hopefully.*

"Great," he said. He pulled me to him and kissed me hard on the mouth. "Let's go."

"Wait," I said, pointing to my watch. "I can't travel yet. It's only eleven-thirty, and the moon cycle isn't open yet."

"Aye, it tis. Scotland is five hours ahead of Gitmo."

My watch was still set to the central time zone. Disappointment hit my heart like a tsunami, flooding away all the possibilities that Caiyan wanted anything other than what booty benefitted him—stolen, female, or otherwise. I snatched my hand away from his kiss.

"Is that why we came to Scotland?"

He ran a hand down my arm. "Jen, ye have been the only one I was willing to give up being a defender for."

"I know," I said, lowering my gaze.

"But my way of life might be more difficult to change."

I was trying to understand as he tipped my chin upward. His eyes stayed with mine, pulling me into a pool of deep-green, sensual acceptance. We walked hand in hand down a long hall toward his final destination.

The hall emptied into a small open courtyard. Stone walls covered with English ivy surrounded the space, and it was a tight squeeze for a blind landing. "I understand why you didn't want me to land here without seeing the spot first," I said as I gestured toward the courtyard. "Landing in the moat might actually have been a possibility."

"Aye, I was more concerned aboot ye crashing through the four hundred-year-old stone walls," he said, playfully pulling a strand of my hair. "It's safe to call your vessel here."

I did as I was told and reminded him I had to be back in time for my meeting with the WTF. He assured me this was an in-and-out trip.

My outhouse appeared in the center of the courtyard, stirring up a slight wind as it settled on the cobblestone ground. The smell of the early-morning dew as it clung to the ivy-covered walls reminded me it was almost sunrise and would be an hour later when we landed in Berlin.

We decided on a secure landing spot in a cluster of trees located in a park. Our main goal was some sort of building he called a bunker. The words *Horst-Wessel-Stadt* were listed above the area, indicating a borough of the city.

"What year am I shooting for?"

He paused for a moment, rubbing his chin between his thumb and index finger. "Maybe ye should give me yer key and let me drive."

We both knew this was a bad idea. My vessel was very persnickety to outside travelers. I knew that Caiyan's experience would make hitting our destination easier, but there was no guarantee my vessel wouldn't throw us both out on our asses. Besides, I felt safer wearing my key. I had control.

"I think I'll keep the key, but thanks for the offer."

He grimaced. "OK, let's go. Nineteen forty-five."

I tried to remember any important details of that year. Jake always prepared me for my travels with intel about my destination and what to expect from the time period. My world-history class in high school had been right after lunch, and napping had taken precedence over listening. I knew I should have paid attention. Caiyan distracted me with a long, deep kiss with lots of tongue. I was going for the buttons on his shirt when he swatted my hand away.

"Time's a-wasting if ye want to be back to report for duty." Caiyan was antsy, but I put the blame on traveling without his key.

He was right. If I didn't want Jake to know I had traveled, this was going to be a quickie. I prayed the guys in the travel lab were preoccupied with following the brigands and wouldn't notice me blipping up on the screen.

We climbed in, and I took a deep breath. Caiyan interlaced his fingers with mine, and I felt a warm surge cascade through my body. We were good together, and my vessel felt the connection. It swept us away with me concentrating hard on the spot in the picture.

The landing was the easy part. When we stepped from my vessel, due to the time difference between Gitmo and our destination, it was early morning. I had skipped about six hours of quality sleep time. Jake was not going to be happy if I was tired.

Streaks of the rising sunlight were trying to make their way through a blanket of angry gray clouds. The rumble of airplane engines could be heard off in the distance.

"Those planes sound really loud," I said, looking up into the sky. We had landed in the park exactly as shown on the map. A grove of mangled trees surrounded a small patch of grass. Towering over the treetops was the luminous form of the gray-brick bunker from which Caiyan wanted to retrieve the painting. It was an ugly building. I couldn't understand why they would keep a precious work of art in such a place, but this was Germany, 1945. I was racking my brain trying to remember what had been happening in 1945.

Caiyan looked dapper in khaki pants, a shirt, and a brown bomber jacket. My vessel had dressed him as Indiana Jones. *Clever*, my inner voice agreed, since we were stealing—correction, *saving*—an artifact.

My clothes weren't so easy to maneuver in. I had on an A-line, gray wool skirt that hit below my knees and a matching jacket with square shoulders. My shoes were cork wedges, and I pranced around a little, trying to get a feel for walking in them.

Caiyan laid a helping hand on my elbow as he guided me over the rubble-laden ground. I decided the park must be going through a renovation as we came to a cemented stone archway and a fountain that had been drained and was filled with debris. Waist-high pedestals were positioned around the fountain, holding statues carved from stone. Most of them were missing key body parts. It was as if the Headless Horseman had been through on a midnight ride.

I passed a stone boy standing next to a dog that was mostly intact. They reminded me of the characters from the bedtime stories my dad read to me as a child. In front of each statue was a limestone turtle. Some of them were missing a shell, or their masonry had become dislodged and crooked. I could imagine that when the renovations were done, it would be a beautiful park. Caiyan was practically pushing me through the sanctuary. As we exited the opposite side through an iron gate, the roar of the airplanes seemed to be getting closer.

"Don't you think those planes are loud?" I almost had to shout the question.

Caiyan looked up to the sky; a worry line creased his brow.

At once, deafening sirens began sounding around us. The air took on a sense of increased consciousness, and I squashed the sudden urge to run as I looked at Caiyan in question.

"Shite!"

I felt the first rumble as the planes dropped their precious cargo. The ground shook below my feet. Caiyan grabbed my hand, and we took off in a dead run toward the building.

"What the hell?" I shouted as I tried to keep up with Caiyan. The planes flew directly over our heads, releasing a bomb that hit one side of the gray building. A round of gunfire started from the top of one of the towers. The gunman hit a bulls-eye, and the plane began a fiery descent, spiraling to the ground and exploding on impact.

"Holy shit! What's going on?" I asked, again raising my voice to be heard above the chaos. We were standing at the bottom of a steep, rocky hill. Bombs and bullets were raining down on us like lead confetti at a New Year's Eve celebration. We needed cover and fast.

"There!" Caiyan shouted and pointed at the entrance to the gray cement building at the top of the hill. People were running toward the building in what looked like a stampede of fear. The entrance was on the other side of the hill in the direct line of fire from the planes. We would never make it there safely. Caiyan motioned for me to go up the hill in front of him. I started up the steep incline, sidestepping my way against the slick grass and rocks. Caiyan was a few feet behind me. I stumbled and lost my footing about halfway up. Tumbling ass over elbows, I passed Caiyan on the way down and came to a halt at the bottom of the hill. A sharp pain smacked me in the back of the head.

"Lass, are ye all right?" Caiyan was standing over me. He bent down and cradled my head in his hand.

"World War II was in 1945," I gasped, trying to catch my breath.

"Aye."

"And we're in Germany." Then my world faded to black.

Chapter 6

I woke with a foggy recollection of what had happened. A searing pain shot through my temples, and I tried to focus on the voice speaking to me.

"Jen, are ye hurt?"

My vision cleared, and Caiyan was hovering over me. I tried to sit up, but a wave of nausea rolled around in the pit of my stomach, causing me to stay down. Caiyan began speaking to me in a language I couldn't understand, and the face of an older woman peered around him. She spoke to me, but I couldn't understand her. The ringing in my ears was causing everyone to sound funny.

I heard myself say, "I'm fine."

"Sehr gut," he said, eyeing me cautiously.

What the heck did he say? my inner voice questioned. I tilted my head so I could get a better view of my location. I was in a tunnel of some sort. The entire tunnel consisted of dingy yellowed-painted brick. Hammocks were strung like bunk beds three high and endlessly down the tunnel. People were crammed in the hold, and I was lying in a single cot at the end. Small lights emitting an eerie yellow glow were spaced along the cracked brick in the ceiling overhead. The pungent smell of blood, combined with sweat and dirt, made me gag.

Caiyan leaned over me, and the woman moved in front of Caiyan. Her ivory skin was weathered and wrinkled, possibly due from stress instead of age, but her eyes held a kindness that made me feel at ease. She was examining me; however, I had a gut feeling she wasn't a doctor. She reached up and removed something from behind my head. It was a rag soaked in blood.

Was that my blood? I tried to sit up, but the woman pushed me back down and replaced the bloody rag with a clean one. Caiyan spoke to her in the strange language, and she backed off.

"Have I been shot?" I reached for my head.

"No, ye hit yer head in the fall down the hill," Caiyan said, but his accent was strange. How hard had I hit my head?

My memory came back to me in one sharp pain. I had been falling down a hill as bombs dropped around me. I remembered Caiyan kneeling over me, holding my head with the look of sheer terror on his face.

Suddenly my vision became crystal clear. We were in Germany during the end of the Second World War. Hitler was on the rampage, trying to hang on to the last hope of world domination.

"What the fu—" Before I could finish, Caiyan started tsking at me and telling the woman his fraulein was confused.

"I'm not confused, you jackass," I said, my voice rising an octave. The woman's eyebrows shot up, and she moved to another part of the tunnel.

"Shh. Keep your voice down, or you will draw attention to us."

"What were you thinking?" I asked in a hushed tone. "We're in Berlin, in the middle of one of the worst wars in the history of the world."

Caiyan leaned down and whispered to me, "How's yer German accent?"

I thought about the question. Caiyan was speaking English to me but with a German accent. I hoped the woman didn't report me to the Gestapo. The headlines would read, "Crazy American Woman Caught Napping behind Enemy Lines."

We hadn't covered German in linguistics, because I wasn't supposed to be here. The only person I could think of who spoke German was Helga, the clinic's massage therapist. I had known her only a short time, but she'd taught me a few words, mostly curse words. I might be able to copy her accent.

"Ya," I said, nodding.

"That's my girl." He helped me sit up and I immediately felt woozy. After he laid me back down, I felt better. Concern and a hint of irritation showed in his eyes as he stared down at me and ran a hand through his dust-encrusted hair. We were stranded in an enemy country, and I needed to know our plan of exit.

"What's our MO?" I asked, using the WTF slang for "game plan."

"You are a sick cousin, and I am taking you home to Milan," Caiyan said with the perfect German accent.

"My Italian is worse than my German."

A crooked smile hinted at the corners of his mouth as he took me in his arms. "When they let us out, I am going to ask to speak with the commander."

"I think we should just head back home."

"No, we need to get what we came for," Caiyan said, a little too demandingly.

"This is war. We aren't just fighting a brigand. We could die more ways than one."

"We're already inside. It shouldnae be a problem to grab the art on the way oot the door."

Jeez, he acted as if the Nazis were going to hand out shopping bags on the way into their treasure room. "We're going home," I said firmly.

He crossed his arms over his chest and looked me right in the eye. "Then ye will have to go withoot me."

"You don't have your key. That means I'm in charge, and I say we are going."

He stared at me with hard-set green eyes. "Ye are impossible, ye know that?"

"Careful, your Scot is coming out," I said, knowing that when he got agitated, he had a harder time controlling his native tongue.

He had raised his finger, pointed it at my chest, and opened his mouth as though he was about to set me straight when the door to the tunnel opened. Three soldiers entered the room armed with rifles.

They were dressed in gray military uniforms, minus the swastika arm-bands that appeared in all the World War II movies I had seen. They ordered Caiyan to come with them. Caiyan was speaking German and pointing at me. An argument started between the soldier in charge and Caiyan. Two of the soldiers grabbed Caiyan and pushed him toward the door. He threw a glance at me over his shoulder.

I stood a little too quickly, trying to help him, and faded to black once again.

⟶

A clanging noise pounded against my eardrum. I felt my world go from black to gray to yellow. The face of the older woman appeared in my line of vision. She spoke to me in harsh, clipped words that I didn't understand.

I remembered the Nazis taking Caiyan. I needed to get out of here. Not an easy feat when I couldn't get vertical. I struggled to sit up, slapping away the old woman's hand. Caiyan was nowhere. I felt light-headed, but as my vision began to clear, so did my head.

"Bloody hell," I said, and the woman gasped.

"Shh," the old woman said. "You don't want Luftwaffe to know you are English."

"I'm not English; I'm American."

Another gasp from the woman. "An American, even worse. Now your president has died, I am sure the führer will win war." She spoke in broken English, and her eyes cut to the other inhabitants in the tunnel.

I brought my hand to my head to try and calm the pounding.

"You hit head during the bombings. You have quite ze goose egg." She pointed toward the back of my head. Her accent was thick and rich, not German, maybe Slovakian. I couldn't really tell. My head ached, and I felt like I was hearing her words underwater.

"Do you know what happened to the man that was with me?"

She shrugged. "He was taken to commander in charge. If he was American, he is probably already dead."

My heart beat faster, and my inner voice started to cry. There was no telling what nationality Caiyan was claiming to be. He was fluent in several languages, German among them. He wasn't Hitler's blond, blue-eyed poster boy, but his dark hair and strong jawline might pass as Italian. I needed answers.

"Where am I?"

"We are in *Flaktürme*." I cocked my head in question at the name, and she explained. "They are towers Luftwaffe occupies to shoot planes from sky before they drop bombs. It is safest place in city."

"Can we leave?"

"The Luftwaffe will open door when it is safe."

A young girl with bright-blue eyes brought the old woman a cup of water, and she helped me drink it. There was something familiar about the girl; her eyes reminded me of someone. The water tasted like rust, and I choked trying to swallow. The girl took the cup from me and smiled and then said something to the woman. The woman translated. "She likes your hair. She thinks it's a pretty color."

My hair—I ran a finger through it and felt the matted wet of sticky blood. *Caiyan better be alive, so I can kill him.* Who in their right mind travels into the onslaught of a world war? For a piece of art? I hated the fact that a priceless piece of art might be lost in a bombing or a fire, but I wasn't willing to risk my life for it.

Damn Caiyan. I'd thought we were moving forward in our relationship, but once again his priorities were cloudy.

"How long was I unconscious?"

The woman conferred with the girl again and said, "A few hours."

"Hours—oh, my god!" I was going to miss my travel time at Gitmo. Shit! *No, wait; when I return, I will have been gone for only a few hours.* My inner voice sighed with relief. If I could find Caiyan and get the hell out of here, no one would be the wiser. Jake and General Potts wouldn't have to know a thing. My inner voice reminded me I had to complete my travel cycle. Time continues until the moon begins to wane. Double shit. A small tear leaked out of my left eye, and my inner voice kissed my key good-bye. I wasn't going to give up that easily. I still had time.

"Thank you," I said to the woman. "Are you a doctor?"

"No, I'm Anna. I run a *Konditorei*." I raised a questioning eyebrow at the foreign word. She stumbled through her words as she searched for the right one. "A *Bäckerei von Süßigkeiten*."

"A bakery?" I asked. "The place you make cakes?"

"Yes, yes," she said, waving her hands with the excitement that we had found the correct translation. "Before war, it was best bakery in Berlin." Her eyes lit up as she spoke of her bakery. "But now, well…" Her sentence faltered, and the light in her eyes faded.

"Jennifer Cloud." I offered my hand to her, and she reached out and grasped it. "I'm traveling through Berlin with my cousin."

"Not a good time to be traveling," Anna said, and we both let out a strained giggle at the absurdity of my statement.

A large bang sent a sharp pain shooting behind my right eye as if it had been speared and plucked from the socket. The noise was from the returning three soldiers opening the door to the tunnel. They gave an order in German, and we filed out. The strap on my shoe was broken, and it made a slapping noise as it hit the side of my leg. I kept my head down and followed the people out of the tunnel and into the hallway. *Snap, slap, snap, slap.* I bent over to try and fix the strap, and a guard bumped his gun into my butt.

"*Gehen*," he ordered, which I assumed meant to move it.

Another soldier was waiting in the hall and spoke to the beefy guard who was poking me in the ass with the barrel of his rifle. The accent was not the strong, complicated sound of German but the fluid tongue rolling of Italian. I kept my head down to avoid eye contact with the soldiers and to keep the ringing in my ears to a minimum. The two soldiers said a few strong words to each other, and then the soldier in the hall grabbed my arm and shoved me down another hallway.

Now I was separated from the only woman who could speak English and being manhandled by the Luftwaffe. I was taken to another tunnel and pushed inside by the man. Was he going to rape me? Gertie had a book on anti-Semitism, and it described the women who were raped and tortured by the Nazis. The soldier had his back to me and was peering out the door before he shut it, obviously checking to make sure his comrades wouldn't interrupt. I jumped on his back and started pounding him with my fists.

"Jesus, Jen. Are you nuts?" He pulled me off in a swoop of his strong arm. I felt the heat and saw his face in the same instant. Marco.

I stopped fussing and wrapped him in an embrace.

"If I *were* a Nazi, he would have had you executed for assaulting an officer."

"I thought you were going to torture me."

He bit his bottom lip, and I felt as if that might not be out of the question.

I was so happy to see him. "What are you doing here?"

"I should ask you the same question." He stood back and folded his arms across his chest.

"I brought Caiyan here to save some art that will be destroyed by a fire."

"You're nuts. This is World War II."

"I was a little fuzzy on the details of the landing location." I changed the subject before he could start in on a lecture. "How did you find me?"

"Pickles caught your unplanned trip on the travel screen. Luckily, he was paying attention and came to me before he told Agent McCoy."

"So Jake doesn't know I'm here?" I grinned in anticipation of getting back before I was outed and mentally thanked Pickles, the navigator in the travel lab, for watching my back.

"Not yet," Marco said.

"When did you get here?"

"I landed just as the action began." His voice became more animated as he described the scenario. "Scared me to death. Bombs fucking dropping everywhere, and Caiyan was carrying you like a corpse."

"I fell, and I don't remember anything until I woke up here."

"He disappeared inside the Flaktürme, and I snatched a uniform off an Italian soldier who had fallen victim to a very large brick wall demolished in the raid."

"You took the clothes off a dead guy?" I made a face.

"You're complaining about my attire?"

We heard voices in the hallway, and the door opened. Marco turned and ripped my top, pinned me against the wall, and kissed me hard on the mouth. I pushed at him, and the soldiers laughed. Marco said something in German, and they left. The heat between us soared, and he stared hard at me.

"We're lucky they didn't want to join in the fun. Let's get the hell out of here."

He grabbed my hand, but I hesitated. He paused and turned, giving me a questioning expression.

"I can't leave him here," I said.

He sighed. "That asshole is going to get us both killed."

"Please, Marco."

"Jen, we are at the epicenter of World War II. Do you know anything about this war?"

I shook my head. My knowledge of the details of World War II was limited. I knew Hitler was the main bad guy. I thought the Italians and the Germans were on the same side. England, Russia—no, make that the Soviet Union, China, and the United States were allies. "We won," I finally answered.

Marco frowned. "You should have paid attention in school." He looked up at the ceiling as if it could cave in any second. "We're in the middle of the worst bombings in Berlin's history. This city was bombed for thirty-six straight days. There are only eight days left, and this city will be nothing but ruins."

That explained the headless statues in the park. I couldn't leave Caiyan here without a way to get home. We were going to have to find him and force him to return with us.

"Let's go find Caiyan and go home."

Marco scowled but cracked the door and signaled that the coast was clear. We were at the bottom of a staircase. We climbed up a floor and tiptoed down a long hallway. At least, I was tiptoeing. Marco was just walking. *Snap, slap, snap, slap.* Marco stopped.

"What's that noise?"

"My shoe is broken." The floors were covered with grime, and I wasn't about to take them off.

He read my mind, and leaning down, he tucked the strap into the back of the shoe. Satisfied with his cobbling, we went left down an adjacent hallway and halted. Six men sat on the floor, gagged and with their hands tied behind their backs. None of them were Caiyan. Their uniforms were embroidered with RAF badges—British air force.

"We should release them," I said.

"No. We're not changing the past. Or did you forget the long grounding you had from our *last* travel?"

I didn't look the men in the eyes. Maybe they would make it out on their own. We went up another flight of stairs and passed a small window. The tunnels were underground. The window was filthy, but I could see this was the first floor of the Flak tower. The commanding rooms of the Luftwaffe. As we drew near a room at the end of the hall, I could hear a static-filled rendition of Beethoven's Fifth Symphony being played from a radio. Who was listening to the radio during an air raid?

We heard voices, and I recognized one as Caiyan's. He was speaking German. Marco put a finger to his lips, and we pressed against the wall, listening to the men speak. If someone came down the hall, we were done for.

"He is telling the commanding officer he's here to move the art," Marco relayed.

"I didn't know you spoke German."

"There's a lot you don't know about me. What do you want to do?"

"He can't travel; he doesn't have a key."

Marco looked as if leaving Caiyan in 1945, in the hands of the Nazis, was the perfect place for him.

"Has he been here before?" Marco asked.

"Why?"

"It seems as if they are talking like they know each other. My German may be rusty, but I think Caiyan just called him *old friend*."

My inner voice began to inquire how Caiyan might have traveled without his key. One bitchy, brother-snatching transporter came to mind. I'd thought Mahlia and Caiyan were on opposing sides after we'd taken her brother hostage during my second unofficial travel.

If Caiyan needed to travel, he could have used any number of other transporters. I didn't know why he would have contacted Mahlia. It was probably Ace, but surely Ace would have told me.

"Earth to Jen," Marco said, waving his hand in front of my face while the other held firmly on to his weapon. I shook my head, blaming my head injury for the lack of concentration. "We know what he's after. Let's see if we can find the hidey-hole and keep it company."

Caiyan sounded like he had the Nazi convinced he was legit, so I agreed with Marco. Caiyan would eventually end up in the room with the painting. We made our way back down the stairs and to the other side of the bunker. As we turned the corner, we spotted a guard standing outside a heavy metal door. We ducked back into the adjoining hallway before he saw us.

"Do you think that's the hidey-hole?" I asked in a whisper.

"I'm pretty sure that door is not hiding the mess hall."

"We can't wait here—we'll be seen." I looked over my shoulder at the long hall behind us. If someone came down the stairs, we were in plain sight.

He looked me up and down as if sizing me up for wingman duty and then assessed the guard again. "It's only one guy. I'm going to take him out. When I do, you grab his feet, and we will move him into the room."

"OK, do you want me to hold the gun on him?" I asked, reaching for Marco's gun.

"Definitely not," he said, shaking his head and slinging his gun to his back. "I've already been shot once in my lifetime. That's plenty, thank you very much."

I rolled my eyes at him, and he said, "Wait here."

He made his way down the long hall and to the guard. Marco approached, and the guard did the whole Nazi salute thing. Instead of returning the gesture, Marco waved his hand as if he were doing a Jedi mind trick, and time slowed, except for Marco. In a millisecond, he had removed the guard's gun and knocked him unconscious.

I ran down the hall. "That was amazing."

"I have other talents that are equally as amazing," he said, picking up the comrade under the arms and jerking his head toward the man's feet. "You grab his legs and help me get him in the room."

I unlatched the heavy door and held it open with my backside as we carried him inside and shut the door.

"Holy Treasure Island," Marco said as he dropped the man on the floor. I turned to see a room filled with enough stolen booty to make even Long John Silver jealous.

Chapter 7

The tunnel was longer than the one Caiyan and I had fled to for safety, but it had the same dingy yellow walls and the stench of war. The hammocks were missing, but the tunnel was filled top to bottom with artifacts. Paintings still in their gilded frames were stacked on tables and leaning against walls. Bronze and marble statues were crammed in the back of the room. Tapestries were rolled up and piled pyramid-style on top of one another. Tables, chairs, dishes, and the remnants of people's lives torn apart by war were stashed in the bottom of the Flak Tower like discarded newspaper.

We walked through the room in awe at the splendor that crowded the room. Delicate bone china was stacked on tables, and I was surprised it had survived the invasion without a crack. I picked up a pretty cream-colored plate with tiny roses sketched around the edge. These were special, like the dishes Mamma Bea used at Thanksgiving. Marco was admiring the statues that lined the wall.

"Jen, these statues. Well, their dudes are…small."

I carefully returned the plate and walked over to him. He was staring at the pubic area of a statue of a naked man.

"I think I read somewhere that small genitals were considered majestic."

Marco snorted. "Would you like to find out how majestic I am?"

I started to object and then stopped myself. Marco felt my hesitation, and a wide grin spread across his face. "When we get back home, I should probably collect my payment. You have a tendency to get into trouble, and I would hate to miss an opportunity."

He put a hand on my shoulder, and a zing of heat shot to my doo-dah. My inner voice started counting off all my missed opportunities in life, and I shut her in the closet. Which reminded me...we had an unconscious man spread-eagle on the floor. If the Nazis came in and found him, we would be next in line for the firing squad.

"What should we do with him?" I asked, focusing the conversation back on our current problem.

"We need something to restrain him." Marco began searching the room.

I spotted an Oriental rug leaning up against the wall. Perfect— and it would keep him bound as well. "Over here."

Marco and I unrolled the rug and contemplated how to get the comrade on top of it. He was tall and lanky, not a fat man, but the dead weight was heavy to push. I squatted down and tried to flip him over onto the rug. He didn't budge.

"A little help would be nice." I watched as Marco removed his rifle.

"I thought SuperJen had this one," he said, squeezing my bicep. His jaw dropped in astonishment at my new upper-arm tone. "Impressive." He helped me roll the man over until he was on top of the rug.

"I think you should change into his clothes, so we can sneak out of here." Marco helped me remove the man's clothes, except for his underwear. Ick. We decided to leave him with some dignity. Stuffing his sock in his mouth to prevent any unwanted yelling for help, we rolled him up like a cannoli. I made sure he could get air and prayed he wouldn't be heard through the thousand-year-old rug. It probably had come from the Ming dynasty, so I guessed a little slobber from an unconscious Nazi wouldn't damage it too much.

"I'm going back on guard duty. You put his clothes on and see if you can flatten out those tits. If they think you're a dude, maybe we have a chance to get out of here." Marco slipped out the door

I shook the soldier's clothes out. They smelled of sweat and the dust that hung in the air from the raids. I quickly pulled on the clothes. The heavy jacket also hid my boobs. I tucked my matted hair up into the wool-lined helmet, which looked like a salad bowl. The wool scratched at the back of my neck as I fastened the strap under my chin. The pantaloons were a bit long but would be tucked inside the tall brown leather boots. I sat on the floor to tug on the first boot, but my toes crumpled against its toe.

"What the frig?" I asked out loud, examining the boot. The man had very tiny feet for his height. I shoved my foot in the other boot and stood, gingerly walking around as I tried to stretch out the boots. This was no good. I looked like one of Cinderella's stepsisters trying to shove my foot in the glass slipper. I opened the door.

"This isn't going to work," I said to Marco as I tiptoed around the room, demonstrating my inability to wear the boots.

"What's wrong?" He peered through the doorway to identify the problem. "Why are you walking like those boots are six-inch stilettos?"

"For one thing, if they were six-inch stilettos, I could walk much better than I can in these boots. They're not my size."

"The comrade has small feet." Marco grinned. "I guess we could cut off your toes."

"Very funny," I said as voices echoed from the adjoining tunnel.

"Hide!" Marco slammed the door in my face.

Hide? I stood staring at the closed door. Hide where? I ditched the small boots in a nearby vase and grabbed my clothes. The rows of chairs, tables, and art would act as a cover, but if anyone looked behind them, I would be spotted. On the floor leaning up against one of the tables were several large, framed works of art. I ducked under the table and pulled one of the paintings in front of me.

This was good. I had a straight view of the door, and unless the painting was moved, I was hidden. I was about to breathe a sigh of relief when I noticed the comrade's rifle. I had left it leaning against the wall by the door. If they came in, they would see it on the way out. Damn. I retrieved the weapon, ducking back into my hiding space just as the door to the room swung open. Great. I was hiding, and now I was armed. This would make it much more difficult for Caiyan to explain his "sick cousin" if I got caught. I quickly tucked my knees to my chest and made myself as invisible as possible.

A short, stout man dressed in the standard Nazi uniform entered, followed by Caiyan. Marco was left outside the door to guard the precious cargo. They spoke in German, and I could hear the excitement in Caiyan's voice as he took in all the purloined treasure. He didn't even give Marco a second look as he walked into the room.

The small man pointed at different objects, and Caiyan was nodding as they made their way toward me. I kept very still and clamped my mouth shut. I was afraid to breathe. The comrade came over to the painting and put his hand on the broken gold frame.

My inner voice was hopping around crying, *Oh shit! Oh shit!* My knees began to tremble, and my mantra started playing in my head: *I'm Spunky, and I'm fierce, and I'm smarter than most men. Bad guys run and hide, 'cause here comes SuperJen.* It was a stupid little ditty I had used in my childhood superhero games, but it was on automatic playback when I needed immediate courage. I pulled my knees tighter to my chest and aimed the rifle at the man's thigh.

Caiyan bent down to get a better look at the painting. His brows shot up as he caught sight of me, and I glared at him. He immediately moved away from the painting and drew the comrade's attention elsewhere. They spoke for a few minutes longer and then exited the room. Caiyan gave me a backward glance as he left, and I stuck my tongue out at him.

I collapsed against the wall, and a feeling of relief washed over me. Marco entered the room shortly after and came over to help me from my hiding space. My legs were shaking, and I mentally told myself to get a grip.

"What if they return?" I asked.

"They won't. Apparently your boy Caiyan has made a deal with the accountant. That was the little man with him earlier." Marco shifted and huffed as if all this was a total waste of time. "They're going to his office to discuss the details of which things the accountant is taking for himself."

"Caiyan is helping the accountant steal from the Nazis?"

"Yep, and you want to bet there is something in it for him too? You still want to help the bastard?" Marco asked, keeping his voice low.

I shrugged. I couldn't leave Caiyan here, but it was obvious he had been planning this entire heist. "Now what?" I asked.

"I overheard the accountant tell Caiyan a truck would be here to retrieve some of the items and take them to a mine."

"A mine?" I asked, tugging on the strap of the comrade's helmet, which was starting to chafe my chin.

"That's where they stored most of the priceless art and other stolen items until after the war. Didn't you see the movie *Monument Men* with George Clooney?" Marco adjusted the strap on the rifle and fumbled through the pack on his hip. "Most of the things taken by the Germans were stolen from Jewish art collectors and Polish museums. The big players, like the Louvre, were quick enough to get all the treasures out before the Germans invaded."

Marco extracted a cigarette and a book of matches from his pack. "Ah, thank you, my fallen comrade." He put the cigarette between his lips and lit it.

"I thought you were going to quit smoking?" I asked. After he was shot, thanks to me, he had suffered some damage to one of his lungs.

"You make me nervous," he said as he took a long drag on the smoke.

I thought about reaching up and taking a puff of the cancer stick myself. I was frazzled.

He dropped the cigarette and stomped it out with his boot.

"Why did you do that?" I asked, wondering if the waste not, want not adage applied to cigarettes. "You only took one drag."

"You looked like you might want to start smoking, and I felt guilty." He smiled, and the dimple in his chin winked at me. He was gorgeous—even in this dimly lit hall with dust floating thick in the air. I asked myself why I was so into Caiyan and not Marco. *Maybe I should give Marco a chance.*

He eyed me. "I don't know what is going on in that head of yours, but I'm starting to get scared."

"Don't worry. I have no idea what's going on up there either." I tapped my temple while my inner voice made a list of seven things she wanted to lick off Marco when we returned home.

"The way I see it, we wait for the truck. When they come to load the stuff, we make a break for it. With or without lover boy."

"You know that's not an option." I huffed at him and paced up and down the hall. "I can't leave him. Now that he knows where I am, he will come back for me."

"And then I can bash him over the head, carry him out of here, and go home."

"Maybe," I said, and Marco looked hopeful. I wasn't sure if it was the head bashing or the getting out of here that he liked more.

I pushed him toward the door. "You'd better get back out there in case any other Nazis want a tour of the merchandise."

"What are you going to do?" he asked.

"Check on the comrade, change back into my civilian clothes, and plan our escape."

"Aye, aye, Comandante."

I used one of the confiscated mirrors to examine the current condition of my appearance. A small goose egg was tender at the base of my skull. The ringing in my head had subsided, and my nausea was gone. My inner voice gave me the thumbs-up, and I agreed it was a good sign—probably not a concussion. My hair was matted where the wound had bled a little, and I had bobby pins poking out haphazardly from my head. I coiled my hair back into the small bun and secured it with the pins. My broken shoes would have to do for now. I frowned at my reflection in the mirror. How was I going to kick-butt in broken shoes? My frown changed into a smile as I realized I was planning my outfit for butt-kicking. Maybe, I will make a decent WTF traveler after all.

I had just finished fastening the buttons on my jacket when I heard a commotion outside the door. I ran for my hiding spot, but before I could duck for cover, Caiyan burst into the room. Marco was following him, and they were growling profanities at each other.

"Would you two please stifle it?" I said as I wedged my way between them. "Caiyan, we need to go home."

His green eyes were fuming and softened only a bit when he pulled his gaze from Marco to me. "The comrade thinks you are my secretary."

"What happened to the sick cousin?" I asked.

"New plan, and it doesnae include this wise guy," he said, throwing a thumb toward Marco.

"Look," I said, poking a finger in his chest. "It may take all of us to get out of this mess you have gotten us into, and I'm in charge, so he stays."

Caiyan smiled at this and crossed his arms over his chest. "Don't ye jest love a woman in charge?"

Marco grinned, and suddenly they were on the same team. Both smiling down at me like there was no possible way I was in charge. We didn't have time to squabble about the details, because the sound of boots clicking on the stone floor resounded off the brick walls. Marco took his post at the door, and Caiyan and I waited outside the door with Marco, as if we were waiting for permission to enter.

The commanding officer in charge of the whole shebang came stomping down the hall, followed by the crooked accountant and two members of the Luftwaffe I would describe as bodyguards. The commander shot a curious look at Marco, but Caiyan interceded, directing the commander's attention toward me.

Caiyan spoke a few words in German to the commander, and introductions were made. I was Fräulein Ingrid Svenson. Now I was Swedish—jeez, my heritage kept growing with Caiyan's nose. I heard my name, and the commander looked me up and down and then licked his lips. Not good. My inner voice whispered the words *sex slave*, and I felt my knees wobble.

As we entered the room, the men spoke only in German and only to Caiyan. The accountant lifted a large ledger book he had been carrying under his arm and handed it to Caiyan. He opened it, skimmed through the pages like he knew exactly what he was doing, nodded, and then passed it to me and said something in Swedish.

I nodded and began to peruse the book. German. Everything was in German. How was I going to know what items they wanted on their truck?

Caiyan peered over my shoulder. He pointed to a number on the side of the register and spoke to me in Swedish. I examined the beautiful porcelain vase next to me. Written on the bottom was a number. Across the top of the register was a word that was possibly the place the art had been taken from, because I did recognize some of the words in that column. Kaiser-Friedrich was one of the German museums Caiyan had told me the art had been removed from and taken to the Flaktürme for safety.

There was also a list of names and what I would refer to as neighborhoods: Kreuzberg, Charlottenburg, Schöneberg, Spandau, Mitte. Each number corresponded to a very detailed description of the stolen item. Whoever was in charge of pilfering the loot had been smart enough to realize that one day these precious items would need to be returned to their rightful owners. The numbers were in sequence. My inner voice wiped her brow—thank goodness.

"Vat are we doing?" I asked Caiyan quietly while the commander was talking to his comrades.

"We are taking the art to a safer place," said Caiyan.

"Vat about our sick cousin?"

He rolled his eyes. "We are documenting everything. The orders are directly from the führer," Caiyan said through clenched teeth. He turned, flashing a smile toward the commander, who had started issuing orders to the soldiers. "Act like a secretary and use the ledger. It has a list of everything in this hold."

"Vat do I do?"

"You'll check off what we take to safety. And quit saying *vat*. You sound like a vampire."

"Everything?" I asked, gazing at the full tunnel of stuff. Apparently, we were supposed to make sure the paintings, sculptures, and artifacts listed in the book made it on the truck, while the tables, chairs, and other pieces of lives were left behind to be destroyed by the fire. Of course, I had to give the commander a break, because he didn't know the flak tower was going to catch fire, destroying the contents, just like he didn't know his beloved führer was going to commit hara-kiri real soon.

"Aye, except you and I are looking for two specific paintings."

"You should drop the *aye* if you want to stay alive."

He smiled. "Touché."

"What do these paintings look like?"

"The first is the Madonna holding a child by Giovanni Bellini, and the second is a portrait of a woman wearing a gold dress."

The commander came over and said a few words to Caiyan. Then he and his men turned on their combat-boot heels and left. Caiyan and I stood alone in the treasure room.

"That's it?" I asked. "He's just going to leave us alone in here with all this?" I waved my hand toward the tower of vases and chairs.

"We're not free to leave." Caiyan pointed at the door. "There's a guard outside to make sure we don't take anything before the truck arrives to transport these to the mine."

"The guard is Marco," I reminded him.

"What's he doing here?" Caiyan grumbled.

"He's here to save me."'

"Ye don't need saving. Yer with me, and since when does Marco travel?"

"Since he started working for the WTF." I took a deep breath. I might as well tell him. Now was as good a time as any, and he couldn't scream at me, because of the tight quarters. "I'm transporting for him."

"No yer naugh."

"Yes. I am. Orders from Jake—and besides, I can transport for whomever I want."

"No, you cannae."

"You're not the boss of me."

"Jen, I have seen the way he looks at ye, and I don't like it."

"Why?" I tilted my head, looking up at him. "Because it's the same way you look at me?"

His green eyes contemplated my words, and the scar that split through his upper lip became more prominent as he pressed his lips together. "Maybe."

"Marco has a few new friends," Caiyan said nodding toward two guards that had arrived. "They're the movers."

Marco was keeping the soldiers occupied sharing cigarettes. Most of the items were packed toward the back of the room, so there was a bit of a distance between us and the door, which the commander had ordered propped open. I was afraid the soldiers might hear me speaking English or see us swipe the paintings.

"How are we going to sneak these paintings out the door?" I asked in my library voice.

"Patience," he said, frowning at me. "We have to find them first. You start on that side of the room, and I'll start here. As ye pull items, check them against the list. If they're on it, move them to the middle, so the movers can start loading the truck." Caiyan started toward the back of the room and stopped midstride. "Jennifer, what's rolled up in this carpet?"

I came up behind him and saw our captive was wiggling a bit. "Um, that's the Nazi who was guarding the door."

Caiyan frowned at me and uttered a few words in Gaelic. He gave the carpet a swift kick, and it stopped moving. Together we dragged the carpeted Nazi behind a rather large chifforobe.

"Back to the search, darling." Caiyan began to help me, and together we spent a few hours lugging precious art to the door for the soldiers to move to the waiting truck.

Most of the paintings were wrapped in brown packing paper, but I managed to pull the paper back enough to get a glimpse inside. These were lovely works of art. Many were portraits I assumed had been plucked off walls where families had been looking at them for generations. Caiyan started on the opposite side of the room, and I wandered over to see if he had found anything. He was examining the contents of a small gold pouch.

I walked up behind him and said quietly, "I don't think the painting's in there."

He startled and dropped the gold pouch on the floor, spilling a collection of marbles that rolled haphazardly over the floor. "Shite!"

"No, I believe the word is *Scheisse*."

"Smart ass." We bent down to gather the marbles, and Caiyan picked up a bright-red marble.

"That one is pretty," I said.

"This is no marble." He held it out for me to see. It was a cushion-cut ruby ring the size of a cherry tomato.

"Oh, it's beautiful." I slid the ring on my finger, and it was a perfect fit.

"Whoever the owner was must have hidden the ring in with the marbles. It was in the box there." He pointed to a gold box on the table next to me.

"Is there a number on the box?" I asked.

"No." Caiyan picked up the box, peered at the bottom, and then grinned.

"You can't take it," I said, pulling the ring from my finger and returning it to the pouch.

"Why naugh?"

"Because it belongs to someone else, and you can't take it back through time."

"Let me worry aboot the details, lassie."

If the box didn't have a number, it would probably be lost in the fire and buried. My inner self was wagging a finger at me, so I promised I would research the ring when we returned. He tucked the pouch into his jacket pocket, and I helped gather the remaining marbles.

We continued our search for the paintings, and an hour later, I hit pay dirt. The large gold frame was cracked, as though a vandal had ripped it from its home, but the painting inside was magnificent. The serene look on the Madonna's face as she held the small child made my biological clock strike twelve.

"I've got one," I called.

Caiyan came posthaste and nodded reverently at the art.

"How are we going to get it out of here, and then what are we going to do with it?" I asked, sizing up the situation. "It's quite large."

A cocky grin spread over his face, and with full Scottish accent, he said, "I remember ye askin' me that before, and ye didnae have much problem."

I gave an exaggerated eye roll as I helped Caiyan remove the broken frame, keeping an eye out for the movers to return from dropping off the last load we'd given them. Caiyan extracted the painting, rolled it up inside a tapestry, and added it to the other items waiting to be taken to the truck. I assumed we would be collecting the tapestry before it was taken to the mine. I returned to my quest of finding the items the accountant wanted on the truck, and Caiyan returned to his search for the woman in gold. As we were going through the pieces, I noticed Caiyan checking inside the drawers of the dressers and other confiscated furniture.

"Are you looking for something in particular?" I asked, checking that the guards were out of earshot.

"No, jest making sure we don't miss anything."

"Caiyan, all these things are supposed to be lost. When they turn up, we are going to be in serious trouble."

He shrugged. "We're saving precious art."

I'd had to endure months of Jake drilling into my head how important it was to keep the past as it is. And here I was, on an unauthorized travel after being grounded, screwing up the past. Our time was limited here. He didn't have a plan, and I was not getting trapped between moon cycles during a war, even if we were about to declare victory.

Caiyan took the book from my hands and set it down on a table that probably had belonged to a nice Jewish family. He pulled me behind a stack of stolen goods, reached up behind my neck, and pulled me to his lips. All thoughts of spending more time with Marco flew south for the winter.

"What are you doing?" I asked after the caress of his lips had my thighs trembling.

"Ye had that look in yer eye like you were considering bolting and leaving me here."

"I would never do that."

"One day ye might have to, but right now, I wanted to make sure ye remembered how I feel about ye."

As I was leaning in for a second round of glorious kisses, a flash of gold over Caiyan's right shoulder caught my eye. On top of the chifforobe, leaning upright against a small statue of a naked woman, was the lady in gold. "Is that your painting?" I asked, pointing at the top of the chifforobe.

Caiyan's head whipped around, and he almost knocked me over as he maneuvered over crates and other art to get the picture. It was smaller than I'd expected, which was why I hadn't noticed it before; I had been looking for a picture the size of the Madonna. As Caiyan brought it down to eye level, I saw what made the painting so valuable: she was wearing a key.

"Really?" I asked, waving my arms in disgust. "All this was about you getting a key?"

"I've been researching this for some time," he said, staring at the picture. It didn't have the same artistry as the Madonna and looked almost as if it had been painted by a family friend instead of a seasoned artist. He stroked the key around the woman's neck, and my guilt-o-meter pointed red.

"Do you know where it is?"

"Nigh, but now that I have found the painting, I have an address."

I bit my bottom lip. If Caiyan took that key, who would be losing their key in the present day? Caiyan ran a hand down my cheek, and I released the lip I was holding prisoner.

"There has naugh been any activity on this key. I have done extensive research, and there has never been a WTF who wears it. If it belongs to anyone, that person's a brigand."

"You should have told me you were after a key."

"Would ye have brought me here knowing what I was coming for?"

I wasn't sure. I wanted Caiyan to have a key so we could be a team again, but traveling to Germany during wartime was not only dangerous but also plain stupid.

"That's what I thought." He acknowledged my silence as my answer.

76

"You lied to me," I said raising my eyes to meet his steely green ones.

"Naugh, I didnae," he said. "I intend to save the art, regardless if I get the key."

"OK, I'll help you. Then we are going home."

"Aye, we will."

We looked the painting up in the register. The accountant hadn't designated it as one for the truck. Caiyan memorized the name and address, then removed the painting from its frame, and tucked it inside his jacket.

The sound of the guard's boots clicked on the concrete floor of the tunnel. I grabbed the register and the nearest object and hoisted it back to the moving area.

The guard came up and wrinkled his nose at me. "Nein!"

He shouted a few more words at me, and I looked at the object I was carrying. I'd thought it was a bowl, but after his little fit, I figured out it was an antique chamber pot. An item a Jew had taken a poo in was apparently not high on his list of priceless possessions. I flipped open the book with some force and scanned the numbers for the object. It was listed. Next to the number was the name Rodin. Seems like the famous sculptor was a fan of creating beautiful pissers.

I pointed to the number and smirked at the guard. He spouted a few words I was pretty sure were curse words, snatched the pot from me, and turned on his heel and left the room.

Caiyan cut his eyes at me. "Try not to irritate the guards."

My inner voice shot him the finger, and I continued to look for as many chamber pots as I could find.

Chapter 8

We found all the items the accountant had requested, and the truck was loaded, but the amount of precious cargo left behind was staggering. Caiyan had told me there would be a fire, and I wanted to try and shove as much in the truck as possible. I added a beautiful bronze statue, but the accountant was firm and had it removed when he checked our load. Caiyan explained I'd misread a number and apologized to the man, giving me a wary glare in the process.

Before we left the treasure room, I made Caiyan unroll the unconscious soldier from the Oriental rug. The man couldn't be left to die—who knew how long it would take for the Nazis to find him? I loosened the binding on his hands, and we scooted him against a wall. Caiyan insisted on leaving the sock in his mouth. I agreed. If he woke up before we were out of town, his capture might be difficult to explain to the accountant.

The soldiers escorted us outside to the waiting vehicle. The truck was army green with a long, covered bed and a Mercedes emblem on the hood. One of the Nazi soldiers drove, and Caiyan and I rode up front with him. Marco and two other soldiers rode in the back.

We made our way slowly, driving over rubble and the remains of what used to be a vibrant city. Most of the buildings were block-style with apartments on the upper floors and storefronts along the street level. Apartments were missing the upper floors, which lay crumbled in mountains of bricks and debris at the base of the buildings. Other buildings looked as though they'd had a large bite taken out of them, and the furniture that remained in the rooms was visible from the street.

We entered a section of Berlin that showed minor damage from the bombings. Many of the buildings had businesses still in operation, and people stared at the truck as we drove by. We had driven a few blocks when Caiyan said something to the driver in German and pointed to a small shop located on a side street. The driver raised an inquisitive eyebrow at Caiyan and turned down the narrow lane. He pulled the truck over next to a building that had a few chunks knocked out of its façade but was in much better shape than the rest of Berlin. A line of people hugged the side of the building. Their thin frames and dark, sunken eyes embodied the effects of a devastating war. They commented and gestured toward the truck as we exited to the street. I noticed the sign on the small shop read *Bäckerei*.

Caiyan got out, and I followed. Marco jumped down from the back of the truck. Caiyan stopped and stared at Marco for a second, and I thought he was about to order him back in the truck.

"Where she goes, I go," Marco said, cocking his head in my direction.

I assumed Caiyan decided it was not worth the fight, because he ordered the rest of the men to guard the truck.

The door to the shop was open, and we squeezed past the line of patiently waiting patrons. I wondered why we were stopping here, but I didn't want the people to hear me speak English, so I kept quiet. The displeased looks on the patrons' faces when we cut in line was making me a little nervous, but Marco angled his gun in their direction, and they backed off like frightened schoolchildren in the presence of the headmistress. Caiyan stopped, and Marco closed the distance between us. I felt like I was being sandwiched as we stood in the center of the small bakery.

The lighting was dim, and a lone bulb hung overhead with the remnants of what used to be a light fixture. The shop was still receiving electricity, and the light from the large windows in the front of the store illuminated the shelves that lined the back wall. A small marble counter and an empty glass pastry case separated us from a woman working behind the counter. The shelves were bare except for a few basic ingredients stored in bags and canisters.

Two other employees were busy handing out half loaves of baked bread to the people and accepting ration coupons in return. I examined the pictures hanging on the wall, while Caiyan tried to get the woman's attention. The pictures were black-and-white photographs showing the bakery in 1940. The bakery was bustling with patrons. The glass case was full of pastries; loaves of bread filled the racks of shelves; and a smattering of tables and chairs were outside, lining the sidewalk. To my surprise, another photo showed Hitler himself enjoying one of the mouthwatering pastries.

As the woman turned toward the light, I recognized her from the Flaktürme. It was Anna, the older woman who had helped me. She smiled and greeted us in German. Caiyan looked surprised to see Anna. He asked to speak with her; at least, I think that's what he asked, because she had one of the other employees take over for her and came around the counter.

Caiyan introduced Marco and said a few more phrases in German I couldn't decipher. She ushered us into a back storeroom where the war rations were kept. In the middle of the room was a long farm table with a beautiful cake being assembled on a lead-crystal, pedestal-style cake stand. It was a tower of bread-like pastry with chocolate frosting piped around the edges. Tiny flowers made of sugar were being added to the cake by a young girl standing on a wooden supply crate. The young girl had also been in the Flaktürme. I had a hazy recollection of her bringing me water.

"That's a beautiful cake," I said, motioning toward the cake. Caiyan smiled and interpreted, and I could tell he was complimenting her work as well. Her honey-blond hair hung in a long braid down her back, and a red blush colored her face at Caiyan's words. Even young girls were prey to his charm. The girl responded.

"She's putting the finishing touches on a gift," he explained. The girl said something to Anna in German.

Anna beamed and explained in English it was for the chancellor's birthday. Since the chancellor was fond of her pastries, cakes, and sweet breads, he had allowed her to have the ingredients she needed to make a cake for him.

The young girl smiled at us, and Anna explained the girl was her granddaughter, Isla. Anna offered us a cup of ersatz coffee, and although I felt a sense of urgency in Caiyan, he accepted the offer. We sat in wooden chairs around the table. Isla helped her grandmother serve the coffee, bringing each of us a cup and saucer made from fine bone china.

Marco took the cup from Isla, staring intently at the young girl. Isla went back to her cake decorating. Anna smiled at her and told us Isla was nine. Her daughter, Isla's mother, worked at the Italian embassy in Paris. Isla had attended school in Paris and spoke perfect French.

Marco joked with her in French, and the girl beamed, looking over her shoulder and replying in rapid French. Marco and Caiyan laughed. I only caught bits and pieces of the conversation. I could translate and read French, thanks to Rosetta Stone, but my Texas accent made it hard to sound legit. Anna sensed my inability to follow along in either German or French and switched back to English for me.

"When war broke out and France became occupied by Germany, my daughter felt it safer for Isla to be in capital city under Nazis' protection and sent her here to live with me."

I cringed at the last words. Berlin was probably the worst place to be, and my inner voice said a silent prayer the girl and her grandmother would live.

"Where is her father?" Caiyan asked, and Marco set his cup down in the saucer so hard I thought he'd broken it. I raised an eyebrow at him, and he shrugged.

"Isla's father is fighting for Wehrmacht in the Kriegsmarine," Anna said. She looked torn, but then lifted her chin high. "He will be home as soon as the führer wins war. Isla's parents will be home soon. I am sure of it."

It felt strange sitting in the back of the bakery sipping coffee when a war was happening around us. Anna touched my hand as if reading my mind. "Sometimes it's nice to have a dose of normal during a time of tragedy."

Isla set down her pastry tools and stepped down from the crate. She gave her grandmother a hug and whispered in her ear. Anna laughed and nodded. The girl's face lit up with delight as she scampered from the room and returned a moment later with a small box. She opened the box and offered its contents to Caiyan. He pulled out a chocolate brownie. He grinned at her, and then she offered one to Marco and me. The blush crept back into her cheeks when Marco made a yum sound.

I knew the feeling. These two guys were masters at making a girl blush. The girl giggled and placed the box on the table next to Hitler's birthday present.

I took a bite of the brownie and was surprised it tasted of cinnamon and raisins but also had a funky aftertaste. Marco saw the distress on my face and said something to the girl in German.

She replied, "*Tollatsch*" and continued speaking in German, ticking off what I assumed to be ingredients on her fingers.

He nodded and finished his brownie. I finished mine to be polite, but that funky taste stayed in my mouth, and I wished I had a Dr. Pepper chaser.

"What can I help you vith?" Anna asked. "I am afraid I don't have much. The führer only allows enough supplies for me to make bread and pastries for his needs."

Caiyan checked to make sure no one else might overhear. He pulled the painting from his pocket and showed it to Anna. She gasped and came closer to examine the picture.

"Where did you get that?" she asked, running a hand over the painting as if it were made of the finest china.

"Yes, where *did* you get that?" Marco chimed in as he moved closer to the painting.

"From the Flaktürme. Is it yours?" Caiyan asked Anna, holding the painting at the ends to keep it from rolling back in on itself.

"It is my mother." A small tear slid down her cheek, and she wiped it away with the back of her hand. "She was a wonderful woman, always loved to bake. The picture was confiscated by the Nazis from my apartment above the shop." She pointed to a door that was cracked open. The bottom few steps of a steep staircase could be seen through the opening.

"They took almost all our valuables. It was our contribution to war." Anna spoke with the tone of a woman trying to be supportive of her country but not fully accepting the demands made on her. Anna took the picture from Caiyan and sat down at the table.

Isla peered over Anna's arm and placed a comforting hand on her grandmother's forearm.

"She is beautiful," Caiyan said.

"My father painted picture. He was an artist at heart but worked as Berlin's city building director. He designed Märchenbrunnen for my mother, because she loved the fairytale stories."

The Märchenbrunnen was the park where Caiyan and I had landed with all the sculptures destroyed from the bombings. How sad something so beautiful was the innocent bystander of one man's greed—not to mention the millions of casualties.

"The Nazis took anything that was of value, but since mein führer has a fondness for my sweets, I was allowed to keep my shop, and they provide me with raw materials I need to bake." Anna laid her fingers across her lips and then turned away, almost as if she were committing a crime. "The führer has been very generous, and I am able to feed my granddaughter and keep her safe."

"I'm particularly interested in the necklace your grandmother is wearing," Caiyan said.

Marco stepped back. The look of contempt on his face added to my guilty conscience. I assumed he had realized Caiyan was after the key, not the painting. It was my fault Caiyan didn't have his key. Marco needed to understand I had to help Caiyan get a key.

Anna looked intrigued. "Why are you interested in necklace?"

"I collect antique jewelry. I am willing to pay you a very large sum for the necklace."

Marco and I looked at each other. Marco smirked.

"Do you have it?" Caiyan asked.

"Maybe." Anna met Caiyan's eyes as if questioning his credibility. She laid the painting carefully on the table and folded her hands in her lap. "Mein führer was also asking about the key."

My mind was spinning. How did Hitler know of the gift? Did he *have* the gift? Did she just say *key*?

Caiyan picked up on the clue as well. The excitement of having a key within his grasp caused his eyes to gleam with a sense of determination. This might be Caiyan's new key if we could get Anna to give it to us instead of the führer. Did Anna know of the vessel?

Caiyan's wheels were turning, and I knew he was working out a plan to get the key and find the vessel. I felt like we were about to search the bakery for any old cupboards that might be large enough to be a vessel. Marco hadn't said a word since Anna had used the word *key*. He seemed agitated, as if Caiyan finding the key was interfering with some master plan.

"The necklace is not worth much, and has been in my family for generations." She eyed Caiyan's empty throat, and in that moment, I understood. She knew about the gift. I pulled at my shirt collar and exposed my key. Her eyes grew wide.

"We have to tell her who we are," I said, touching Caiyan's sleeve. "Who knows what path we've disrupted by being here? If Hitler gets the key, it could change the entire world."

Caiyan nodded. I reached forward and placed my hand on hers. Nothing, not even a tingle. Sometimes the gift was subtle, and my reading skills were still new to me. I shook my head and released her hands.

Caiyan began speaking to Anna in German. I guess he felt he should make sure Anna understood she might have a mystery gift wound around her genetic code that could allow a person to time travel. Anna was nodding, and I could tell she knew the history by her hand gestures, and she was intrigued to meet a time traveler. I could also tell Caiyan was making his case for her to give him the key. She began wringing her hands. Choosing between her beloved führer and Caiyan was a difficult decision.

I glanced at Marco and wondered if I would have to make a difficult decision.

Marco pressed his lips together and shot me an icy glare. I was about to ask what had his tighty-whities in a twist when a commotion began in the outer room.

Caiyan's head jerked up, and Anna barked an order at her granddaughter, who ran to the staircase and closed the door behind her. Anna fled to the front room, and we followed.

Three soldiers entered the small shop and stood at attention. The people in the shop had made themselves scarce, and I could see out the window a small congregation of them huddled together outside the bakery, watching as more soldiers stood guard around a fancy automobile. I watched as Anna took her place behind the counter, and her employees stood behind her. An officer came in and inspected the bakery.

After the officer had declared it safe, he left, and the soldiers lined up and stood at attention.

In less than a minute, the officer was back and took his place in the lineup. A man stood in the doorway, and the soldiers gave a click of their heels. There was no formal announcement as I'd envisioned when I'd studied this man. Adolf Hitler was about five foot eight, taller than I had expected. He had the tiny mustache just as he did in all the pictures I had ever seen of him, and he wore his short, dark hair perfectly combed across his forehead. It fell to razor-sharp precision above his left eye.

Marco and Caiyan both shot up to attention, arms out in the mandatory salute. I wasn't sure what to do. Did I salute? I watched as Anna greeted the führer with the salute, so I did the same. He walked into the shop and halted when he saw Marco, almost as if he was startled by his presence. He ignored Caiyan and spoke a few words to Anna. Their words were clipped and harsh. I couldn't figure out if they were arguing or just having a normal conversation. Hitler had no intonation to his voice, so every word sounded like an order. She gestured toward us, and I understood the German word for *friends*. I held my breath. If we were caught, Anna would also be arrested for helping us. Caiyan and I were going to have a serious discussion about imperiling others when we returned home. *If* we returned home.

Hitler barked orders at his soldiers, and they had their guns on Caiyan and Marco. Caiyan cut his eyes at my open throat, and I quickly buttoned up my blouse, hiding my key. If Hitler did have the gift, he wasn't taking my key.

Hitler walked around the shop, eyeing us curiously. He started toward the back room, and Anna stopped him. I caught the word *present*, and I assumed she was explaining his birthday cake was unfinished. He moved her hand and proceeded into the back room, returning a few moments later with the painting of Anna's grandmother. Damn— Caiyan had inadvertently left the picture lying on the table. In his opposite hand, he held the box of Isla's chocolate cakes.

He placed the box on the counter and paced across the center of the room, tapping the painting and pausing in front of each of us. I shuddered at the proximity, knowing the evil this man had produced. Slowly, he turned toward Anna and asked her a question. She shook her head as she responded. I could tell from his mannerism he was asking about the key and wasn't happy about the answer.

He walked around the room, stopping in front of the counter. He helped himself to one of the *Tollatsch* in the box and took a big bite of the cake.

Anna froze as if the führer had made a bad decision. Her eyes grew large, and she was explaining something to the führer. She said the same word the girl had spoken earlier: "*Tollatsch*." Anna tried to give him another box of sweets, but the führer would not relent. He insisted on the cake as he continued his pacing around the room. Stopping in front of me as if noticing me for the first time, he reached up to my neck with his chocolate-covered fingers. I grabbed his hand, and his mouth twitched back and forth like a rabbit. Hitler gave more orders, and one of his men grabbed me around the neck, pointing a gun to my head. Caiyan and Marco struggled in my defense, but the soldiers maintained a hold on them.

He reached again for my shirt. Anna shouted something in German, and the führer smiled. Instead, he picked up my hand and kissed the top of it like he was Prince Charming. A sharp zing shot to my elbow. SuperJen wanted to pull her hand away in disgust, but my inner voice didn't want to get shot and held firm.

I felt the tickle of his little mustache and noticed it had slipped slightly away from under his nose. I had never read anything about Hitler's mustache being fake. He hid the misplaced mustache with a cough. His hand politely covered his mouth and adjusted the slipping facial hair back into position as he stood. He snapped orders to his men, who clicked their heels and said the German form of "aye, aye, Captain."

Anna removed her apron as the führer left the shop. The guards waited while she gathered her purse. She said something to the two workers, who were standing huddled in the corner, faces as pale as the moon. They nodded and began cleaning as if the Gestapo would be eating directly off the counter.

The soldiers released me. Anna turned and shook my hand, sliding something into my palm as she placed her opposite hand on top of the handshake in a mock gesture of friendship.

"Be safe," she said under her breath in English, and the soldiers escorted her into the waiting convoy.

Caiyan, Marco, and I stood in the center of the bakery, not sure what had just happened.

"You were after a key this entire time?" Marco asked, keeping his voice at a low growl so the workers would not hear.

Caiyan ignored his question. "I'm going to find the girl." He went upstairs to find Isla, slamming the small stairwell door behind him.

"Is that what you want?" Marco asked, looking at me with steely eyes. "He doesn't give a rat's ass a woman was just taken hostage because of that damn key."

"Now what do we do?" I asked, focusing on the current problem. "If Hitler gets that key, it could change history in a big bad way."

"You know, the führer seemed very familiar," Marco said, stepping farther from the counter as the lingering patrons began making their way back into the bakery for their rations. The show was over, and many of them were speaking in hushed, excited voices about the visit from the führer.

"Didn't you study him in world history?" I asked.

"Yes, but there was something about him that was familiar, like that feeling you get when you've met before."

"He has the gift. I felt it all the way up to my elbow."

"Jen, that's bad. We might all be Communists when we return, thanks to your boy."

Marco was right. Caiyan had gone too far in the search for a key. This was exactly what Jake had warned me about, changing the future and affecting the lives of millions. We had to fix this before we could return. I wished I hadn't slept through my world history class. I was trying to recall anything I knew about Adolf Hitler.

"You know, he looked exactly like all the pictures in my history books, except for the fake mustache," I said.

"What do you mean?" Marco asked

"His mustache wasn't even real." I described the way his little mustache had slipped around during the kiss. "He made this quirky little motion, like a rabbit, and then the thing started to slip off."

As I described the mustache, I felt the paper Anna had given me in my hand. I rolled it against my fingers, trying to decide if I should give it to him.

"Jen, when are you going to read that paper you have in your hand?"

Busted. Marco didn't miss much. I shrugged and held up the small piece of paper. It was part of an index. Written in German. I handed it to him.

He looked at it and rubbed his chin.

"What does it say?" I asked.

"It's a page torn from a ledger. A list of patrons and their allergies, likes, dislikes." Anna must have kept a list of her customers so she could recommend which items they could eat. Then his eyes widened. "Shit."

"What's it say?" I asked, peering at the paper in Marco's hand and trying to decipher the German script.

"Hitler is a vegetarian, and he doesn't eat raisins, because they give him uncontrollable gas."

"So?"

"So…those cakes we ate were *Tollatsch*. They are made with pork blood and animal fat."

My inner voice turned green and barfed. "And they had raisins," I added.

"Damn." Marco stomped his boot on the floor. "*Toches.*"

"What is *Toecheese*?" I asked.

Marco's mouth turned up at the corners in a suppressed smile, but before he could answer, Caiyan came down the stairs with a stunned Isla.

"Why don't you ask him?" Marco bobbed his head in Caiyan's direction.

My anger had reached its limit. Now a kind German woman was probably standing in line for the firing squad, and Caiyan was playing let's-find-the-vessel. I marched up to him and practically shouted, "Who is TOECHEESE?"

The patrons in the shop stopped talking and stared at the blond girl spouting English. Caiyan pulled me into the back room, followed by Marco and Isla.

"Who is Toecheese?" I repeated, placing my hands on my hips.

A small smile pulled at the corner of Caiyan's mouth. It was the side where the scar cut across his upper lip and made me want to kiss him. My inner voice reminded me I was angry with him. He caught the glimpse of affection, and his eyes got all cloudy.

"Oh, for Christ's sake," Marco said, looking at me as though my common sense had just caught the last train out of Berlin.

"Toches is a brigand. But I rather prefer yer pronunciation of his name. We haven't come across him in years. In fact, I thought he wasn't traveling," Caiyan said. "He has an uncanny gift of imitating people. I dinnae recognize him."

"He makes that quirky motion with his mouth. Like he just ate a sour pickle," Marco said. "It's hard to forget the brigand who killed the former boss of the WTF."

"Who was the former boss of the WTF?" I asked.

"We don't know if he killed Agent Grant," Caiyan said to Marco, answering my question at the same time.

"Agent Grant from the British Secret Service?" I asked, alarmed. "Jake told me he retired after the British government had cutbacks."

"That's what the WTF wanted you to think," Marco snapped. "They never take the blame when they screw up."

"If ye had been traveling at the time, ye might have a say in the matter." Caiyan's voice rose, and he moved to stand chest to chest with Marco.

Marco looked like he might engage his weapon and take out the Scot.

"That quirky motion—it's his tell." I stepped between the two men and interrupted the stare down. "When Toecheese saw Marco, his mouth contorted, and he put his finger to his mustache. It was probably the reason it slipped from his face."

"Didn't Hitler's men know he wasn't the real deal?" Marco asked, stepping back and giving everyone some space.

"Hitler was known for using a doppelganger to do his day-to-day functions," Caiyan said. "If there was an assassination attempt, it would be futile, and the real Hitler would be safe in some underground bunker." He placed a hand on my elbow. "He could spend his days plotting his world dominance, while the imposter risked his neck riding in parades and awarding medals to the Hitler Youth."

We stood around digesting this information.

"So there's a chance the real Hitler doesn't know about the key or time travel?" I asked.

"Knowing Toches, I'd bet he's keeping that information to himself." Caiyan rubbed his chin.

"I guess both of you were after the same prize," Marco said, resting his arms on the strap of his rifle. "And he won."

"He doesnae have the vessel," Caiyan said.

"Neither do you." Marco nudged me toward the door. "We need to go. Jen's in enough trouble."

"First we have to help Anna," I said. Marco stopped midstride, and the men nodded in agreement.

"Where do we start?" I asked.

"Hitler's at the Reich Chancellery. The soldiers would expect Toches to take his hostage there," Caiyan said.

"I agree. Hitler didn't leave his bunker the entire month of April until he…" Marco made a slashing motion across his throat with his finger.

"We need to ditch our escorts and make our way there." I glanced over at Isla. She was sitting with her legs drawn up in front of her, and she had her arms wrapped around them. I walked over, sat next to her, and placed an arm around her for comfort. A warm sensation flooded me. I looked up at Caiyan, and his eyes met mine.

"Scheisse," he said with that faraway look like all his plans had just gone to shit.

Chapter 9

We headed into the main room of the bakery, where a few patrons were whispering. Isla looked worried, and Marco bent down to tell her something in German. She thanked him with a big hug. Caiyan gave her a peck on the cheek and said something in German that made her blush.

"What did you tell her?" I asked Marco after I told Isla good-bye.

"I promised her we would find her grandmother and told her to hide in the basement, not the attic, when the Russians invade Berlin."

Caiyan nodded as we stepped outside the bakery. A camera flash went off, causing me to see spots. Caiyan stepped up and grabbed the photographer by the shirt collar.

He was a skinny guy with a press badge on his military jacket and a large box-shaped camera strapped cross-body style, probably following Hitler around hoping to photograph him in action. Little did he know he wasn't stalking the real deal. He tried to squirm out of Caiyan's grasp as Marco relieved his camera of the film. They had a few words, and the photographer removed his boots. He gave Caiyan a disgusted scowl and scurried off in his stocking feet. Caiyan picked up the boots and handed them to me.

"Put these on. Ye cannae go traipsing aroond Berlin in yer broken shoe."

I took the boots, removed my shoes and slid them on. They were tall, black leather combat boots and they fit perfectly.

"Now what?" I asked, noticing one of the soldiers had exited the truck to smoke and was leaning restlessly against it. We had a truck full of priceless antiques, a crooked accountant demanding we take them all to a mine, and a fake Hitler running amok with a stolen key and a grandma hostage. The question was answered in minutes. The air-raid sirens began to sound again. The people outside the bakery ran for cover. Isla and the workers took refuge in the basement of the bakery.

"Why aren't they going to the Flaktürme?" I asked.

"It's too far," Marco said. "These planes are close. We need to find Toches."

"You want to go out in the middle of an air raid?" I asked, my knees shaking.

"If we dinnae go, we might not make it oot of here," Caiyan said. He shouted and motioned to the men in the truck. I assumed it was to take cover, because the men scattered. The three of us jumped in the front seat of the truck, and Caiyan drove like a madman to find Toches and Anna.

A building in front of us suffered a direct hit, and rubble went flying, hitting the windshield of our truck with the sound of a machine gun. A cloud of smoke rose from the ground, obscuring our brigand. As the dust settled, we made our way slowly toward the Reich Chancellery.

"*There!*" Caiyan shouted and pointed at a blurry black blob through the haze. The car carrying Toches was stopped at an intersection, waiting on a flock of fleeing people to get out of the way. The sirens were deafening, and the sound of the second wave of planes was getting closer. The debris and dust began rising from the piles of rubble like an evil smoke snaking its way through war-torn Berlin.

The Toches car started again, and we followed. Trying to get the fake führer to safety was a chore. His car didn't maneuver over the rubble as easily as our truck did. Caiyan sped up, and I thought a few pieces of our precious cargo may have fallen out into the street as we rounded a corner. The ground was vibrating as planes dropped bombs in the distance, and they were heading in our direction.

A truck came out of nowhere and sideswiped us, sending us barreling through a blockade and toward the back end of the Toches motorcade. Pedestrians were running for shelter. I covered my face as Caiyan jerked the steering wheel to the left, and we slid sideways before slamming into something hard. Marco and I were ejected from the truck.

I heard a woman scream, and something wet spewed across my face as I hit the ground. I couldn't see, and a sharp pain was shooting through my right leg. Caiyan's voice called out to me. I was lying on the ground, trying to see him through the thick fog. I managed to wipe the wet out of my eyes and saw red running down the front of me. My hands were also covered in red. I started screaming, and Caiyan was at my side.

"Are ye OK, lass?"

I felt Caiyan's hands on me, checking my body for injuries. I focused as he helped me sit up.

"I'm…I'm covered in blood!" I shouted.

"Jen, relax—it's jest paint," Caiyan yelled into my ear.

"Paint?"

"Aye, the truck we hit was hauling paint fer the bomb shelters. The walls are painted so the people can see their way in the dark."

I took a closer look at my hands, and they seemed to have a fluorescent tint to them. "We didn't hit anyone?" I asked, trembling. "I heard a woman scream."

"It was you screaming," Marco said as he joined us. He had a small cut on his face but was otherwise unharmed.

"Are ye hurt anywhere?" Caiyan was running his hands over my legs.

I winced when he touched my ankle. "My ankle hurts, but I think I'm good."

They helped me stand, and my ankle was a little sore. Probably a sprain, but I could walk on it. I tried to wipe my hands off on my skirt, but the paint was drying quickly.

"I can't get the red off," I said.

"That's OK," Marco said, handing me a handkerchief from his pack. "You look good in red."

———

T he front end of our truck was crumpled and spouting smoke from under its hood. We had missed Toches's car and hit a parked cargo truck head on. The truck was unoccupied, but the back had been full of barrels of paint, which had spilled all over the street. When we hit the truck, it rammed into the back of the Toches motorcade. His car had sustained a minor scrape during the crash and was stalled out in the intersection. The soldiers had bolted, seeking cover and leaving Anna standing next to the car. Toches was MIA.

"Are you OK?" I asked when I reached her.

"Yes, I am fine," she said and squeezed my arm. "My mother told me one day someone would come and ask for my magic key. She told me to give it to them only if they seemed trustworthy. I thought Mein Führer was trustworthy, but look what he has done to my country." She gestured at the fallen buildings and the people running to save their lives. "He is going to Märchenbrunnen. The key is under turtle."

The sound of approaching aircraft had me worried.

"We're getting the hell out of here, with or without you," Marco told Caiyan as he grabbed my hand and yanked me in the direction of the park.

"I've got to find Toches before he gets the key," Caiyan yelled at Marco.

"He doesn't have the vessel," I said, trying to calm the two men over the air-raid sirens and the distant sounds of more oncoming aircraft.

"Yes, he knows of vessel." Anna began to sob. "He threatened to kill my Isla if I didn't tell him."

"Don't worry; we'll find him," I said. I told her Isla was taking shelter in the basement of the bakery. Anna nodded and gave me a long hug. Thanking Caiyan and Marco, she hurried off in the direction of the bakery.

"Get to the park. I'll meet you where we landed," Caiyan said. "Just give me some time to find him before he takes that key."

Marco helped me walk a few steps. We weren't that far from the park. "You've got twenty minutes, and then we are gone."

Caiyan nodded and then went to the back of the truck and pulled out the tapestry with the Madonna hidden inside.

"Are you fucking kidding me?" Marco asked. "He's going to steal that painting. Jen, he never changes."

Caiyan took off at a dead run with the tapestry clamped under his arm, leaving Marco and me alone.

Marco helped me as I limped to the park. Antiaircraft guns shot at the planes from the top of the Flak tower, and a low-flying plane dropped a bomb that had a direct impact on the tower. I thought about all the people taking refuge there. The Flak tower didn't budge, though the ground was shaking with fright, and buildings were toppling over in surrender.

Just as we reached the park entrance, a bomb exploded nearby, knocking me off my feet and away from Marco. A huge pile of debris separated us. The building adjacent to where we were walking began a crumbling descent.

"Look out!" Marco yelled as the building fragments tumbled between us. We found each other across the hill of debris, and he motioned for me to meet him in the park.

"I'll go around." I gestured and hobbled the opposite way, looking for an entrance. I finally found a gaping hole in the fence, climbed through, and headed in the direction of the fountain.

The air was thick with the fog of war, making visibility difficult. I moved slowly, not only because my ankle was sore, but also because I was trying to keep from falling over uprooted trees and debris. As I rounded a corner, I came face-to-face with Toches. We practically bumped into each other. Dangling from his scrawny neck was a gleaming key. I thought it resembled a cloud. The tiny diamonds fell like snowflakes, accumulating in a blanket of sparkles along the base of the medallion. He saw me staring at his key and pulled his coat around his neck.

"I know what you are," he said, his accent sounding a little less German.

"I know what *you* are," I said, my voice sounding a little more frantic. "A murderer."

That quirky, twisted smile consumed his lips. He reached up and ripped off the mustache. "Is that what they told you?" he asked and tried to push past me. "Out of my way."

He underestimated my strength, and I pushed back. He wasn't a big guy, so my push moved him back an inch or two.

"I've got to get out of this shithole!" he screamed, his face turning beet red, and he charged at me.

"Not with that key, you're not!" I braced for impact. "It doesn't belong to you."

I dropped my shoulder linebacker-style to offset his hit, but he dodged right at the last minute, and I ended up flat on my face. I turned in time to see a glorious red sleigh appear. I had to blink twice to be sure I wasn't hallucinating—Santa would have been envious of the beautiful vessel. With debris from the bombing raining down on us, it almost looked like it was snowing.

My first impression was all girl, definitely more *yang* than *yin*. This was the vessel of a transporter, not a defender.

Toches was caught off guard at first. I didn't know what he was expecting, but he slowed down long enough for me to make my move.

I leaped at him, grabbing him by the legs, and we tumbled to the ground.

"Let go of my legs!" he screamed. He clawed at my arms, trying to break my hold. He grabbed my hair and yanked hard. I screeched in pain, and he pulled his legs free, giving me a good kick in the head as he stood and tried to make a run to the vessel.

I rubbed my head, trying to lessen the blow. Out of the corner of my eye, I saw a flash, and someone was running at Toches. He saw it too and made an Olympic effort to run for the sleigh. He jumped inside and was searching the interior, looking for the ancient word of the Ancalites that would propel him to his destiny.

I struggled to my feet just as Toches gave me an evil smile followed by a finger wave. Time seemed to slow as Marco made a flying leap and tackled him in the sleigh. They fought for a brief second—and then *whoosh*. They were both gone, and I thought I heard sleigh bells.

⌒〜〜⟶

*M*y head was pounding, and I felt the force of each explosion as the bombs tore the city apart. I needed to get to the other side of the fountain for the rendezvous with Caiyan.

As I approached the remains of the Märchenbrunnen, I saw a figure on the other side of the empty fountain. The upper half of his body was bending into the pedestal of one of the turtle statues. As I came closer, I recognized the tight ass sticking up in the air as belonging to Caiyan. He rose from the base as if his Spidey sense had told him I was near.

"Good. Yer here."

"You can stop looking. Toecheese has the key."

"Damn, do ye know how many turtle statues are in this fountain?" Caiyan paused and dropped his head down on his arm, exhausted from the scavenging. "Weel have to catch Toches back home." Caiyan glanced behind me, and a faint look of alarm crossed his face. "Where's Marco?"

"Toecheese took Marco."

"What?" Caiyan gave me his undivided attention. I explained about the sleigh and both of them vanishing into thin air. I also told him my theory about the sleigh being a transporter's vessel.

"Huh, I didnae know it was a transporter's vessel. That'll make it difficult fer him until he has it trained." Caiyan resumed his digging. I bent over the hole and saw he was using a small shovel to dig a hole in the dirt-and-rubble-filled base of the turtle statue.

"If you would pause from your thieving for a moment, I would like to go home and find Marco."

Caiyan bent and picked up the tapestry, checking to make sure the painting hidden inside was secure. "I'm saving the art," Caiyan said as he laid the tapestry gently in the hole. He reached into his pocket, retrieved the pouch with the ruby ring, and dropped it in the hole.

"Are you nuts?" I asked. "Did you hear me? Marco just disappeared with Toecheese, and that painting isn't going to last seventy years buried in the dirt until you can recover it in the present."

Caiyan stood, wiped both hands on his jacket, and placed them on my shoulders. "'Tis valuable, and I will find another way to get it when things are not so…dangerous."

I stood with my mouth hanging open. *Come back here?* Who was this man who risked his life to save a painting? A glint of something shiny caught my eye. On the ground at my feet was the painting of the woman in gold. Anna's mother was staring up at me. "Wait!" I cried before Caiyan could fill the hole. I handed him the painting.

"Toches must have left it behind." He rolled it up, tossed it in with his other treasure, and began covering it with dirt and rubble from the surrounding ground.

At least the woman in gold would be safe from any brigands trying to hunt down Anna for the key.

"Please, lassie, help me move this turtle back to its original spot." He strained as he tried to heave the stone statue into place. I pushed from the back end, and we managed to get the rectangular base of the turtle statue aligned with the stone pedestal carved into the fountain.

Caiyan held his palm up for a high five to celebrate our accomplishment, but the air-raid sirens began crying out their miserable warning, and his face changed from victorious to serious. "Jen, call yer vessel."

I looked around to make sure it was all clear.

"It doesnae matter if someone sees. They willnae be around to claim witness." I placed my hand to my neck and summoned my vessel. My outhouse appeared under the only undestroyed tree left in the park.

We made a run for it. Bombs dropped around us like hail from the planes overhead, and gunfire lit up the sky from the Flak towers. We jumped into my vessel together. I covered my ears against the roar of the plane's engines and screamed my word. I heard Caiyan yell, "Not Gitmo!" But it was too late; I was driving my vessel to the safest place I knew…and destroying Caiyan's chance of traveling in the process.

Chapter 10

My vessel landed. I didn't want to look at Caiyan. I knew he would be mad, but I was mad too. He had put our lives in danger with his stupid attempt to get a new key. I glanced at my watch and saw it was 9:00 a.m. It had been around three in the afternoon when we'd left Berlin. The time change, combined with the time-travel lag, was going to kick my butt. I turned toward Caiyan. He was slouched against the wall of my vessel, wearing a stony expression. He seemed disappointed in me. *Well, it goes both ways, buster.*

"Jen, ye brought me to my prison." His Armani suit was covered in mud. My vessel knew he had hurt me, and it had backed me up by changing his clothes but leaving him filthy.

"I know. I think maybe it's for the best." I bit my bottom lip.

Before we could sort out our differences of opinion, Jake yanked open my vessel's door. He stood staring at us.

"McGregor—that figures. I should have known you'd be the instigator. Both of you, out now!" He was angrier than I had ever seen him. I felt like Maverick and Goose in the movie *Top Gun* when they got busted for buzzing the tower. Caiyan climbed down from the platform. He didn't turn to help me down as he normally did when we traveled together.

"You're late!" Jake barked. He squinted at me. "And why are you red?"

I looked down at my hands and saw they were still tinted with the red paint. I guess there are some things even my vessel couldn't remove. "It's paint," I said as I clumsily tried to maneuver out of my vessel, thankful I was back in my sexy red dress. My ankle was swollen and painful, but I refused to ask for help.

Jake and Caiyan both stared as I flashed a long leg while stepping down from the landing square.

Jake motioned to two rather large men in black suits who were standing behind him and then turned on his heel and left the hangar. The men escorted us to the blue room.

"Do ye gorillas jest hang out in here waiting for someone to land?" Caiyan asked along the way, causing one of the men to tighten his hold on my arm. They deposited us in the room and then stood at attention on either side of the door frame, just in case one of us might try to make an escape from the most secure prison in the world.

The credenza, which normally held only a fresh pot of coffee, was loaded with pastries and kolaches. My stomach rumbled, reminding me it had been a long time since I'd had anything to eat.

"Sit, both of you," Jake said as he shut the door behind him but remained standing. Both of us sat down across the table from each other. My hunger was silenced by guilt.

"You're not supposed to be traveling," Jake said, pointing a finger at Caiyan. "And you"—he turned toward me—"*you* were supposed to report for duty at six hundred hours. What the hell were you thinking?"

I was thinking I was in love and was trying to help the man I loved. I started to speak but shrugged instead. "Are you going to take my key?"

"I can't!" Jake almost yelled the words, but his self-control grabbed him at the last minute. "I've got brigands that need to be followed. The moon cycle's been open for nine hours, and I had to put your entire team on hold until I knew if you would need help in Berlin."

Caiyan and I both stared at the ground. I was trying to decide if I should tell Jake about Marco. Would he be in trouble for coming to rescue me? If Jake took Marco's key away, he would race without the extra protection from his key. But how was I going to rescue Marco without help from Jake and the travel lab?

"Mitchell Mafuso has been traveling back to 1990. I can't even send *you* back then," he said, pointing at me. "It will have to be Campy, and he's not ready to travel alone. The Cracky clan has another traveler, and now they are dividing up and going back to different times. Not to mention Rogue is back, and God knows where *he's* going to end up." Jake dropped his arms to his sides.

This was good and bad. Good, because they needed Marco, so they would help me find him…and bad, because we had so many brigands to chase.

Caiyan started to disapprove about sending Campy when Jake cut him off. "What do you know about Mitchell's sister, Mahlia, and Germany in 1945?"

Caiyan grimaced and looked down at his hands. He glanced at me out of the corner of his eye.

"What do you mean?" I asked.

"Mahlia has been going back to Berlin to the year 1945 the last few travels. We didn't have a WTF agent available to track her, but since lover boy here snagged you to the same time period, I thought he might know something about this."

"Do you?" I turned and raised an eyebrow in his direction.

"She might have been helping me locate a lost key." Caiyan sighed like he had been caught with his hand in the cookie jar.

"You've been traveling?" I stood. Now I was mad. "With Mahlia?"

Caiyan remained silent. He was apparently debating how much he wanted to tell me. I knew that look of indecision.

I aimed my anger at Jake. "Why didn't you tell me?"

Jake shook his head. Holding up both hands in front of him, he said, "He doesn't have a key or a vessel, so he doesn't show up on the travel screen." Jake put his hands on his hips and smirked at the fact Caiyan had been caught and I was pissed. "It's almost like a NAT going back in time."

"Before ye were hired…" Caiyan gave Jake a nod and straightened in his chair. He cocked his head to the side as if he had a perfectly good explanation for this mess. "I found a key in the possession of another WTF traveler. We are to report any unclaimed keys to authority, so I did. When the traveler was confronted, he claimed it had been taken by a brigand. My boss at the time, Agent Geoff Grant, asked me to follow up on the key if I ever received any information on its whereabouts, so I did."

"What key is this?" Jake asked, taking a seat at the table.

"The Sleigh key?" I asked Caiyan, and he nodded. I described the key to Jake, but before I could explain whose neck it was hanging around or tell him about Isla and Anna, Caiyan interrupted me.

"I was purchasing some art from a gallery in Berlin. There was an exhibit of lost treasures from World War II. These pieces were though' to be lost in a fire that occurred in the Flaktürme Friedrichshain in Berlin. I saw a painting of a lass in a gold dress wearing a key. I recognized the key and did some research. There's no record of any travelers using that key."

"That doesn't mean it's not in use by a brigand," Jake said. "Did Mahlia know what you were searching for?"

"She did, and who cares if a brigand loses a key? It's why we are here, aye?"

"What did you promise her?" I asked, and he flinched.

"Any of the lost art she wanted. We planned to hide it under the Märchenbrunnen and retrieve it later."

That explained how he'd conveniently had a shovel to dig the hole in the park. It was obvious to me that Mahlia was after the key.

"Why would she let you walk away with a key?" I was standing as I shouted the question. I felt cheated and lied to and *mad*.

Caiyan's head jerked up, as if yelling at him was against the rules.

Jake raised a calming hand in my direction, and I huffed as I sat down, causing the legs of my chair to squeak against the floor.

"Why did you use Jennifer instead of Mahlia this trip?" Jake asked.

"I can answer that." Gerald, one of the defenders on my team, casually strolled into the room. Gerald, who preferred to be called Gerry, was a dwarf, standing at four feet and five inches with reddish-brown hair and a bad attitude. His small stature kept him on the spy-and-tell side of the WTF and away from the horrid task of capturing a brigand.

"Were you eavesdropping?" Jake asked.

"Absolutely," the dwarf said with a smile. "It's my specialty."

"OK, so tell us," Jake said.

Gerry greeted Caiyan with a nod as he slid into the chair next to him. "Yesterday, I was down in the Flatiron district having lunch at Eisenberg's Deli. You know, I was sitting at the counter eating my tuna on rye, and who should walk in but Mahlia and her evil brother Mitchell. They grabbed the table directly behind me."

"Did they recognize you?" Jake asked.

"Not a chance. I tend to blend. Anyhow, I was sipping on my lime rickey when I overheard Mahlia say she couldn't possibly travel this weekend because she was onto something big, and Jennifer Cloud's brother, Eli, was going to get it for her."

"Does Mahlia dating Eli have anything to do with your trips to Berlin?" Jake asked Caiyan.

"Mahlia is dating Eli?" Caiyan asked, and his gaze shifted to me. "Did ye know aboot this?"

I squirmed in my chair. "Yes, I was going to tell you, but then you almost got me killed, and it slipped my mind."

He stood, chest thrust out and nostrils flaring, as he pointed at me and shouted, "When a brigand is crossing the line into yer family, ye need to tell yer defender."

"I'm surprised you didn't get that information firsthand, seeing as you've been all cozy with Mahlia yourself. Besides, you're not my defender—Marco has that job now!" I stood, and we faced each other across the table.

Jake and Gerry watched as if they were in the front row at Wimbledon. "I've got ten bucks on the blonde," Gerry said.

"She's after more than jest Jennifer's brother, I guarantee," Caiyan said, taking his seat. I followed.

"Do you have any idea what that might be?" Jake asked.

Caiyan shook his head. "We have a bigger problem." I didn't think there could be a bigger problem than Caiyan lying to me, risking my life, and traveling with the bitch from hell—who was currently, as Ace would say, shagging my brother.

"Please, enlighten me," Jake said, waving an exhausted hand in the air

"Toches is traveling again, and he has the key from Berlin and Marco."

"Marco?" Jake asked, turning toward me. "Pickles told me he saw you blip to Berlin, and he was worried when you didn't return for the meeting. I assumed McGregor was involved. He didn't mention Marco."

"Marco was rescuing me," I said, frowning at Caiyan. I explained about meeting Anna and Isla, the fake Hitler, the fight between Marco and Toches, and the sleigh. I didn't bring up the bombs or the art Caiyan had confiscated. No need to stress out the boss. My inner voice tucked away the information on the stolen art for safekeeping.

"I don't have much intel on Toches. He hasn't caused any problems since I was put in charge," Jake said.

"Apparently, he was stuck in 1945," I added.

"Someone must have taken his key in the past before he received it," Jake said.

"Aye, and now he has the Sleigh key."

"Your team should be arriving soon," Jake said, scooting his chair back and standing. "Get something to eat. The travel lag is going to kick in, and I don't need you falling asleep until I figure out what to do. I'll be back in a moment."

Caiyan and I stared each other down as we waited for the other members of our team to arrive. Travelers were sorted in teams, and ours included Brodie and Ace; Gerald and his transporter, Tina; Campy after he completes his training; and formerly me and Caiyan, currently replaced by Marco.

Each team was based on the brigands they were assigned. Now, thanks to Caiyan, Toches became a new brigand added to the mix in our already filled bowl. Ace rolled in a few minutes later, followed by Brodie. They both gave Caiyan a knuckle bump, showing their support for his presence. Ace grabbed a coffee from the credenza. Brodie sat down across from Gerald, wearing a big shit-eating grin.

"What are you so happy about?" Gerald asked.

"That's the smile of a guy who is getting shagged," Ace piped in, taking the seat next to Brodie.

"Must be nice." Gerald looked at Caiyan and me. "I guess the two of you are taking a break. How about it, sweet muffin? Ever shagged a little person?"

I groaned and stood to get a cup of coffee. The travel lag was starting to affect me, and I would be napping soon if I didn't infuse my veins with caffeine.

Gerald let out a sharp wolf whistle. "You know what they say: big things come in small packages."

Caiyan grabbed the dwarf by the shirt collar and tossed him across the room. He took out two rolling chairs and bumped up against a filing cabinet.

Marco entered as Gerald was flying across the room. "Cool! Midget tossing—can I play?"

Relief overcame me as I rushed forward and threw my arms around his neck, hugging tightly. "You're here?"

"You didn't think that little weasel was going to take me, did you?" Marco asked, grinning and sending an admiring glance down the neckline of my red dress.

"What happened?" I asked, taking a few steps back.

"I'll say this: kicking someone's ass while traveling through time is freaking awesome!"

"Where is Toecheese?"

"When we landed, he was unconscious." Marco cracked his knuckles.

"So ye jest left him with the key?" Caiyan asked, flipping his hand in the air in disbelief. "Why didnae ye bring him here?"

"My main concern was my transporter, Jennifer," Marco said with an annoyed glance at Caiyan, and then his eyes gently found mine. "I had to make sure you arrived safely."

Marco walked over and offered Gerald a hand, which the dwarf took, and Marco lifted him to his feet.

Although Gerald was a nasty little prick, I couldn't help but be concerned. "Are you hurt, Gerald?"

The dwarf stood, brushing himself off, "Only my pride and my ass. But you could kiss it and make it all better."

I ignored the comment and finished making my coffee. Marco sat down next to Brodie. I grabbed the plate of doughnuts from the credenza and placed them on the table in front of Marco, who immediately grabbed one covered in sprinkles. I took a seat next to Marco. Caiyan growled, and Gerald made a face at him.

Jake returned and scouted the room, making note of everyone present. He didn't look surprised to see Marco, which meant Marco had already made his presence known to Jake.

"OK, everyone, settle down." He tapped on his laptop, and a picture of Toches came up on the projection screen on the far wall of the room.

"This is Kishin Toches," Jake started, but Gerald giggled.

"That's Yiddish for *kiss my butt*." He slapped his knee. "His mamma must have really hated him."

Jake glared at him and noticed the chair next to Gerry was empty. "Where's Tina?"

Gerald did a palms up. Tina was Gerald's transporter and was always late. She rushed in a minute later. Her dark bob framed the sides of her face, which was flushed from the exertion of punctuality.

"What did Kishin do?" she asked, observing the face on the screen as she took her seat.

"Do you know him?" I asked.

"Yes, before I became Gerry's transporter, he was the main brigand that my defender followed."

I didn't realize she had transported for another defender. She looked to be in her late twenties, but I supposed she could be older. She always wore black and rarely any makeup. She sometimes masqueraded as a young man if the need arose.

She fidgeted in her chair. "He had a sad life. His grandfather died, leaving him a key when he was only thirteen years old. His parents died under unusual circumstances not too long after that, and he kind of lost his mind. He's a slippery fellow. We never caught him, but a few years ago, he just disappeared."

She dropped her head, and her eyes squinted shut. "Then my defender was killed by one of the Cracky clan, and I haven't seen Kishin since. I would really like to get those damn Crackys thrown in the brig and tomb all their keys."

Everyone at the table was nodding. I didn't know any of the Cracky clan. Brodie and Ace had been the key duo to keep an eye on them.

We filled the team in on our trip to Berlin, and I told them I thought Isla had the gift.

"If she does have the gift, we have to get that key back to her," Marco said.

Why was Marco so adamant about returning a key that had never been in use? A year ago, Marco couldn't have given a flip about anyone but himself. I'd had to kidnap him to get his help, and now he'd joined the WTF and had a serious calling to risk his life to return a stolen key? My inner voice was holding up a sign that read *Marco loves Jen.* I called bullshit on that one. He wasn't doing all this because of me. Something was off.

"I did some recon on Anna and Isla," Jake said, tapping a few buttons on his computer.

I felt Marco shift uncomfortably beside me.

"Are you OK?" I asked him.

"Yeah, we should really try to get the key back to that little girl."

"Are you saying you want to go back to 1945?"

"If it means doing the right thing." Marco looked away when he said the last words, and I couldn't help but think there was more to this story.

Jake spoke to the group. "The bakery suffered a direct hit in the war. Anna died in the bombing, and I can't find any information on Isla."

109

Marco jumped to his feet. "That's not possible."

"I'm afraid it's what our records show." Jake scooted a paper across the table for Marco. "It's a miracle the three of you didn't die in that air raid. It was the worst of all the raids on Berlin."

"This can't be happening," Marco said, pacing around the room. Everyone turned to stare at him.

"Spill it," I demanded. "I know there's more to this key than Toecheese."

"I will tell you, but…" Marco stopped pacing and stood with his hands on his hips, staring defiantly at the group. "I can't tell you who the Sleigh key belongs to."

"Why the 'ell not?" Ace sat back with his arms crossed. "Does he travel? Maybe he could join us?"

Brodie jumped in. "Absofuckinlutely. We're bustin' our arses every moon cycle. We need the help."

"I agree," said Jake. "Why doesn't this person travel?"

Marco crossed his arms over his chest, and the dimple in his chin deepened as he held his jaw firm.

"The mystery traveler can remain anonymous, as long as we get the key away from the brigands," Jake said. "Tell us what you know about the Sleigh key."

"OK, here it is," Marco said slowly. "When my grandfather was in his early twenties, he traveled back in time and met the lady in the gold dress."

"The one in the painting?" asked Ace.

"Yes. He fell in love with her, but he was already married in his present time. I think my father was about two years old. My grandfather traveled back each month during the moon cycle to see her. When she became pregnant, he knew he couldn't continue with his double life. He told her about time travel and gave her the key to give to their child. He promised to return when he could. Her parents forced her to marry a captain in the German army, and then she had Anna. I don't know all the details, but the woman and her husband were killed in the bombings during World War I. My grandfather didn't know Anna was still alive."

Marco pulled up a chair and dropped his head between his hands. "Anna was sent to live with relatives in Czechoslovakia, who owned a bakery. After she married, she moved to Berlin, had a family, and opened her own bakery. The bakery was bombed in World War II, but Anna and Isla opened a new bakery together after the war. My grandfather and his business partner, Henri Cordero, visited the bakery in 1965. The picture of Anna's mother was hanging on the wall, and Isla had the Sleigh key. It's how they connected the dots." Marco leaned back in his chair. "You see, Isla married Henri Cordero, and a year later they had a daughter, my mother."

Silence filled the room. If Isla died, what happened to Marco and the owner of the Sleigh key?

"Whoa, that's some heavy shit," Gerald finally said, breaking the silence. "Isla is your grandmother?"

"And your mom is also your half cousin, sort of?" Tina asked, rubbing her temples at the heavy task of trying to connect the branches of Marco's family tree.

"In a very distant way, yes. If they died, what happens to me?" Marco asked.

"We 'ave until the moon cycle ends to go back and save 'em," Ace said.

"It's impossible," Jake said.

"Why?" I asked.

"We have no way to tell if Isla was killed or if Anna died before you returned to our time, and you can't be in both places at once."

"Then send someone else!" I demanded.

"It would be a suicide mission," Marco said. "You saw what was happening when we left. The Red Army is in the middle of a hostile takeover of Berlin. Landing a vessel in the middle of that would be a miracle. I wouldn't put another traveler's life in danger to save mine."

I shot Caiyan an evil glare, and he changed the subject. "Why was the key naugh in the Flaktürme?" Caiyan asked.

"It was never in the Flaktürme." Marco shrugged. "My mother is on the board of directors of NEMO."

"NEMO, like the movie?" asked Gerald.

"No, the Network of European Museum Organizations," Marco answered. "She loaned some family items from our vault to the German Historical Museum in Berlin for an exhibition. The painting was included. I went to the museum to retrieve the painting before a random brigand might come across it, and the museum curator was in a frenzy, because the painting had been stolen." Marco cut his eyes at Caiyan.

"Borrowed," Caiyan grumbled under his breath.

"Shortly after, I was informed Jennifer was in 1945, and I connected the dots."

"How are we going to save Marco?" I asked.

"Maybe we can git the little girl the key," Brodie said. "Ya told us no one used the key, right?"

Marco nodded.

"Weel, if we take 'er the key and explain things, she can still meet up with Marco's grandpa."

Jake thought about this for a minute. "Let me do some recon on Isla. If she wasn't killed in the bombings, I might get clearance to send a traveler back to take her the Sleigh key at a later date."

"What if she was killed?" Ace asked.

"One thing at a time," Jake said.

"First we have to get the key," I said.

"Where's the key now?" Jake asked.

"That idiot Toches crashed us on the beach. Right out in the open, for cripes sake." Everyone seemed alarmed at the picture Marco had painted. "Surprisingly, we were on the Mafusos' private beach in Amagansett." Marco added sarcastically. "You know the house—the one where I got shot." He glanced my way and then continued, "As you know, they're the title sponsor for my racing team, and if they found out I'm now WTF, well…" Marco hesitated before he spoke again. "I don't think it would be wise to let that happen."

"What did you do?" Tina asked.

"I ran for cover in the trees and left Toches lying unconscious on the beach."

Jake's cell phone chirped as Marco finished his account of what had happened, along with another sprinkled doughnut. Caiyan remained unusually quiet.

Jake read his text and grimaced. "The Mafusos want a trade."

"What kind of trade?" Brodie asked.

"They said they want the Tribal key."

"Is that the Thunder?" Gerald asked. "I've never heard it referred to as the Tribal key."

"Ye betcher ass it's the Thunder," Brodie said, scratching his bearded chin. "It's from the Cracky clan, and they can't 'ave it. I stole it fair and square."

There was something about the last few words that made my gut tighten. If Brodie had stolen the Thunder key, and Toches had stolen the key from Berlin, it seemed like someone along the way would be affected. There were so many reasons we didn't have history on those keys, only one being that the people who owned them knew nothing about the gift.

"How did they know we 'ave it?" Ace asked.

All heads turned to Caiyan.

"I didnae tell them," he said.

"You were all hot and cozy with Mahlia. Maybe you let something slip in the heat of passion," Marco said.

Caiyan jumped to his feet, knocking his chair back in the process. "I have never let anything slip in the heat of passion, ye jackass."

Silence overtook the room. I heard Ace swallow hard. Caiyan was pressing both hands hard onto the table, and he leaned down, supporting himself with his arms.

"I was not sleeping with her," he said, turning his face toward me. His green eyes were hard. "It was jest a business deal."

Jake looked over at Caiyan. "Sit down and explain what happened during your trips to Berlin. Maybe you can shed some light on why Toches landed on the Mafusos' beach."

Caiyan sat slowly. "As I told ye before, I saw the key and researched the location. It should've been in the Flaktürme. In my previous travels, I was meeting with the accountant and arranging for the transportation of the stolen art for him. Mahlia was posing as my assistant.

"Several months ago, Mahlia and I were invited to a dinner at the Reichskanzler, what we call the Reich Chancellery. All of Germany's upper class was present. I think Hitler switched with Toches during the party. Hitler's girlfriend was an avid art collector and had me caught up in conversation most of the nigh'. Mahlia must have recognized Toches and made him a deal."

Jake stood, slowly letting the tension in the room settle. "They want to arrange a meeting at Jen's cousin's wedding."

"Melissa Jo's wedding?" I asked. "Why would they want to meet there?"

"Because they have Eli." Jake handed me the phone with his camera app showing a picture of Eli. He was wearing the same clothes from yesterday, except his necktie was currently being used as a gag, and his hands were tied in front of him.

I gasped, and the other travelers gathered around me, looking over my shoulder at the picture. I heard Caiyan cuss in Gaelic.

"Why would they want Eli?" I asked as Eli's panic-stricken face stared back at me from the small screen.

"Maybe because they can use him as a threat against us," Brodie said.

"He's not one of us. They can kill him," Gerald piped in, and my hands started shaking.

Jake came around and squatted next to me. "They won't hurt him, because they want the Thunder, and it's a direct violation of the WTF agreement with the Mafusos."

"But Toecheese wasn't involved in the agreement, was he?" I asked. I shuddered at the thought of my brother being killed over a key.

"He'll be fine," Jake said, gently removing the phone from my hands. "I don't know why they want to meet in Mount Vernon at your cousin's wedding. Maybe they feel like we can't interfere if there are family members we are trying to keep in the dark about your gift."

The thought of my parents or Mamma Bea finding out I can time travel made me cringe. My father would order me to stop traveling, and my mother would tear up every time I left for a travel. I didn't need my family questioning every move I made. It was a pretty good plan on the Mafusos' part. My mental unraveling of my family dynamics came to a halt as Jake started giving assignments.

"I need the four of you at the wedding. We need to get Toches before he screws up something major," Jake said, pointing at Brodie, Ace, Marco, and me.

"What about the Cracky clan?" Ace asked. "We've been searching for the vessel. Do you think the Mafusos 'ave it?"

"Maybe," Jake said. "I'm sending Gerald and Tina to Ireland to monitor the Cracky clan. Gerald, go talk with Pickles and Al to see if any of the Mafusos have made an appearance recently in the little town where we got the Thunder. Jen, Marco, and I will meet with the Mafusos. Brodie and Ace can keep an eye on things. Since Jen's family is already familiar with the three of you, you will attend the wedding. Jen, make sure they get invited."

Gerald hopped down from his chair and snagged a kolache on the way out the door.

I nodded and made a mental note to instant message Melissa Jo when I got home.

"What aboot me?" Caiyan asked.

"Tina can give you a lift home, and for god's sake, no traveling, or I'll throw you in the brig," Jake said. "I'm going to confirm your story with the general. If it doesn't play out the way you say, you can count on another year of NAT, even if we have a key for you."

Caiyan's mouth turned down in a deep grimace, and he pushed his chair back hard as he stood and left the room without even a glance in my direction. I thought he'd gotten off easy for the chaos he'd caused.

Jake jerked his head at Tina to follow him, and Tina scurried after the stormy Scot.

"The two of you," Jake said, pointing at Brodie and Ace. "Go to the travel lab to get the coordinates on Toches. If he is wearing the Sleigh key, we should be able to locate him on the map while the moon cycle is open." Jake informed us that our instructions would be sent to our secured e-mail accounts after he discussed our plans with the general and arranged the meeting. He ordered Marco and me to go home and get some sleep.

"We don't have much time," I said.

"Both of you need to get some rest. If I find Isla, I will send you back to fix this mess."

Revealing the WTF to a NAT in the past was a big violation. If I was right and Isla had the gift, she wouldn't be a NAT, but would she start traveling or use the gift and change the present?

If Isla had the gift, it would explain why Marco had amazing power: it came from both of his parents' bloodlines. I was confident General Potts wouldn't risk losing a traveler with that kind of power. My inner voice was down on her knees, reciting the rosary.

"Do you think General Potts will allow us to break a law of the WTF?" I asked.

"Sometimes it's better to ask for forgiveness," Jake said and began clacking away on his laptop in search of the missing Isla.

*M*arco seemed a little unsettled as we left the blue room. Brodie and Ace were walking ahead of us. Brodie was obviously upset about having to trade the Thunder key. He and Ace had been working hard to find the vessel in hopes that the WTF would give Caiyan the Thunder key. I knew it hadn't been easy for Brodie, who was accustomed to working with Caiyan. They had a Han Solo–Luke Skywalker kind of relationship. The four of us were a good team. I was Princess Leia, and I guess that made Ace Chewbacca. The replacement of Caiyan with Marco was going to stir up the force for sure.

Marco walked through the entrance to the hangar, and I laid a hand on his forearm. "I'm sure we will get the key back and find Isla."

Marco shrugged. "This is the reason I didn't want to travel. I'm not a huge fan of dying."

I nodded. When a key was stolen, chaos followed. Even a key that was hidden away and not used by a traveler had caused a life-altering situation. My reason to protect the keys from the brigands became crystal clear. "I think I'll pop in on Albert and Pickles to see if they found Toecheese."

Marco stifled a yawn. "My grandfather told me his one regret was that he had fallen in love with a woman from the past and changed the way her life should have been." He bent down and gave me a peck on the cheek. "Later."

I turned and caught up with Brodie and Ace, who had stopped and were arguing about the Thunder key. "I say he screwed us," Ace said. "He knew we were tryin' to find that damn vessel to get 'im reinstated."

"Caiyan would never slice us in the back like that, mate," Brodie said.

"He's always lookin' out for number one. See how he did poor Jen, shagging that tart." Ace had his hands on his hips standing firm and defending my honor.

"Do you think he was shagging her?" I asked as I joined them.

They both jumped, surprised to find me standing behind them.

"Crikey, Jen, I didn't know you were there," Brodie said.

"Of course not, luv." Ace put a protective arm around my shoulders. "I just meant the bloke is a little dodgy at times, and I think you deserve better."

Brodie didn't look as certain.

I loved visiting the travel lab. The layout was similar to the command center of the starship *Enterprise* in the *Star Trek* series. My bet was whoever had designed the lab had been a Trekkie. Albert was the agent in charge of following the brigands. His partner, Pickles, was the navigator. Pickles had the gift of foresight. He could see where the brigands decided to travel moments before they engaged their vessels and entered the travel portal. This gave us an advantage over the brigands.

Albert was waiting for us at the entry to the lab. His white lab coat hit just below the knees, and his striped oxford shirt with pens lining the shirt pocket was haphazardly tucked into his navy slacks. I never asked him why he wore a lab coat. He didn't spend his days treating patients like my brother did, mixing chemicals, or dissecting frogs, but his pockets were always full of this and that, so I assumed it was so he could keep all his necessities close at hand. His long gray beard was tied at the tip with a red bow. It reminded me of my Mamma Bea's Yorkies. They were yappy little dogs that always had bows secured behind their fluffy little ears.

"Al, my man, what's up wit' the bow?" Brodie asked, giving Albert a high five.

Ace laughed. "Are you supporting one of those charitable groups?"

Albert flushed and winked at me. "Italina thinks a little decoration is nice."

I liked the way Albert called Aunt Itty by her full name. The way it rolled off his tongue sounded very romantic, like he was referring to a Romanian princess instead of Caiyan's great-aunt. She was a sweet, absentminded little old lady who had been a fierce traveler in her day. She had some history with Albert that was unknown by me but had caused a rift my last time travel when they'd made a connection. It was nice they had mended their prior disagreement and had been seeing each other.

"Is she here?" I asked, surprised, because Jake didn't like her coming to Gitmo. Things tended to go awry when she was around.

"No, we Skype," Albert said, removing the forgotten bow from his beard.

I laughed and stood on my toes to kiss his cheek. Pickles was busy hacking something out on his keyboard. The large screen located across the front wall was full of blinking black dots. Jake was right; the brigands were out of control.

Brodie, Ace, and I sat down in the three chairs facing the big screen. Albert was leaning over Pickles's shoulder, asking him questions about something on his screen.

"I've got it!" Pickles shouted and stood at his desk. He used a cane now and came over to point things out on the screen. "Here," he said, pointing at a black dot blinking inside the borders of New York, "is your brigand." His strong island accent filled the room and made me think of a font that had curlicues on each of the letters. "Dis is de guy."

"Great, let's pop over there and grab him," Ace said. "We can be back in time to 'ave a nice dinner and return the key to Isla."

"Dar's one problem." Pickles pointed at several black dots very close to the one marked as Toches. "These are all Mafusos."

My heart skipped a few beats. What were they all doing in present time? There was an open moon cycle, and the Mafusos usually took full advantage of the time to travel back and cause chaos.

"Why didn't they go back?" I asked.

"Mahlia has been traveling back to 1945," Albert said. "Terrible time to travel, as you already know." He raised his eyebrows at me. "We're not sure why she didn't go back this travel cycle, but she is staying present time."

I knew why. Because Caiyan wasn't around to escort her, and she was holding my brother by his necktie.

"Mitchell has been going back to 1990, but he also stayed behind."

"I don't know why these buggers aren't traveling. If they break the agreement and cause an infraction in the present, we could have serious problems," Ace said.

"I hate losing the Thunder to that mob of lunatics," Brodie said.

"Me too." I sighed, feeling the drain from the travel to Berlin.

"Doll, you need to get some rest," Ace said, giving me an arm to lean on.

I agreed. I needed rest, especially if we were about to fight brigands. I said my good-byes and set my course for home.

Chapter 11

ertie was at work when I arrived at home. I couldn't decide if I was tired or hungry, but inspecting the contents of the fridge made my decision for me. It was empty except for half a carton of milk. Gertie and I needed to go grocery shopping. Attack Cat gave me a swat as I passed by the couch on my way upstairs to crash. I skirted around him and gave him a finger wag for trying to snag my red dress.

I woke up a few hours later to the grumbling of my stomach. I showered and rummaged through my closet for my Dallas Cowboys sweatshirt and gray sweatpants. The smell of pepperoni pizza wafted up from downstairs. Good. Gertie was home, and she had pizza. I pulled my hair into a top bun and slipped on my Chuck Taylors. Clean, comfortable, and free of red paint, I went downstairs to find Gertie and Aunt Itty drinking wine and watching the Sci-fi series *Firefly* on Netflix. Aunt Itty was perched in the comfy overstuffed chair with her feet up on the matching ottoman. Attack Cat stretched out in her lap as she stroked his gray fur.

They shouted a greeting at me as I poured myself a glass of wine and joined Gertie on the sofa. A large box of pepperoni pizza was open on the coffee table. I grabbed a paper plate and helped myself to a slice. Gertie had a bowl of popcorn in her lap and various boxes of movie-watching-approved candies in a basket on the floor at her feet.

"I see you ladies have all the necessities at hand," I said as I shook a handful of Reese's Pieces from one of the boxes onto my plate.

"Shh, this is the good part," Aunt Itty said, leaning closer to the flat-screen TV. I had used my first paycheck from my time travel to get rid of my old console TV and purchase a fifty-five-inch flat-screen display for our den. I figured Gertie had helped me out in my first time travel, so I should buy something both of us could enjoy.

I propped my sore ankle on the coffee table and sat back to enjoy my pizza and try to forget about Caiyan's lies.

Gertie and Aunt Itty watched as the handsome captain of the *Serenity* ordered his first officer, who just happened to be a woman, to back him up in a fight against the inhabitants of an outlaw planet. They worked well together. He was the witty brains who kept the bad guys distracted while his wingman—or in this case, wing*woman*—took them down.

I tried to imagine Caiyan and me working together like Captain Mal and First Officer Zoë. The picture became fuzzy as I finished off my first glass of wine and imagined Caiyan's hand making its way inside my blouse instead of handcuffing the bad guy.

"Earth to Jen," Gertie said, waving a hand in front of my face.

"Sorry, I got caught up in the show." I refilled my wine glass from the bottle on the table.

"Sure, it's a great show. Too bad it only ran one season." Gertie sighed and popped a Milk Dud.

"I just love that Captain Malcolm Reynolds," Itty said. "He's sassy and smart all in one. But he should really make a move on the companion—you know he really likes her."

"That would just complicate things," Gertie said. "That's why he and Zoë work so well together. Since she is married to the pilot, they don't have that whole sex-gets-in-the-way thing."

"Do you think that's what's wrong with me and Caiyan?" I asked, interrupting their movie-review session.

"Oh no," Gertie said. "I think y'all are great together. I mean, you don't have to do all the complicated stuff like conning, killing, and ass kicking. You just let Caiyan take care of that, and you bring 'em home."

"Horsefeathers!" Aunt Itty shouted, causing the cat to startle and leap off her lap. "I'll have you know, in my day, I had to take down plenty of brigands!"

"You did?" I asked, not sure if this was one of Itty's fantasy moments or an actual recollection of fact.

"Why, yes, dear." She adjusted her glasses and sipped her wine. "My defender was more brains than brute, but we were a good team."

"What happened to him?" I asked, wondering who her defender was.

"Oh, you know, he broke my heart, and I went home to Scotland. My parents had hoped I would marry the local boy, and when I returned home, they sealed the deal. I stopped traveling when my daughter was born. We moved to America, and that was that."

We were interrupted by the doorbell. "That should be the pizza I ordered," Gertie said.

"You ordered *more* pizza?" I asked.

"That'll be the dessert pizza," Gertie said, licking her lips. "A hot-chocolate brownie pizza covered with marshmallows and chocolate drizzle."

"Yum!" Aunt Itty toasted Gertie with her glass of wine.

"I'll get it." I went to the door and was greeted by a pimply pizza-delivery boy, who gave me a large pizza box in exchange for a ten-dollar bill.

He looked down at the money. "This is the second time I've been here tonight," he huffed.

My wallet was empty. I dumped my change purse out into his hands, which granted him another fifty cents and a cherry Life Saver. "Gee, thanks, lady," He slumped off, and I stuck my tongue out at him. *What is it with men? I give them all I have, and they still want more. Geesh.*

I stopped by the kitchen, grabbed dessert plates, and passed out the brownie pizza as I listened to Itty tell Gertie about her family. I knew her grandson Liam had been killed in Operation Desert Storm. He had refused to wear his key for protection and had lost his life defending our country. The keys didn't work like a Kevlar vest, but I felt like they enhanced our senses and could have helped save Liam's life.

"When President Johnson developed the WTF, they sought me out again. My husband and daughter had both died of cancer. Liam's father had run off with a floozy, and I was the only one Liam had to take care of him, so I refused." She took a big gulp of wine to wash down a tear. "I was really getting too old, anyhow; my landings weren't what they used to be."

We toasted Aunt Itty. I told them about Caiyan taking me to Berlin and the horrors of the war. We finished off the brownies and two bottles of wine and then moved on to a bottle of Glenfiddich Caiyan had given me for a special occasion. I asked Itty if she knew why Caiyan would get Mahlia to take him back to Berlin.

"My nephew has always been attracted to the ladies," Itty said, licking the last bit of chocolate brownie from her fingers. "His good looks and Scottish charm draw them like the royals to a polo match."

"I thought he had given all that up for me," I said. My lips felt a bit swollen as the words came out of my mouth.

"How come you don't give Marco a go?" Gertie giggled. "He's BEooootiful."

"I agree that boy has muscles in all the right places," Aunt Itty said. She tried to coax the cat back into her lap. "Here, pussy, pussy."

"That's what Caiyan probably says to Mahlia." Gertie laughed, downed her Glenfiddich, and threw another peanut M&M in the blue bowl on the coffee table. It was her way of tracking how many glasses of alcohol we drank. We each had a different color bowl. My red bowl was starting to fill up.

I frowned at the comment about Caiyan and finished off my glass. *Plink.* Gertie added another M&M to my bowl. She was probably right; perhaps I *should* give Marco his payment. I mean, Caiyan hadn't even spoken to me after our meeting. I was tired of his arrogant Scottish ways. *Wait here, Jen. Be root back, Jen. Jen, ye jest wait here and let me kiss yer breast before I ride off into the sunset and take Mahlia to Berlin fer the last god-knows-how-many travels.*

"I'm goping to visit Narco—I mean, Marco," I announced, jumping to my feet and swaying slightly.

Gertie and Itty raised their glasses in a toast. "Go for it, girl!"

As I stumbled to get my jacket from the peg on the wall, I heard Itty say, "Do ye think we shoob let 'er drive?"

"It's OK," Gertie slurred. "She's not going far. I hab her car keys."

She held up my keys in victory as I exited the house and staggered toward my vessel.

I focused really hard on the rooftop garage where Marco stored his vessel. It was always a hard landing in such a small space with no room for error. If I missed, I could end up dangling from the Empire State Building—but the word *hard* made me more motivated to see what he had under all that sex appeal. I was confident Jake would find Isla and save Marco's future, but there was a slim possibility this might be my last chance to pay my debt to Marco. If Caiyan was going to go flitting to the past with Mahlia, maybe our relationship wasn't what I'd thought it was. My inner voice gave me the thumbs-up and did a shot of tequila.

I landed with a scoot and a thunk. Not bad. I pushed open the door to my outhouse, and a whoosh of cool air hit me. I stumbled out, tripping over the threshold. I caught myself before I fell facedown on the cement floor. Not a good way to start my first rendezvous with the blond giant.

I managed to pull myself upright and ran my fingers through my hair. Top bun—I forgot. Not my best look. I pulled out the hair elastic and shook my head, feeling the world go a little wonky. I stabilized myself and sashayed past Marco's vessel, running my fingers along its tail fin on my way to his back door. The car shuddered, or at least it seemed that way in my drunken state. My hand was lifted to knock when the door swung open. Marco stood there naked from the chest up, his key glowing in the darkness, wearing boxers and a half-cocked smile.

"Do yoob just open the door fir anyone?" I asked, trying to enunciate. My mouth felt fuzzy, and my head was light.

"You set off the alarm when you landed." He had obviously been asleep, and the scent of sleepy Marco intensified my level of intoxication.

He moved aside, and I shuffled into his warm lair. Closing the door, he leaned against it and looked me up and down. "What did I do to deserve this visit?"

"I'm ready to pay my doobs…my dues," I said, opening my arms wide and smiling.

"Jen, have you been drinking?"

"Maybe jest a little bit." I held up my fingers, indicating about an inch of drinking. "But I'm good to go." My inner voice kicked back in her chair and nodded approvingly as I walked up to him and wound my hands around his neck.

"I don't think we should have sex with you in this condition," he said, placing his hands on my arms, ready to extricate them from his neck.

"I don't want to have sex—I want to *fuck*!"

"Oh, damn," he said. "I'm a goner." He kissed me long and hard on the mouth as he flipped our position, and then I was the one backed up against the door. Heat shot through my arms as he pinned them above my head with one hand, and I felt his other hand creep up under my sweatshirt. This was so hot. My head was doing that spinny thing as Marco and I realized at the same time I wasn't wearing a bra. The stroke across my already hard nipple had me moaning as I ran my tongue up the curve of his neck.

He released my arms, and I grasped the hard, muscular mounds of flesh most people call an ass. He had a super ass. *Yep, I bet Superman's ass felt just like this.* He groaned, and I could feel his arousal pressing against my thigh. My legs gave way beneath me, and he lifted me off the ground.

I wrapped my legs around his middle. We were both sweating. My heart was pounding, and then I had a vision of me kicking ass like the first mate on the *Firefly*. Marco was my defender, and we made an excellent team. He didn't hold me back the way Caiyan did. We were flying through space, right toward the burning sun. It was so hot. We were going to crash, and I screamed.

Hot was all I remembered. I woke up in Marco's bed wearing only my panties. The bedroom was dark, except for a sliver of light coming through the slightly open door.

I heard voices in the outer room over the clanging in my head. *Did I have sex with Marco?* I couldn't remember. Damn. One minute I was drowning in his kisses, and the next minute I was in his bed with a lingering feeling I had been on a spaceship.

I swung my lead-filled legs over the side of the bed. The clock on the nightstand read 5:00 a.m. What time had I arrived? I couldn't remember. I stood slowly. My ankle felt better, surprisingly. My head was a different story. I searched for my clothes. Nada. Maybe he had torn them off me. I wrapped the blanket around my bare body. I opened the door and shuffled down the hall. I passed by a mirror mounted on the wall. My eyes were bloodshot, and I tried to swat down my hideous hair, which was standing on end. The voices caught my attention. I took a deep breath, and my Medusa-possessed body stepped out into the living room. Marco was sitting on the couch, and across from him was Jake. *Crap!*

Jake had his back to me. Marco stood, turning toward me with a small smile on his face. He was showered and dressed in standard Marco wear of jeans and a T-shirt. His blond curls were still slightly wet from a shower, and I had that uncomfortable feeling I was in trouble.

"Sleeping Beauty has risen," Marco said, coming forward and kissing me on the cheek as he passed into the kitchen.

"Jake, what are you doing here?" I squeaked. My throat was as dry as the Arizona desert.

"I might ask you the same thing." Jake stood and turned toward me. His eyes widened at the sight of me, but he didn't remove that annoyed frown he gets when someone has royally pissed him off.

He watched as Marco returned with a glass of scotch, a bottle of water, and two aspirin.

"Hair of the dog," Marco said, handing me the scotch.

I took two sips and felt my stomach roll. Marco rescued the glass before I dropped it on his Persian rug.

"Maybe just the water," Jake said. "She never really did well the morning after."

I drank the water, and my throat felt a little better. "Why are you here?" I asked again.

"Pickles caught you landing in SoHo. I thought I should come rescue Marco."

I licked my lips and looked at Marco sheepishly. "Did he get here in time?"

Marco looked hurt. "Jen, you don't remember?"

I really couldn't remember a thing. After the hot kisses, my memory was a blank. Maybe that was part of Marco's power. Could he wipe memories?

"I'm a little fuzzy."

Marco leaned in and whispered, "You were fantastic."

That didn't really answer my question.

"We have to get to Gitmo. The meeting's in an hour." Jake tapped his watch.

I took the aspirin and borrowed Marco's shower. By the time I extracted myself from the glorious steam shower, my clothes were laid out on the bed, clean and folded. I dressed and finger combed my hair. My reflection in the mirror showed dark circles under my eyes. A veil of embarrassment covered my face like the pimples on the pizza-delivery boy. I sighed. I might as well get the dreaded walk of shame over with. I was surprised Jake hadn't called my mother to report her slutty daughter shacking up with various men.

My legs felt less like lead and more like Jell-O as I made my way toward the kitchen. Marco and Jake were sitting at the kitchen table, running over possible scenarios of why Toches was teaming up with the Mafusos.

"I got you a present," Jake said when he noticed me standing in the hallway. In the middle of the table was a bag of McDonald's french fries and a Coke. Best hangover cure ever. Jake may have been my boss, but he was also my best friend.

I smiled, sat down at the table, and enjoyed that first taste of french-fry heaven. Marco excused himself to get ready to travel to Gitmo, now that his houseguest had vacated his bedroom. Jake gave me a few minutes to enjoy my fries while he made some notes on a small notepad.

"Who brought you here?" I asked Jake.

"Ace, and he's plenty mad I interrupted his night out on the town, so you will have some groveling to do." Jake snatched a fry and checked his smartphone. "Time to go. I have things to do before I meet with everyone." Jake tucked the notepad into his jacket pocket and stood. I scarfed a few more fries and took a last sip of the Coke.

Marco met us in the hallway, and I kept my head down. Avoiding eye contact was the easiest for me right now. Jake and I left Marco to lock up and climbed into my vessel.

I felt ridiculous. Flying off to Marco had not been the right thing to do when I was mad at Caiyan. I let out a big, deep sigh.

Jake patted my knee. "Don't worry. Marco didn't have his way with you."

"How do you know?"

"I called Gertie, and she told me how many M&M's were in your bowl."

"And?"

"And I know you, Jen. You probably threw up on the poor guy. That's why he was showered by the time I got here and your clothes were in the washer."

The memory came flooding back, and Jake was right. I dropped my head in my hands and groaned.

Jake gave a little chuckle. "Marco has good sense. He won't invade Caiyan's territory until it's completely safe.

"I'm nobody's *territory*."

"This is not your normal club scene, and these are not normal people." Jake searched my face to see if his words of warning had made an impact.

They rang loud and clear: *I needed to be careful.* I knew Caiyan had his own agenda. He had killed before, but I also knew he loved me in his way and wouldn't hurt me intentionally. It was good and bad. I was glad I hadn't missed out on great sex, but I still owed Marco a debt. My inner voice held an ice pack on her head as Jake and I jetted off into the darkness.

*J*ake left me in the blue room, and Marco came in a few minutes later. He stood at the door, staring at me.

"Um, I'm sorry about last night," I finally mumbled.

He grinned. "It's not every day I get to kiss an amazing girl."

"You think I'm amazing?"

"Anyone who can projectile vomit across an entire lane of traffic is pretty amazing."

"I did that?"

"Yes, you ran to the window, climbed out on the fire escape— which I thank you for—and heaved over the railing."

"I don't remember doing that."

"When I got you back inside, you started to cry because you'd thrown up on the Dallas Cowboys, and you were afraid Jerry Jones would be upset. And then you took off your sweats and passed out."

"That's it?"

"That is it." Marco sat down, and I noticed he had dark circles under his eyes too.

"You didn't get much sleep."

"No, but it's all good. I think you needed to let off some steam. I was happy to help out."

Jake returned with his laptop and some files. The three of us waited in the blue room for Ace and Brodie. The magic pastry fairy had left buttery croissants and a full pot of hot coffee. My stomach churned a little at the pastry, so I opted for the coffee.

"I still don't understand why they want to meet at my cousin's wedding in Mount Vernon," I said as I poured myself a cup of coffee.

"I'm not sure," Jake said. He was leafing through a stack of papers when Brodie and Ace walked in. Brodie stood at the credenza scarfing down a croissant, and Ace made a beeline for the coffee. He poured a steaming cup and added a dash of Coffee-Mate, then made himself comfortable in the seat across the table from me. He took a sip of the coffee and sighed.

"Rough night?" I asked.

"The roughest. I was in Las Vegas for a sneaky peek at Steve Wynn's new nightclub Intrigue. He's 'aving the grand opening next week and wanted a few close friends to do a test run." Ace cut his eyes at me. "Of course, I had to stop right in the middle to escort Agent McCoy, but all is well. I returned and partied my ass off until I had to leave and come do my civic duties."

Jake stopped what he was doing and gawked at Ace. "You stayed out all night before a mission?"

"It'll be all right, mate," Ace said, taking another sip of coffee. "A little java juice, and I'm good to go."

Jake just stared like a mother at her wit's end with uncooperative children. He shuffled his papers, ignoring Ace, and focused on the task at hand. "The happy couple is getting married at the cowboy church."

My head snapped up. "The cowboy church?"

"Yes, why?" Jake looked at me, alarmed.

"The cowboy church is an all-horseback venue. The entire bridal party will be on horseback. The bride, the groom, everyone."

"What about the guests?" Brodie asked, grabbing one of the armless chairs that normally stood against the wall, flipping it around backward, and straddling the seat.

"There are bales of hay for the guests to sit on," I said, recalling the only other time I had attended a wedding at a cowboy church.

"Why is this the first I'm hearing of this?" Jake asked me. "Didn't you read the invitation?"

"I was included on my parents' invitation. I communicated with Melissa Jo about adding the extra guests through Facebook."

"The meeting is to take place during the wedding reception. When the choir from the Holy Tabernacle of the Nuwaubian Nation sings—"

"What?" I interrupted. "That can't be right. That's an African American church in downtown Dallas."

Jake glared at me. "Jen, do you know the groom?"

"Well, no. I haven't spoken to Melissa Jo in years. She is a few years older than me and moved to California to go to Berkeley."

"Let me introduce you to the groom." Jake stifled a grin as he slid a photo from his file across the table to me. "Your cousin Melissa Jo is to marry Kanye Washington, a.k.a. Emperor KW Smooth Dog."

I picked up the photo of Melissa Jo with her arms wrapped around a dark-skinned man. The photo showed the smiling couple standing in front of a club. Gold chains and medallions hung around Smooth Dog's neck and rested on his belly, which I could see protruding through the thin black shirt.

"I know this guy," Ace said. "He's a gangsta-rap artist."

"Oh, yeah," Marco chimed in. "What was that song he released recently?"

"'Pimpin' Is Hard Work,'" Ace said.

I was holding my head in my hands—not only because of the hangover but also because this was going to be a disaster.

"What's wrong, love?" Ace asked. "Do you 'ave a headache?"

"Yes, I mean, no, y'all don't understand. This wedding is the first time my redneck relatives have had the pleasure of an outsider joining the family."

"Whaddaya mean *outsider*?" Brodie asked, a look of confusion clouding his face. "Your family is going to be upset because your cousin is marrying a black man?"

"No," I said, sighing. "It will be the first man ever marrying into the family who doesn't worship country music. My entire family knows every word to 'I Was Country When Country Wasn't Cool.'" I stood and began to pace. "When I travel to Mount Vernon, I change my radio station from top forty to country classics miles from arriving. The only crossover music they have ever allowed was Elvis, and that practically took an act of Congress, because my dad was such a fan. I don't know what my cousin is thinking, marrying a rapper. My family is going to be at DEFCON three, and the Mafusos are demanding a meeting?"

"Did you get the invites?" Jake asked.

"Yes, I added Marco as my date, and Gertie added Brodie." She was thrilled Brodie was going. "I assumed Mahlia is going as Eli's plus-one." Then I unloaded the bullet. "And...um...since you were already invited to the wedding, I added Ace as yours."

Brodie let out a bark of laughter and slapped the back of his chair.

Ace grinned. "Well, Agent McCoy, I guess you get to find out how it feels to be the object of my adoration, or maybe you can admire me. We need to work out the details."

Jake just sat dumbfounded.

"I didn't know how to get Ace invited otherwise," I said. "Melissa Jo doesn't know him. You were only invited to the wedding because Melissa Jo's sister Amy was in charge of the guest list."

"I declined the invitation. I was planning on setting up a stakeout to keep an eye on everyone, then joining you for the meeting."

"Well, I accepted for you and added Ace. Besides, you were at most of my family events growing up, and Amy has always had a crush on you."

"Oh, the poor dear will be heartbroken," Ace said, patting Jake's hand.

Jake snatched it away, and Ace explained he was just getting into character.

"How are they going to pull this off?" I asked. "Won't it look suspicious when Eli shows up with his hands tied behind his back and guns drawn?"

"The Mafusos made it clear Eli was willing to cooperate and have this matter settled without the use of force."

My brother was cooperating as a hostage? That didn't sound right. Eli wasn't one to be bullied around. He was in great shape, and I was betting he would make a run for it as soon as the chance presented itself.

"Where are we going to make the exchange?" Brodie asked.

Jake spread out a map, showing the distance from the cowboy church to Aunt Elma's house. "While the choir is singing, the Mafusos will meet you in the garden at Elma's house." Jake pointed to the hidden garden area at the back of the property. "After the choir sings, the bride and groom will cut the cake here." He indicated the big red barn. "That will keep the guests occupied."

"How many Mafusos are coming?" I asked.

"Mahlia will be there. Mitchell and…" Jake hesitated before saying the last name. "Gian-Carlo, according to my contact."

"Gian-Carlo?" Marco grimaced. "The elder is coming out for a key exchange. It's rare he comes to America. Normally, he manages his evil deeds from Italy."

"The Thunder key must be more important than we realized," Ace said.

"They will only allow Jennifer, me, and one other to keep the odds even," Jake said. "I need you at the exchange." He raised his eyes to meet Marco's. "If things go south, you are the only one who can add a few seconds of safety for Jennifer."

Marco nodded. "They will know I'm WTF."

"Welcome to the family," Brodie said, giving Marco a brotherly pat on the back.

"Most likely they'll have a few goons as backup," Ace said.

"And so will we." Jake indicated the areas on the map where he wanted Ace and Brodie to provide cover.

"Toches will be there," Marco said. "If he has to give up the Sleigh key, he will be there to take the Thunder."

"They didn't say who was getting the Thunder." Jake said and checked the map to confirm all our bases were covered.

We dispersed after making plans to meet at the wedding. I felt like we should have done a hands-in, all-for-one and one-for-all team huddle at the end. I shook off the feeling of uneasiness as I headed home in my vessel. I had worked my butt off training to be the best WTF traveler, and the Mafusos had caused enough problems. I was in the best shape of my life. I was a tough bitch. This time I was ready for them.

Chapter 12

Aint Elma's house was a cute white-framed farmhouse tucked back into a cluster of hundred-year-old trees. After she'd passed away, the house was given to Gertie's mom, my aunt Trish. She had married well and moved to New York City, but she kept the house for family gatherings and such.

Recently, Mamma Bea had moved in after an altercation with a neighbor in her assisted-living condominium complex. The complex had politely asked her to leave, and she had told them she didn't need any assistance living *anyhoo*.

The Mafusos wanted the exchange to be at the family house during the reception. I couldn't wrap my mind around why they wanted it to be there. I knew they were holding Eli hostage, but having the rest of my family around didn't make sense to me.

Exposing my gift to my family would be worthless. My parents might be difficult to deal with at first, but they would eventually get over it. The Mafusos could have a sit-down with my Mamma Bea. She would deem them nuttier than a five-pound fruitcake. My family has its share of lunatics, and having someone tell Mamma Bea her granddaughter was a time traveler was mild compared to what some of her other relations had done.

There was Uncle Durr, who claimed he could read minds. He wore a purple cape and had convinced the entire town he was legit until

Mamma Bea discovered him hiding microphones all over town in an attempt to pick up bits of idle gossip. She threatened to expose him, and he complied but still wore the cape. Aint Loretta Lynn was often seen around town wearing aviation goggles and a bomber jacket and telling everyone she was Amelia Earhart. A time traveler would be bragging rights in this family.

Nope, this didn't make sense at all. They needed something from me, and I would have to wait and see what that something was at the wedding.

My parents were intent on us attending family functions. Melody, my older sister somehow managed to tap out of these events, leaving Eli and me on the receiving end of cheek pinching and smothering hugs. My mom insisted Eli and I ride with them to the wedding. I told my mom Eli had to pick up his date at the airport, and before she could start with the inquisition, I explained my date would ride down with us instead. My mom was thrilled when I explained that Gertie's stepdad's nephew, Marco, was my date.

Marco wasn't thrilled about riding in a car instead of going by vessel, but I explained it was to keep my parents from growing suspicious about Eli. It would be a nice distraction if he rode down to Mount Vernon with us.

Marco showed up at the house punctually and oozing sex appeal. His jeans were a pair of faded Levi's, and his sport coat was brown and cowboy cut over a cream-colored vest and crisp white shirt, finished off with a smart tie. He looked amazing. The $4,000 chocolate gator boots peeked out from under the leg of his boot-cut jeans. Luke Bryan had worn a similar pair to the CMAs last year.

"Wow," I said as I admired his boots. "I didn't realize you did western."

"I do a lot of things you don't know about." He raised a sexy, dark eyebrow at me.

I took a step back, knowing my parents were about to arrive, and they didn't need to see Marco in his naked form…which was the state he'd be in if he got any closer to me.

A horn beeped, and I received a text from my mom, alerting me to their presence: *Running late. Meet us outside.*

Marco and I left the house, and as I was locking the door, I said, "Please don't mention I have been to your house in SoHo." We took a few steps toward the car, and I saw my mom's head snap up in excitement at the fact her youngest daughter had a date. "And Marco, don't say anything about Caiyan. I haven't gotten around to introducing him yet." Marco nodded, and we walked a few more paces. "Oh, and Marco—"

"Jen," he said, putting an arm around my shoulders. Heat shot down to my boy howdy and out my toes. "I've got this. I'm good with parents."

I sighed as he opened the door of my mom's red BMW sedan. My dad refused to buy foreign cars, but my mom was nonpartisan. In her book, comfort was more important than politics. My parents greeted me, and I introduced Marco. They had met once before at Gertie's mom's wedding to Marco's uncle Vinnie, but it had been a while.

My mom blasted questions at Marco most of the way down to Mount Vernon about his job as a race-car driver and about his parents and New York things they had in common. It wasn't until Marco gave me an elbow in the ribs that I realized she was asking me a question. I pulled myself from the window and focused.

"Jen, have you lost weight?"

I realized that the results of my intense workouts at Gitmo had been covered up by baggy sweatpants, my main state of dress on the rare occasions I made it to Sunday dinner. I had gone to Mass with them on Christmas Eve, but once again, I'd had on a thick pea coat.

For the wedding, I was wearing my Marc Jacobs floral sleeveless dress with a jean jacket and cowboy boots. It was one of those rare April days when the temperature was a breezy seventy degrees. My jean jacket was lying on the seat next to me, and my arms were exposed. She hadn't noticed my toned biceps; she thought I looked skinny.

"Um, yes, I guess. I have been trying to work out more."

"Good for you." Mom reached over the seat and patted my knee. "Eli is making a good impression on you. He exercises every day."

My inner voice was sticking out her tongue at my mom.

She whipped her head around with an amazing amount of flexibility and looked Marco over. "How about you, Marco? Go to the gym in New York?"

Was she kidding? The guy was ripped.

"Yes, ma'am. At least three days a week, and I run five miles every day."

"Good for you," my dad chipped in from the front seat. "It's important to keep in shape."

Now my dad was double-teaming us.

"How are your eating habits?" my mom asked Marco. "I just finished editing a cookbook for the Healthy Chef—you know, Teresa Cutter. She has some great tips for eating healthy."

"Mom, please stop with all the questions. Marco isn't going on the auction block." She acted as if any second the cattle truck would pull up and take Marco off to auction.

After that my mom shot off a few questions to me about my job at the chiropractic office and if I knew anything about Eli's new girlfriend. Oh, I knew about her all right, but nothing I could share was the truth. My mom got tired of her interrogation and turned back around to finish her crossword puzzle. Marco and I checked for updates on our secured e-mail. Dad sang with George Jones, and the rest of the ride was peaceful.

My dad parked the car in a small parking lot designated for guests. Marco and I walked a few steps behind my parents up the small hill to the wedding ceremony. I was clutching my jacket and fiddling with the clasp on my shoulder bag as we approached the chapel.

"Is it the wedding or the church that scares you more?" he leaned in and asked me.

I elbowed him, and he chuckled as we continued toward the cowboy church. The church consisted of a small white chapel with stained-glass windows and an arched belfry.

I knew the church held about two dozen people and had been designed in the days when cowboys had needed a church they could attend and then return to their morning chores. Church service on horseback had provided them the best of both worlds. The pastor held Sunday service inside for those people who wanted to sit indoors, and it was broadcast through a PA system to the outside cowboys. A small arena off to the left hosted weekly bull-riding and equestrian events. Baptisms took place in the stock tank, and sermons were kept to a minimum. If all the members of the congregation were on horseback, the preacher would give his sermon from the front steps of the church.

Today, there was an arched trellis set up under a large oak tree to the left of the chapel. The tree was known as Hangman's Tree and had Bonnie and Clyde's initials carved in the trunk.

Family members sitting on bales of hay came forward to welcome us. Mamma Bea embraced me in a hug, and her White Shoulders perfume encircled me like an invisible coat of armor. I didn't know what the Mafusos had in mind, but I felt immediately stronger with family around. Maybe this was to my advantage after all.

Gertie was in the wedding, and Brodie arrived a few minutes after us via vessel, which he must have landed a good mile away, because he was out of breath when he caught up to me.

My cousin Hildy headed straight for us, and I introduced Brodie to her before she could wrap me in one of her famous squeeze-the-breath-of-life-out-of-you hugs. She was a pale, heavyset woman who currently had her short hair dyed a deep plum—the perfect complement to Uncle Durr's cape. I introduced Hildy to Brodie and explained that Brodie was Gertie's boyfriend. He turned a nice shade of pink and extended a hand to Hildy.

"Well, landsakes. My little Gertie got herself a man. I never thought I'd see the day." She ignored the hand and wrapped Brodie in a tight squeeze that resembled a polar bear hugging a wiggling fish.

When Brodie finally broke loose, she turned her attention to Marco, who took a step back. "Nice to see you again, Hildy."

She moved her mass forward faster than seemed possible and got Marco in a full-body hug, picking him up off his feet. Brodie let out a bark of laughter, and I was thankful cousin Hildy had her arms full of hot men and just gave me a wink.

Jake joined our little group, carrying a large, wrapped package. Hildy gave Jake a side hug and raised a dark-purple eyebrow my way. My family was used to me dragging Jake to weddings, reunions, and funerals. They had been dumbfounded a few years back when I'd shown up with a broken heart instead of a ring on my finger. They hadn't forgiven Jake since. I shrugged, and she wandered off to find other family members to torture.

"Is that a present for Melissa Jo and Kanye?" I asked.

"No, it's the Thunder key," Jake said, lowering his voice. "I was afraid to leave it in the car with Toches running amok, Caiyan still searching for a key, and the Mafusos causing a pain in my neck."

Marco leaned forward and said, "I haven't seen a sign of any of them."

My parents strolled over and greeted Jake. I heard my mom ask why he hadn't brought a date. Jake shrugged helplessly. My dad changed the subject and asked Jake about work. *Thank you, Dad.*

"Where is Ace?" I asked him after he had made polite conversation with my parents, and they'd wandered off to chat with members of Kanye's family, who were huddled together and looking like a herd of lost sheep.

"He told me he had an errand and would meet me here. Which normally I would not have allowed, but the thought of spending three hours in a car with Ace was more than I wanted to experience." Jake rubbed the back of his neck and looked at his watch.

Poor guy was under a lot of pressure to make this exchange happen without a catastrophe. He had brigands, travelers, and NATs to worry about. Any one of them could cause problems, and keeping the exchange under the radar was going to be a challenge. I felt as if I were Harry Potter trying to keep his magic hidden from the muggles and Jake was the minister for magic.

"I'm surprised you drove," I said.

"Had to." He held up the box. "The general didn't think keeping the key in my pocket was wise. Ace dropped me at headquarters in Dallas, and I secured the key in a locked box and drove down."

"And this way, you arrived separately from Ace, minimizing the family gossip chain." I laughed. He knew my family well, and I wouldn't be surprised if Jake had suggested the idea to General Potts.

My mother was catching up on the latest gossip with Aint Loretta Lynn, who had ditched the aviation goggles but still wore the bomber jacket. My dad was slapping backs with his cousin Buster Keaton. Mamma Bea had a sense of humor. She had named all her children after her favorite celebrities, except my dad, who was named after his father, John Wayne. Go figure.

"Jen and I are going to find out where the wedding party is and see if anything seems off," Jake said.

"I heard someone say the groomsmen were in the back of the church, and the bride was getting ready in the small house in the back pasture that doubles as a bridal venue and the pastor's parish," I said.

"Marco, you and Brodie take the groomsmen. Scout the area and let me know when Ace arrives."

Marco nodded and left to gather Brodie, who was standing next to a rusted-out John Deere tractor and talking to a group of guests. The family of the groom, no doubt. They were dressed to the nines in sparkly, black strapless dresses and stilettos that were going to sink to the sole into the east Texas ground. The rain had come three days ago, providing a nice mushy soil for the wedding party. They were in for a shock when the bridal party arrived on horseback,

I followed Jake around the back of the chapel and walked with him to the parish house.

"You know he's going to show up, right?" Jake asked.

"Who?"

"Caiyan."

"No, I haven't heard from him at all. In fact, we are not currently speaking to each other." My inner voice was binge eating Ben and

Jerry's ice cream but put her spoon down when she heard the news Caiyan might be in attendance.

"I'm sure Ace's errand was to go get him. He may have his faults, but there is one thing I can't deny: he loves you."

"Then why did he drag my ass back to Berlin in the middle of a war and risk my life *and* Marco's life instead of leaving immediately when he discovered the bombing had begun?"

"If Caiyan doesn't have a key, he can't protect you. That worries him more than you think. He has been in touch with me several times over the past twenty-four hours, trying to figure out how to keep the Thunder key."

"Really?"

"Yes, General Potts is starting to realize how much we need Caiyan to travel. He is considering giving him the Thunder if we can find the vessel. Caiyan thought he would have already taken his key back from Mitchell, but we found out Mitchell is not using Caiyan's key."

"How is he traveling?"

"We don't know, but Mahlia told Caiyan he doesn't have it."

Caiyan doesn't know who has his key. He's not able to get his key back, and that's why he wanted the key from Berlin. My mind was chewing over the facts as we came up to the parish house. *He didn't know it belonged to Marco's family. I'm sure he would have left Berlin immediately if Marco had told him the key's history. The painting would have stayed with Anna, and she wouldn't have died.* My inner voice was airing out her kilt, but I wasn't convinced Caiyan and I should jump back on the love train.

The parish house was a small ranch-style house with a long front porch. Rocking chairs provided seating for family members waiting for the bride. It was set up like a duplex, with the right side converted for the bride and the left side a private residence for the preacher. We knocked, and Gertie answered the door. She was dressed in a purple floral sundress and boots. Her red hair was done up in a French braid, and tiny flowers dotted her braid.

"Hi, y'all," she said, moving aside so we could enter.

"You look pretty," I said, and Jake bent down and gave her a peck on the cheek.

"Thanks—always the bridesmaid..." She didn't finish her sentence. "Wait until you see Melissa Jo." Gertie beamed.

We turned into a large room with a sofa and several overstuffed chairs. Two additional bridesmaids were seated, drinking champagne. Melissa Jo was standing in front of a three-way mirror, and her mother was fussing with her hair.

"Jen!" Melissa Jo's eyes lit up as I entered the room. She swatted away the hand placing small flowers in her hair. "I'm so glad you made it."

"You look fabulous," I said, giving her a hug. Her plump figure was molded into a lacy V-neck wedding dress that not only slimmed her wide hips but accentuated her full bust. Melissa Jo introduced her bridesmaids. One, the sister of the groom, was a short, thin girl with a giant Afro. It dominated her small, attractive frame and reminded me of Beyoncé's hairstyle in that Austin Powers movie. The other girl was Melissa Jo's sister, Amy. She marched over and reeled Jake in for a full kiss on the mouth and then reprimanded him for not friending her on Facebook. Jake appeared slightly embarrassed by the dramatic display of affection but told Amy he was sorry he hadn't responded and would do so immediately.

I exchanged hugs with Amy and her mom. I introduced Jake to the groom's sister, and Melissa Jo's mom asked when Jake and I were getting married. Jake raised his eyebrow, and I explained our relationship was long in the past, and now Marco was my boyfriend, which sounded weird coming from my mouth.

Amy told us about her recent divorce as she drowned her sorrow in a flute of champagne and began making eyes at Jake.

Melissa Jo plopped her bottom down in a chair so her mom could finish her work of art. Melissa Jo's mom owned the beauty salon in town. Her father, who was known to hold court at the local bar, was currently unable to attend the wedding due to a conflict of interest with the county sheriff.

"Mama is making me look to die for," Melissa Jo said while her mom attached her veil.

I hoped Melissa Jo's statement didn't turn out to be true. There was no telling what the Mafusos had planned. Jake had assured me they should abide by all the rules set forth in the present-day contract. They *were* on our turf, so to speak. Jake scouted the room as the bridesmaids drooled and flirted with him. I made conversation with Melissa Jo and her mother, catching up on the local gossip. Everything seemed in order. No sign of the bitch from hell or any brigand activity in this room.

"Is that present for me and Kanye?" Melissa Jo asked, pointing to the gift Jake had under his arm.

"Yes," Jake stumbled on the word.

"I can give it to the wedding coordinator to take to the reception," Melissa Jo's mom said.

Jake hugged the package tight. "I would like to take it myself. It's very delicate."

"Oh, I can't wait to see what it is." Melissa Jo clapped her hands excitedly, and Jake cut his eyes toward the door.

After the final can of Aqua Net was empty, Jake and I wished her luck and left.

We peeked in the window of the preacher's side of the duplex as we passed. This side was bigger and divided into a bedroom, den, and kitchen. No brigands.

"Can I help y'all with anything in there?" a gravelly voice asked from over my right shoulder, and both Jake and I jumped. A man in white robes, jeans, and cowboy boots had snuck up behind us. Mamma Bea had told us the cowboy church had a new preacher, and this must be him.

"No, my friend and I were thinking of moving to the country and liked the look of your place."

He placed his hand over the Bible he was carrying as if he felt the urgent need to pray. Instead, he motioned toward the church. "The wedding will begin soon. You may want to get a good seat."

We nodded and made our way back to the church, but as we walked past a small barn adjacent to the arena, we heard a commotion.

"I done told you I was not gettin' on that damn horse." A short, round woman in a purple dress and heels stood her ground firmly against a man with skin the color of an eight ball.

His tuxedo was purple suede, and he was sweating bullets even in the cool April air. He wiped his brow with a white handkerchief. The gold chains around his neck had me guessing this was the groom. "Mama, you got to get up on this horse. It's for Melissa."

We stood watching the two go at it, and the preacher came up behind us.

"I don't think she's going to get on the horse," Jake said.

"God always provides an answer." He patted his Bible and began walking toward the couple.

Jake and I got out of the way of God's solution and found seats on one of the hay bales behind my parents. Jake placed the large package on the ground next to his feet. Marco sat down next to me and shook his head at Jake's speculative gaze. Ace and the rest of our little party of pillagers and thieves were running late. I hoped Eli was OK.

A few more guests made their way to the hay bales, but there was no sign of Mahlia or Eli. The whole hostage situation had my stomach in knots. All this was my fault. Maybe working for the WTF was too dangerous, and I didn't have what it took to be a good agent. I mean, here I was sitting at a wedding with most of my family, and the brigands would be a gunshot away. My key might provide some protection for me, but what about my parents or Gertie or Mamma Bea? I was in the middle of rethinking my life's game plan when my mom's head spun around with superhero intuition.

"Finally, your brother is here," she said and hopped up to greet Eli. I hurried after her. Marco followed me, and Jake stayed behind, one hand on the gun hidden in his shoulder holster and the other resting on the package at his feet.

Eli and Mahlia were standing at the entrance to the churchyard. Eli was wearing his favorite black suit, and Mahlia was in six-inch Stuart Weitzman stilettos. I hoped she would get stuck in the soft ground and fall flat on her face. The picture flashed in my mind, and a small smile threatened the corners of my mouth.

"Only good thoughts, Dorothy," Marco teased as he walked with me.

"Yeah, if only the great and powerful Oz were here to lend a helping hand."

My mom hustled over to Eli and threw her arms around him as if she hadn't seen him in years. I stood back and eyed Mahlia, who was greeting my mom with a polite shyness. I frowned at her. The bitch. She had complemented her shoes with a black Italian MILLY slit dress.

While my mom was occupied with Mahlia, I tried to speak to Eli. He looked shell-shocked but not injured in any way.

"How are you?" I asked.

He almost growled the response. "Fine."

"Let's find a seat, lover." Mahlia and Eli interlocked hands, and they went ahead to be seated.

My mom stood openmouthed as she watched Mahlia and Eli greet a few relatives. She twisted her lips and frowned at me. "There's something about her I don't like." She squeezed my arm as she passed to return to her seat.

Even though Mahlia was a fellow New Yorker, I think my mom's gut was telling her Mahlia was no good. I smiled as I watched her walk back to her seat. Eli caught my eye and frowned at me.

"I think Eli's mad at me," I said with an air of confusion.

"I'm sure he's in shock from the experience of traveling in a vessel. Mahlia's making no attempt to hide the vessel or your secret from him." Marco put a hand on my shoulder.

"I don't know. He had the same look his sophomore year when I washed his white football jersey with my red hoodie. His teammates nicknamed him Pinky."

Eli and Mahlia sat with my parents, and they both greeted Jake with smiles, but I caught Mahlia taking a long glimpse at the package Jake had stowed at his feet.

I was dumbfounded. Mahlia mingled with everyone as if we were casual friends. There wasn't a gun pointed at Eli's ribcage, and I didn't see brigands holding sniper rifles in the trees. The only thing keeping

Eli in line was a skinny, tanned, French-manicured hand gently placed in the crook of his elbow.

"Where is Ace?" growled Jake. "I need him here as backup when we make the exchange."

I surveyed the crowd of people who had now gathered for the wedding. Mahlia was the only brigand here. The others were probably setting booby traps at Elma's house. Ace ran in at the last minute, his face flushed from rushing, but his Givenchy studded western shirt, rawhide jacket, and matching boots made a statement. My family was buzzing with gossip as he took a seat next to Jake, giving him a big hug, apologizing for being late, and calling him *pookie*. My dad looked over his shoulder at us and raised a dark eyebrow at Jake.

Jake dropped his head and murmured, "Your dad is never going to look at me the same way again."

"Don't worry," I said, patting his hand. "My dad is very open-minded."

Music began to play over the PA system. Ronnie McDowell's song "Older Women" began as an usher drove a horse-drawn gig cart down the aisle. The woman we had seen arguing earlier was perched up on the seat in her purple, beaded dress and sparkly shoes. She looked pleased with her method of transportation and was assisted out and plopped down on a front-row hay bale. After I had found out about Melissa Jo's fiancé, I had done a Google search. My research on Kanye had revealed he'd been raised by a strong single mom. His father had skipped out early in Kanye's life, but Kanye had had two hit songs and was deemed the next P. Diddy.

A tall brown mare sauntered down the aisle, carrying Melissa Jo's mom. The ushers helped her off the horse. She took her seat on the hay bales as they escorted the horse away.

The music changed, and the preacher rode around from behind the church and positioned his horse front and center. The bridal party followed on their horses with the ring bearer and flower girl riding Shetland ponies. The whole thing was über cute, and Marco elbowed me.

"You're getting that starry-eyed look in your eyes like you are mentally creating a wedding board on Pinterest."

"I like weddings. They're...normally a happy event."

"They make me nervous," Marco said.

"Why?"

"It might be the whole 'until death do you part' thing. How do you know when you've found the right person?" Marco put a hand on my knee. Fire shot through my thigh and caused things to stir, and I removed his hand. I wasn't the expert on relationships. My inner voice was drawing hearts around Marco's name, but I couldn't picture myself walking down the aisle with anyone.

"I would like to think there's a moment when that person does something incredible, and you just know."

"That's beautiful. Do you need a tissue?" Jake asked from the other side.

"Shut up," I said, giving Jake a friendly swat on the arm. I caught an evil look from my mom, who had a finger to her lips.

We watched as the two groomsmen took their places, followed by the groom. Kanye was the epitome of romance sitting astride a tall, white stallion. He seemed stiff in the saddle, as though maybe he wasn't all that familiar with horseback riding. His horse trotted down the with Kanye bouncing up and down in the saddle. When his horse sidestepped and snorted a few times, his eyes widened in fear.

One of the ushers calmed the horse, and the bridesmaids rode in. Kanye's sister, Gertie, and Amy took their horses to the front. The music changed again, and an acoustic version of the wedding march began. We stood as Melissa Jo's horse ambled down the aisle.

She was beautiful. I scanned the crowd. So far only Mahlia was here. I didn't see any sign of Caiyan. Jake had been wrong: Caiyan wasn't the least bit concerned about Eli's hostage situation or Marco.

I turned to look behind me. I recognized almost everyone on the bride's side, mostly family members and close friends. I looked over my right shoulder and scanned the groom's side. A few people had flown in from California and looked overdressed and bored. The guys from Kanye's band sat in the third row behind Kanye's family members, who were seated in the first two rows of hay bales. In the last row was a handlebar-mustached man in a tall cowboy hat. He looked out of place among the rappers and the sparkly dresses. I nudged Jake, and he took a look at the guy.

"I don't recognize him," Jake said and asked Ace to keep an eye on the man at the reception.

We watched as the happy couple exchanged their vows. The horses were considerate; there was no pooping during the ceremony. The groomsmen looked very nervous, as this was possibly the first time they had ever mounted anything other than California beach babes.

The couple kissed and began to ride down the aisle as man and wife. Kanye was grinning ear to ear. As they passed the handlebar-mustached man, Kanye's horse spooked, reared, and took off at full speed with Kanye screaming like a frightened schoolgirl.

Melissa Jo shrieked for help as everyone stood in awe as the groom went bouncing away. Gertie loosened her reins and gave a little nudge to her horse's ribs. "I'll git 'im!" she hollered as she rode off after the runaway groom.

"Save my baby!" Kanye's mom yelled after her.

We watched Gertie ride away, and I noticed the mustached man was missing...and so was Jake's package.

"Jake, the package is gone, and the guy in the back row with the handlebar mustache is missing." I pointed to the empty spot where the package had been.

"Shit, shit, shit, shit!" Jake hopped around as if he couldn't believe it. We stood dumbfounded for a few minutes and then began scouting the area.

A large black mare bolted from the barn with the mustache man on top. He flew by the crowd of people, the package tucked under his arm.

"That man is stealin' a wedding gift," Cousin Hildy shouted.

"That's not the worst part," the preacher said. "He's riding Devil's Tooth. Ain't no one been able to break that horse. He's got Satan's spirit."

The families stood gaping as the horse stopped on a dime and began bucking and snorting. The handlebar-mustached man held on for dear life. The horse decided to try and throw its uninvited rider by racing along the fence line. A figure wearing black leaped from the tree line and knocked the mustached man off his horse.

I recognized the well-built package of Caiyan as the other package dropped to the ground. We rushed over, and the two men had fists flying as my family gathered around. Jake secured the package under his arm.

"This here town is full up of crazy people," the mother of the groom shouted, fanning herself and looking for her son.

"This is Texas, and we're proud of our crazy people!" Mamma Bea stepped up to the woman, and I was afraid there might be a side brawl.

"It's Toches in disguise." Ace bent over and picked up something from the ground, holding the handle-bar mustache at arm's length for us to see.

Ace was right. Toches's ten-gallon hat and mustache were knocked off when Caiyan rocket launched him off the horse. The bastard was trying to steal the Thunder key out from under the Mafusos.

Caiyan was giving Toches a good pounding with his fists. Toches was trying to fight back, but Caiyan outmuscled him.

Mahlia stood on the outside of the group, rolling her eyes, and I noticed my brother stood next to her, arms crossed and a frown on his face. Mahlia didn't have a secret gun pointed at Eli or even a hold on his arm. Why wasn't Eli running to us for safety? Maybe the Mafusos also had someone in the shadows of the trees watching us.

After a few minutes, Caiyan had Toches's arm behind his back and pulled him to his feet.

"Who *is* that handsome man?" Cousin Hildy asked, pointing at Caiyan.

"That is Jennifer's boyfriend," Eli answered.

My mom's head bobbed up. "I thought Marco was your boyfriend?" she asked.

I caught Caiyan's angry glare as I answered, "It's complicated."

Chapter 13

Gertie returned with the groom in tow, and his family surrounded him as he reassured them he was fine. He claimed he'd had control of the beast long before Gertie arrived.

Gertie gave me a wink as she dismounted from her mare.

Jake flashed his badge and informed everyone he was with the CIA, and Caiyan was assisting him in the capture of a fugitive.

The crowd began to clap and shout affirmations. "Praise Jesus. Good job, city slicker!"

Ace yelled, "Way to go, honey."

Jake turned beet red and apologized for the intrusion. He handcuffed and escorted Toches to his car.

Elma's house was a short distance from the cowboy church, and a hay wagon was available for those guests who wanted a full-on country adventure. The bride and groom sat front and center as the guests reluctantly climbed aboard. My family scurried off to the reception, giddy with the excitement of having new gossip to spread around town.

"Is Johnny Cash coming to the reception?" Cousin Hildy asked, batting her false eyelashes at Caiyan.

Caiyan stood next to me in a full-on black suit. He did remind me a little of Johnny Cash.

"You showed up," I said to Caiyan.

"Aye, Toches is veery bad brigand."

"Oh, my sweet Jesus, he's got an accent." Hildy tugged on Caiyan's elbow. "C'mon, sweetie. You can ride on over to the reception with Hildy." Caiyan shot me a pained gaze, and I shrugged. Once Hildy got her mind set, there was no stopping her.

Jake nodded in my direction. We were to meet at Elma's house, and Jake had no choice but to bring Toches. He had the Sleigh key secured around his neck, and he was the only one who could remove it. Now that the family thought Toches was a fugitive, Jake would have to keep him out of sight until the trade. When the Mafusos found out Toches was trying to double-cross them, there would be hell to pay, and I wanted to see it up close and personal.

Ace rode with Jake in case Toches tried any funny business on the way. My parents had happily joined the hayride, leaving Marco and me to ride over with Eli and the evil bitch. I was surprised Eli had driven down. A few more guests followed behind the hayride, leaving the parking lot empty except for Mamma Bea's car and a black Mercedes-Benz SUV. Mahlia and Eli were standing next to the gate talking with Mamma Bea and looking ready to bolt. Brodie was keeping a short distance from the not-so-happy couple.

"Do y'all want a ride over to the reception?" Mamma Bea asked, looking at the black SUV as Marco and I approached.

"We are riding with Eli," I said, pointing at the SUV, and Mahlia's mouth twitched.

"That's a mighty fine ride you have there." Mamma Bea nodded admiringly at the Benz.

"Thank you, ma'am," Mahlia said with a touch of apprehension in her voice.

Mamma Bea looked at her and gave a slow nod. "OK, I'll see you there." She slowly walked down the road to her car and turned at the last minute, giving a wave.

"OK, what gives?" I asked Eli.

"I know all about your secret spy life," he spat at me.

"It wasn't like I could just tell you about it," I said in defense.

Mahlia looked a little pale, as if things weren't going her way. The self-confident bitchy attitude had been replaced by something less confident, almost scared.

"What's going on?" I asked, my gaze switching between the two of them.

Eli unbuttoned his shirt and exposed a key around his neck. Mahlia's key. Marco and Brodie both broke out in huge grins.

"What?" I asked. "Why is Eli wearing your key?"

"How'd ya git that?" asked Brodie.

Mahlia teared up, and Eli frowned at us.

"She always takes it off when she showers." Eli stood, his lips pressed tightly together and frowning.

"Leaving your key unprotected. That's brigand no-no number one. I bet the elder Mafuso was pretty upset with you," Marco said.

"Why didn't you just take it off him?" I asked.

"I tried," she said, swiping at a tear that had leaked down her cheek.

"You have the gift?" I asked Eli. "But didn't Aint Elma try her key on you when we were kids?"

"Are you nuts?" Eli said. "I wasn't going to have them put a girlie necklace on me. I remember Aint Elma touching my cheeks and shaking her head, then trying to put that necklace around my throat. One time, when I spent the night with her, I caught her trying in the middle of the night. It was scary waking up to an old woman leaning over you and trying to dress you like a girl. I told Mamma Bea, and she gave Aint Elma a talking to. I didn't know the necklace had some magical power, and my sister was flitting about the world on her day off."

Mahlia couldn't take her key off Eli, because he had the gift. I didn't know if I should be happy—now Eli would understand how my life had changed—or sad because he looked like he might strangle me.

"What's the plan?" Marco asked.

"Simple," Mahlia said, her bitchy self making an appearance. "We go to the reception at the white house in the woods. We will return Eli safely in exchange for my key. Gian-Carlo has made a deal with Toches to return the Sleigh key to the WTF after we receive the Tribal key."

"Whoa, no one said anything about your key. We will have to talk to Agent McCoy." Brodie strutted around as if he couldn't contain his good fortune. I knew he was thinking this changed the game, and there was a possibility we could keep the Thunder key.

Eli looked hurt. Mahlia had used him so the Mafusos could get the Tribal key. Eli's theft of Mahlia's key was only a small snafu in their evil plan. I decided to inform him of a few rules. "She can't kill you if you're wearing the key, because she will die as well."

"I thought there was more. It was like the thing called out to me, and when I put the necklace on, I had this unbelievable energy. I felt like I could run a marathon. I thought maybe it was the great sex. But normally, I'm exhausted after. When I saw myself in the mirror, I knew it was coming from the necklace, and then she tackled me and tried to force the thing off me."

Marco and Brodie smiled. I rolled my eyes and noticed a small bruise under Eli's right eye that was partially hidden by his glasses.

"Did she hurt you?" I asked.

"Some—probably a cracked rib—but when she took me to see the Elder Mafuso, Gian-Carlo, he asked me to join them."

I took a step back. "You're not going to join them, are you?"

"It's his decision," Mahlia said, butting in. "After we receive the Tribal key, we will have a spare, thanks to Caiyan giving up his key in the name of love." She examined her perfect manicure. "Seems like the WTF is fresh out of keys."

"It's my brother's choice to take off the key." I gave her a small smirk. "We know your vessel. If Eli decides to keep the key, you can say bye-bye to that fancy Harley of yours."

Mahlia's face fell. "We'll see you at the exchange."

Eli crossed his arms over his chest. "I'm standing right here, and I'm capable of making my own decisions."

I knew my brother. It wasn't in his nature to be a thief. He was a doctor, do-gooder, healer. If a choice had to be made, Eli would choose the honest path. Mahlia had picked the wrong guy to wrap her legs around this time.

⌐

*T*he sun was setting as we approached Aint Elma's house, and the sunlight cast a golden glow over the small farm that used to belong to one tough old woman. I hadn't known her well, but when I wore her key, I felt a connection with her. I was curious whether other travelers felt the same pull from their keys. Mahlia's key had called out to Eli subconsciously or telepathically—or had it actually spoken to him? The Thunder key made a noise that sounded like a boom from the heavens. Maybe there was more to the keys than an inanimate piece of moonstone. My inner voice took a memo to ask the other travelers.

Aint Elma's backyard was big enough to hold a wedding party, including a tented sit-down dinner for about fifty people. Guests were directed to enter the reception through the side gate. Tall oak trees wrapped in miniature twinkle lights provided an enchanted fairy wonderland. Marco was slouching along behind me, not nearly as impressed with the venue as I was. I stopped to get a feel for the area, and he leaned in next to me.

"Are you sensing any brigands on your radar?" he asked, leaning in extra close so I felt his breath on my neck, and my toes began to tingle.

"Other than Mahlia, I don't see anyone." We walked together, saying hello to my relatives as we passed. The large white party tent was set up directly behind the house. Tables and chairs were arranged beneath it with a few scattered outside the tent for extra seating. Gertie's mom had used the same setup when she'd married Vinnie the Fish. I tried to imagine marrying Marco here. He could definitely rock a black tuxedo with tails, and I would wear a white Monique Lhuillier wedding dress. I was mentally arranging the seating chart when Marco nudged me.

"Are you sure you're ready for this?"

My mouth popped open so wide I thought my TMJ would lock up, and I would be stuck for the night. "What do you mean?" I managed to get my jaws moving again and crossed my fingers Marco didn't suddenly have ESP.

"If this thing gets out of hand, your entire family will be exposed to your time-travel secrets."

"Let's make sure it doesn't get out of hand." I turned toward the tent and began searching for any uninvited wedding guests.

A special stage was set up in front of the tent for the choir that would perform for the guests during dinner and for the obligatory toasts from the maid of honor and the best man. A few choir members were lingering around the stage, but they seemed harmless. No brigands here.

The reception attendants were lighting patio heaters to keep the night air warm. I pulled on my jacket as I canvassed my surroundings for brigands. To the right of the wedding tent was an old red barn. The last time I had seen it, the double doors were covered in chipped paint and falling off the hinges. The family used it to store odds and ends, rusted-out farm equipment, and items we couldn't get rid of in a garage sale. Tonight the barn sported a fresh coat of fire-engine red paint, and its entire contents had been cleared. The wood floor was swept clean, and mason jars were strung throughout with small votive candles adding a romantic illumination to the old barn.

"It's beautiful," I said, walking inside the barn.

"It ought to be, dawrlin'," Mamma Bea said, entering the barn. "It took me three weeks and four farmhands to get this old barn clean and ready."

"You did an amazing job," Marco said, admiring the wagon-wheel chandelier that hung overhead.

Tiny twinkle lights that mimicked the lights on the outside trees wrapped the crossbeams, and in the far corner was an area set up for a DJ and karaoke.

"Well," Mamma Bea said, leaning in so only Marco and I would hear. "Emperor KW Smooth Dog sent an e-mail saying he would need a place for him and his dog pound to perform."

We laughed, and I honestly couldn't wait to see the looks on my family's faces when he began his gangsta rap.

Mamma Bea opened a trapdoor in the floor of the barn. It led to a hidden room my ancestors had used during Prohibition that also doubled as a tornado shelter. She disappeared down a ladder and re-surfaced a minute later, hauling two jugs of brown liquid. I took the jugs from Mamma Bea as Marco helped her up from the ladder.

"Is that what I think it is?" I asked.

"Yep, Grandpa Cloud's famous moonshine. I hide it in the bootleg-gers' hold, or Uncle Durr would drink me dry. I'm going to mix it in the punchbowl with the lemonade."

Moonshine lemonade. After a few glasses, we would all be rapping along with the dog pound.

The reception was in full swing. A full buffet of fried everything. I was starving, but my stomach was doing flip turns over the approach-ing exchange. Mahlia was keeping within an arm's length of Eli, and Hildy had Caiyan occupied with one of her many lengthy stories. I knew Jake was staked out somewhere with Toches, waiting on the meet-ing, but I didn't see Ace or Brodie. Marco left to walk the perimeter, and I was standing alone, feeling useless. I caught Gertie as she left the buffet table with a plate piled high with fried chicken and waffles.

"Have you seen Brodie?" I asked as she passed and snagged a heart-shaped waffle off her plate.

"He's in the wind," she said, wiggling her eyebrows at me and tip-ping her head toward the treetops. "I'm supposed to keep an eye on things when you go back to make the trade. You know, to keep all us NATs from interfering with the secret-agent stuff."

"Wow, so you know about the meeting?"

"Yes, and no thanks to you. You would think your best friend would know what's going on."

"I'm sorry. It all came to a head pretty quick."

"That's OK. You can make amends by telling me every detail of the night you spent with Marco."

"What details would those be now?" Caiyan asked, walking up next to me.

"Got to go." Gertie took off toward the bridal party and left me with all the details. Damn.

"How's Hildy?" I asked, hoping to change the subject.

"She's got some great stories—long, but interesting." He placed both hands in his pants pockets. "Aboot Berlin—"

"I'm not sure I want to know," I said, cutting him off. A swift wind swept through the trees, and a strand of my hair came loose from my sleek ponytail.

He reached up to place it back behind my ear, hesitated midway, and returned his hands to his pockets.

We stood for a moment in silence. I felt people passing by, and Hildy said, "It's time for the Nuwaubian Nation choir to sing. I heard they're incredible."

That was our cue for the meeting. Marco rejoined us, and the two men had a brief growl at each other. I waited until all eyes were focused on the choir.

"Let's go." I broke the stare down, and we headed through the back gate to the hidden garden. A row of tall, thick bushes blocked the backyard from what most of my family referred to as the pasture. When Aint Elma was alive, the area had resembled a picture from a garden magazine. She'd had multiple vegetable and flower gardens that were interwoven throughout tall trees and an occasional frog pond. The gardens were gone now, and the pathway through the garden was overgrown with crabgrass. As we walked, the singing from the choir slowly faded away. We passed the weeping willow tree where Aint Elma had kept the outhouse before she gave it to me.

"Remember when we met here?" Marco asked, knowing full well he was pushing Caiyan's buttons.

Thankfully, Marco's stroll down memory lane was halted by the glow of a low fire and shadows in the distance. As we walked closer, the figures became familiar. Standing under the canopy of a hundred-year-old pecan tree was Jake. Toches was seated on a wooden bench at the base of the tree with his hands secured behind his back. Ace was hovering over him. Eli and Mahlia were standing off to the side in front of a large stump. When we were kids, Gertie and I had played Knights of the Round Table on that stump, because of its rounded edges and large base. Aint Elma had used it as a chopping block to chop wood for the winter.

As we approached, Caiyan saw the key around Eli's neck. "Holy shite!" he exclaimed. "How did that happen?"

Mahlia looked at the ground.

"Eli has the gift," I told him. "We didn't know."

"What's wrong with this family? How can they keep something so powerful a secret?" Caiyan asked, narrowing his eyes at Marco.

Jake held up a hand, halting what was about to be an unnecessary confrontation. "Here's the problem. Now they want to exchange Eli for Mahlia's key and the Sleigh key for the Tribal key."

"I don't think that is a very fair trade," Ace said, still trying to hold on to the Thunder key for Caiyan.

At once, everyone was arguing their point. A crack of thunder sounded, halting the conversations, and a few minutes later, the Mafuso leader entered the secret garden. It was the garden where I'd first discovered my vessel and the heart and soul of Aint Elma. I felt a tickle of anger in my throat. It was as if the devil himself had penetrated our sacred space.

He approached the group, dressed like he should be attending a charity ball instead of meeting with the WTF. He wore a black virgin-wool Prada suit, a deep-red silk shirt, and freshly shined shoes. His red shirt was open at the collar, and reflecting the flame from the firelight was Caiyan's key.

"Gian-Carlo, ye son of a bitch!" Caiyan shouted and started toward him. Marco held on to Caiyan to prevent him from attacking the old man.

"You didn't think I was going to let Mitchell keep such a valuable prize?" he asked, lowering his chin and staring down his nose at Caiyan.

Jake stepped between the men. "It seems there is another key now on the table for negotiation."

"Yes, yes," he said. "So unfortunate." He placed a hand on Eli's arm. "We would be happy to have you join our family business. Mahlia has taken quite an interest in you."

Ace snorted. "Family business, bloody filchers."

Eli just stood planted, not making a sound.

"We will trade Eli and the Sleigh key for the Tribal key—and Mahlia's, of course."

Toches's head shot up. "I have the Sleigh."

"We had a bargain. Did we not?" Gian-Carlo stood facing Toches. "Although after your attempt to steal the key from under our noses, I might reconsider."

"I was making sure they didn't trick us," Toches whined.

Gian-Carlo crossed his arms over his chest and studied Toches. "You may have the lovely key I am wearing, and I will take control over the Tribal key."

Toches stopped whining and gave Caiyan a smug look. Caiyan grumbled a Gaelic curse.

Jake took control. "OK, first we will exchange the Sleigh key for the Tribal key." He placed the unwrapped box in the center of the stump and used his key to unlock and open it.

Ace removed the handcuffs from Toches, and he reached up, unfastened the Sleigh key, and handed the key to me.

Gian-Carlo reached into the box and lifted out the Thunder. A loud boom rang out from the key, and Gian-Carlo smiled.

Toches started to freak out. He jumped from his seat and flapped his arms like a turkey trying to take flight. "They're scamming us. That's not the Tribal key."

"It's not?" Jake asked.

"No, that's my key, and I don't want it back. You bastards stole it from my ancestors, didn't you?"

"Bloody hell, Toches, we didn't know it was yours," Ace said.

"We though' the key was dead," Caiyan added.

"You took it while I was in Berlin. I was stuck there for over a year!" His face started turning red. "I finally realized what my key had been doing to me, but I was trapped there being Hitler's bitch. I couldn't enjoy my freedom."

"What was your key doing to you?" I asked, watching Gian-Carlo run his hands over the Thunder key.

"The key is possessed," Toches said, his voice escalating a few octaves.

"Possessed?" Gian-Carlo dropped the key back into its velvet bedding and pulled a gun from his breast pocket. Grabbing Jake around the throat, he held the gun to his head. "Now you will return both keys, or I will shoot your leader dead."

My heart sank. I didn't see Brodie in the trees. But what could he do? He couldn't shoot Gian-Carlo; he had the gift.

I heard the distinctive sound of a shotgun being cocked. Mamma Bea stepped into the light with a double-barreled shotgun pointed at the brigands.

"You drop your weapon, Gian-Carlo. I can kill all y'all and not bat an eyelash."

I was in shock. I'd had no idea Mamma Bea knew about the Mafusos, the WTF, or the gift. Gian-Carlo stood still, as if waiting for something to happen.

"Your little brat Mitchell is caught up in the poacher's net toward the back of the garden there, if you are waiting for him to come save ya. You can find him hanging from the old oak tree twenty paces west."

The Mafuso elder released Jake, who returned the favor by pointing his .45-caliber pistol at the Mafusos.

"Easy, Jake," Mamma Bea coaxed, keeping her shotgun pointed at Gian-Carlo.

"Bea, come on now. Be reasonable." Gian-Carlo held his hands up in the air, and Jake removed the gun from his hand.

"I've been reasonable my whole life," Mamma Bea said. "My John was taken from me because I was *reasonable*, and I'll be damned if I'm going to let you bully these young'uns into giving up what's theirs."

"Bea, at least give us Mahlia's key back," Gian-Carlo said.

Mamma Bea paused, thinking about the request. "If you take the key and leave quietly."

"You have my word," Gian-Carlo said, giving Mamma Bea a nod of sincerity.

"Eli, that key don't belong to you," Mamma Bea said. "Give it back to the pretty girl."

Eli paused, considered. He took off the key and handed it to Mahlia. She quickly secured it around her skinny neck, and the key glowed briefly. I frowned. We'd had Mahlia's key and could have sent them away empty-handed, but I knew if we didn't return it, all hell would break loose between the Mafusos and the WTF.

Mamma Bea put two fingers in her mouth and whistled. A few minutes later, Brodie showed up, pushing Mitchell forward. "Look what I found tied up in the trees."

"What about the Sleigh key?" Toches asked, sounding a bit hysterical.

"No Tribal key, no exchange," Gian-Carlo said to Toches. "You can try and get it back from them yourself." He turned on his heel and left, Mahlia and Mitchell trailing after him. Jake and Brodie followed them to assure they left the premises.

I tightened my grip on the Sleigh key, and Ace patted Toches on the back. "Better luck next time, bloke."

Toches went berserk. He rammed me, pulling the Sleigh key from my grasp and pushing me backward into Ace. We both fell to the ground. Marco, Caiyan, and Eli were standing between Toches and the exit to the back gate. Toches made a break toward the wedding reception.

"Damn, you slippery little weasel," I heard Mamma Bea shout as she took off after him. Marco and I ran after her and took opposite sides to find the little freak.

We made it to the reception as the Nuwaubian Nation choir was in full vocal harmony of their rendition of a song from *The Lion King*. The choir was blocking the exit. Toches tried to make his way, pushing and shoving through the choir, and was stopped short by a rather hefty choir member, who gave him a bop on the head with her tambourine. He tripped and fell, losing his grasp on the Sleigh key. The key flew through the air and landed in Gertie's lap.

Gertie picked up the key and saw Toches floundering on the floor. "The fugitive has escaped," she shouted and pointed at Toches.

"It's that present stealer!" Hildy screeched. The choir stopped singing, and guests were craning their necks to get a look at the criminal.

I looked for Marco and spotted him coming out of the barn on the far side of the wedding tent. He was too far away to help.

"Gertie," I called out to her as Toches regained his footing and ran toward her. She jumped up from the table where she was seated and made a quarterback pass over the heads of the guests. Gertie overthrew me, and Melissa Jo intercepted it at the head table.

"I've got it!" she yelled. Toches changed direction and climbed over the head table knocking over glasses as he went. He clawed at Melissa Jo. As he took the key from her, he ripped the bodice of her wedding dress, causing her boobs to pop free and bounce around like large Jell-O molds fresh out of the fridge. Kanye grabbed Toches's right arm and bent it behind his back. I was able to squeeze through the singers and headed for Toches. He sneered at me as he used his free hand to try and secure the key around his neck before I could reach him.

"No!" I screamed as I balled up my fist and rammed it directly into Toches's face. I felt the bones crunch under my fist, and blood began flowing from his nose.

Toches dropped the Sleigh key and fell to the floor clutching his nose. Cousin Hildy promptly sat on him as Brodie and Jake arrived. Jake pulled his gun and pointed it at Toches. This was followed by a serenade of guns being cocked. I looked around, and almost every guest had a gun on Toches.

"Damn!" Brodie said. "There's more heat here than at a five-alarm fire."

"Looks like you're done, Toches," Jake said as he cuffed Toches and brought him to his feet. Toches was using his shirt to try and stop the blood running out of his nostrils.

"Here ya go, doll," Hildy said, giving him the hankie she kept tucked in her bra next to her cellphone.

Jake informed the guests the fugitive would not escape again and thanked them for their contribution. My parents plowed through the gawking guests, and my mom grabbed me and hugged me tightly.

"Jen, are you OK?"

"I'm fine, but you're squeezing the air out of me."

She released me with a once-over, checking for any broken bones.

"Mom, really, I'm fine."

"Way to go, slugger," my dad said, giving me a high five. He told a nearby guest he'd taught me how to throw a right hook. He wasn't completely wrong. He had shown me how to make a fist when I was five. I wouldn't tell him about my kickboxing instructor or the many self-defense training classes the WTF had checked off my list.

The Nuwaubian Nation choir started singing again, and the party resumed. Brodie was allowed to stay with Gertie and keep an eye out in case the Mafusos returned. Jake thought this was unlikely.

I handed Jake the Sleigh key, and he tucked it inside his jacket pocket. I walked with Jake and Ace as they escorted Toches out of the reception.

"I'm going to have Ace take Toches and me to headquarters to sort this mess out. You get the Thunder key and meet me there in half an hour." Jake glanced around. "Where's McGregor?"

Damn. Our eyes met, and Jake turned a little pale.

"Oopsy," Ace said, wincing. "With all the commotion, I forgot all about that key."

Jake stopped and threw his head back as if life couldn't get any worse. I made a sprint for the secret garden. I didn't recall Caiyan being in the vicinity when Toches had made a break for it. I found Eli sitting on the stump, holding the Thunder key's box. I peered inside. Empty.

"What happened?" I asked.

"I don't know. I ran after you, and when I saw you punch that guy in the nose, I came back here. It's all a little surreal."

"I didn't think I could hit someone that hard," I said, sitting down next to him.

"It was pretty freaking awesome." He laughed and then looked down at me. "You have some explaining to do."

"That makes two of us," Mamma Bea said as she walked toward us.

I stared at her with my mouth hanging open.

"What?" She smiled. "Did you think I didn't know about the goings-on in my own family?" I rushed toward her and hugged her. "Come here, dawrlin'." She motioned toward Eli, and he slinked in for a hug.

"I have to report to headquarters, but we can meet later, and I'll explain everything," I said and broke free from the hug.

Marco joined us, and I was curious about how much of our conversation he'd overheard. "Where's the Thunder?" he asked, pointing to the empty box.

"I don't know," I said, but I did know. Caiyan had taken the Thunder key and vanished. "I wonder what Toches meant by his key being possessed."

"If that was his key, he couldn't have killed Agent Grant," Marco said. "Brodie and Ace were in the year 1665 when they took the Thunder key, and nothing has changed."

Marco was right. If a key was taken, as long as it was returned in the same moon cycle, time would remain unchanged. We'd had the Thunder key for over a year. Toches had been stuck in 1945 the same way I would have been stuck in 1914 if we hadn't retrieved my key from Pancho Villa when I first began my traveling. There was no way Toches had killed Agent Grant.

"Toches didn't kill anyone," Mamma Bea confirmed. "He's a petty thief, an excellent pickpocket, and an impersonator. He's not a murderer."

"Mamma Bea, do you have the gift?" I asked.

"No, child, but your Pawpaw John was a fine traveler. We didn't keep any secrets. You go on now and do your job. After this shindig is over," she said, using her thumb to point over her shoulder at the wedding reception behind her, "we can meet and have a glass of sweet tea, talk about the way things used to be."

I nodded and gave her a hug. I'd had no idea my grandfather was a traveler. I had so many questions for Mamma Bea, but they would have to wait. Marco and I avoided the wedding guests by sneaking out the back gate.

"I bet your grandma has an interesting tale," Marco said.

"Yep, I'm gonna need more than sweet tea to get me through this weekend." My inner voice was pouring a mug of Mamma Bea's moonshine lemonade. I couldn't help but agree.

Ace and a blindfolded and handcuffed Toches were seated in the back seat of Jake's Land Rover. Jake was speaking on his cell. I could hear General Pott's booming voice from where I was standing. Jake looked at me and raised an eyebrow. I shook my head, indicating the obvious. No Caiyan and no key. Jake ended the conversation and informed me Eli was requested to report to WTF headquarters.

"That would be his decision." I frowned at Jake. *Did he* have *to run and tell the general about Eli?*

Jake started to argue, but Marco cut him off.

"We need to get the Sleigh key back to 1945," Marco said.

Marco was right. We needed to fix the problem we had inadvertently caused in 1945.

"I'm going to drive up the road," Jake said. "Ace can meet us and take us back to headquarters. The general will make a decision on what to do with the Sleigh key."

Marco scowled but agreed to meet at headquarters. Jake sent a text to Brodie and asked him to pick up his SUV.

After they left, Marco pulled me into his arms. "I'm sorry about Caiyan. I know you were hoping he didn't take that key."

I rested my head against his shoulder. I had been hoping I would find him in the garden. Marco bent down to kiss me, but I stopped him, abruptly pulling back.

"Wait, how did he leave?" We knew the Thunder belonged to Toches, but we didn't know his vessel.

Marco sighed. "Caiyan and Toches go way back. I wouldn't be surprised if Caiyan knew how to find his vessel."

"He never said anything the entire time we had the Thunder key." *He knew it belonged to Toches, the rat bastard. He knew it wasn't the Tribal key. The rat bastard.*

"Caiyan took the Thunder key. Toches isn't going to be happy he's keyless. The Mafusos are going to have to make good on the promise they made Toches, or he's going to cause problems for them, which is good for us."

"Won't the WTF keep Toches in the prison?"

"For what?" Marco asked. "Disrupting a wedding? We have the Sleigh key, and he didn't steal it any more than Caiyan was going to steal it."

"True."

"After they give him a good interrogation, they will release him."

Another brigand for us to keep in line. I sighed, and Marco and I walked down the road to a place we could call our vessels and report for duty.

Chapter 14

We were on the second day of the full-moon cycle, and I felt like I had lived a week in two days. The bombs weren't literally dropping around me anymore, but Eli having the gift was scary. Did I want him to travel? I understood why Jake had been concerned about *my* decision to join the WTF.

What if Eli was killed on a mission or went MIA? My inner voice was plucking newly sprouted gray hairs. I dismissed her and tried to keep my chin up.

When I entered the debriefing room, Gerald was sitting at the conference table. I sat down next to him and let out a long breath.

"Rough day, buttercup?"

"My boyfriend almost got me killed and then ran off with a stolen key. My brother was abducted, and we were all rescued by my shotgun-toting grandmother."

"Just another day at the office, I'd say." Gerald smiled and took a bite out of an oatmeal cookie.

My stomach rumbled, reminding me I was missing the reception dinner. I chose a cookie from the plate on the conference-room table and ate it in two bites.

"I thought you and Tina were in Ireland?"

"We were, but we couldn't find the Cracky clan, and then Tina came down with a bug."

"Weren't you in the fourteenth century?"

"Yes, dreary time. Everyone was wearing black."

"They were probably in black because they attended so many funerals, due to the deaths from the bubonic plague," I said, recalling the intel from Ace and Brodie about the impoverishment and death on their past travels.

Gerald halted with a cookie midway to his mouth. He pocketed the cookie and scooted abruptly off his chair. "I'm going to the infirmary to check on Tina."

He left, mumbling something about fleas and a damn cat.

I was devouring my third cookie when Jake walked in, followed by Marco and Ace. The boys were plotting without me.

Jake was carrying an armful of magazines. He plopped them down on the conference table, and everyone took a seat.

"Here's the deal," Jake said. "You and Marco are going to Berlin to return the Sleigh key."

Had Jake figured out a way for us to save Anna and Isla? The thought of landing during the bombing was scary, and my inner voice was unpacking her gas mask.

Jake jammed the cogs of the wheels turning in my mind. "You won't be going back to 1945. It's too close to your original travel time, and I can't take the risk of you landing in the middle of an air raid or the invasion of the Soviet troops."

"But what about Isla and Anna?" I asked.

Marco turned to me. "Jake found Isla—she lived," he said, grinning, but then his grin faded. "Anna didn't make it. Our facts were correct."

"Why can't we go back and save her?" I asked. "If we hadn't been there, Toches wouldn't have taken her, and she would have lived."

"Jen," Jake said. "We did the research, and we don't know if she died before or after you returned to the present. We can't risk your life or changing the past."

I understood, but I didn't have to like it. I knew thousands of people had died in World War II…but Anna should not have been one of them.

"What year?" Marco asked, sliding one of the magazines over in front of him.

"Nineteen sixty-five." Jake pointed at the stack of reference materials. "Ace will be here to help if you run into trouble. Jen, I expect you to summon Ace if you have any problems."

"Great," Ace said. "Hope you don't 'ave any problems. The last time I was in Berlin, I got arrested."

"What did you do?" I asked.

"I might 'ave caused a bit of excitement on the steps of the Siegessäule."

I raised a questioning eyebrow at him.

"It's the Victory column with the gold woman at the top." Ace smiled and interlocked his fingers, placing them behind his head. "I think it was 1976. The clubs were open all night, and I might 'ave partaken in a few shots of illegal absinthe and tried to shimmy up the pole."

"He forgot to include he was butt naked," Jake said with a hint of a smile. It was the first time I'd caught a glimpse of the old Jake in a while. This job was turning him into a staunch, stiff-necked military man, and it was refreshing to hear him joke with Ace.

"If we go back to 1965, we might be too late," Marco said. He huffed.

"What do you mean?" I asked.

"My grandfather finds the key in April of 1965 when he goes to Berlin on business. He visits the bakery tomorrow and discovers the painting."

"But the painting isn't there," I said.

"That's correct," Jake said. "We have to get you there before Marco's grandfather visits the bakery. Isla doesn't own the bakery; an older German couple owns the bakery that Isla and Anna would have purchased from them and turned into one of the best bakeries in Berlin."

"Where is Isla?" I asked.

"She works at a nightclub called the Eden."

Isla worked at a nightclub. I dropped my head in my hands. We had ruined her life. Isla was supposed to own the bakery with Anna.

I jerked up. I knew where the painting was left in 1945. Maybe it was still there. "I know where the painting is." I almost shouted the words.

"Where?" Three heads turned in my direction.

"I saw Caiyan bury it in the Volkspark Friedrichshain under one of the statues in the Märchenbrunnen Bottomain park."

Jake ran a hand through his already mussed hair. "It's in East Berlin. I can't authorize landing behind the wall in a Communist country. You might as well be back in 1945. This is a quick in-and-out mission."

"But how will she know who Marco's grandfather is?" I asked. "Without the picture, he won't find the key."

"Marco can give Isla the key. You two will have to convince her what to do with it."

"Why can't we go back to another time before the wall is up?" I asked.

"It's mayhem," Jake said. "The Russians invaded Berlin and committed so many acts of treason the government couldn't count them all. It took years for the four allied groups to divide Berlin and become civil with one another. General Potts wants the key placed close to the time Marco's grandfather discovers it to decrease the opportunity of another heist."

"Before we screwed up, Anna and Isla moved back to Berlin and purchased the bakery in West Berlin. Isla went to culinary school in Paris and returned to help Anna run the bakery," Marco said, reminding me that Anna's death changed everything.

Jake stood and spread a map out in front of us. "Truman drops the atomic bomb in August, then all hell breaks loose, and Berlin isn't the same again until 1989, when the wall is finally taken down."

"What do I do?" Ace asked.

"Go to the travel lab. If you are summoned, Pickles can help you with the landing mark."

"Good luck, mates. I hope you don't need my assistance." Ace picked up a copy of *Movie Mirror* magazine and left the room with a casual wave to us.

"You will land here." Jake pointed to a location on the map of Berlin marked Tiergarten. "It's a large park, and the tree cover should provide a safe haven for your landing. This area has an open space that now holds a soccer field. The nightclub is here on Kurfürstendamm. You will have to walk or catch a taxi. After you find Isla, take her to the bakery." He handed Marco and me each a fifty deutsche mark banknote, the German currency used in 1965. "Sorry, this is the largest bill we have in our vault."

I didn't know the conversion rate, but the concerned look on Marco's face told me it wasn't enough money, even in 1965.

"The bakery is here on Friedrichstraße. It's a short walk from the Tiergarten. Go east until you reach the Berlin wall. Follow the wall to Struesemann, and go left until you hit Friedrichstraße. Checkpoint Charlie, the American checkpost dividing East and West Berlin, should be on your left, and the bakery is on the corner."

"We'll be so close to East Berlin." Marco ran his fingers over the map, stopping on the Märchenbrunnen park.

"Under no circumstances are you to land in East Berlin. This is directly from General Potts." Jake stared at me as he said the words. If he were Superman, the message would have been burned on my forehead. "You will go in Jennifer's vessel, together."

Marco folded his arms across his chest in defeat. We had one shot at finding Isla and convincing her to give the key to Marco's grandfather, Giorgio. If all went well, she would fall in love with his business partner, and Marco's lifeline would remain intact.

"You have one hour to learn about Berlin. I will get the Sleigh key and meet you at the landing dock." Jake left the room, and Marco and I sat in silence.

The inability to get the painting was a deal breaker. If we disobeyed the order, we would both lose our keys and our jobs. Jake's unspoken words were left on the table next to the cookie crumbs.

⌒

I aimed for a cluster of trees in the Tiergarten. When we'd reviewed the maps of 1965, Pickles had assured me this area was hidden from view but not so densely wooded that I might ram into a tree. We came to a stop, and I looked over at Marco. I heard music playing and voices of people singing in the distance. I prayed we hadn't landed in the middle of Potsdamer Platz or another highly public place. Marco and I retrieved the money, folded and covered in spit, from our cheeks.

"Jen, I hear music. Where did you land us?"

"Only one way to find out." I took a deep breath, pushed the outhouse door open, and stepped out into the night. Marco followed, and we were greeted with a loud "Heilige Scheiße!"

A stubby, round man was leaning against a tree trunk about ten yards away, pants around his ankles, holding his manhood. He had obviously been in the middle of a piss when we'd interrupted. About thirty feet behind the man, lights were strung haphazardly between trees, providing illumination for a dozen or so picnic tables. Damn Pickles. He hadn't taken into account the night activities of the Germans.

"This wasn't in the plans," I said, thankful we were tucked back in the shadows, hidden from everyone except our local pisser.

"It's a biergarten," Marco said. "Probably temporary—that's why it wasn't in the research."

Marco stepped forward, and I hoped he would pull a red laser from his pocket and wipe the man's mind clean. Marco spoke a few words to the man in German. The man nodded his head and replaced his boy part back into his pants. We watched our friend stumble back to the party.

"What did you tell him?" I asked.

"He asked if you were the green fairy."

"The one from Ace's illegal booze?"

"Yep, I assured him you were indeed the absinthe green fairy, and you were providing a more private place for him to relieve himself." Marco nodded toward my outhouse. "He went to tell his friends."

"Oh, no. Definitely not!" I waved my hand, and my outhouse disappeared into the night.

Marco laughed. Nice of him to find humor in the desecration of my vessel. In the light cast from the biergarten, I looked down at my outfit. The green fairy wasn't too far off. I was in head-to-toe green wool plaid. I removed the hat from my head. It was a cute pillbox-style hat in the same shade of green as the dress. I examined the hairdo with my fingers. It was pulled back with bobby pins on top and done up in a clever knot, while the back of my hair was down. Replacing the hat, I checked out my shoes. Loafers, not my favorite, but functional. The plaid skirt hit above my stocking-covered knee, and a matching jacket completed the ensemble. The night was cool, and I was thankful my vessel had dressed me warmly and fashionably.

Marco was watching me admire my clothes, so I gave him a quick catwalk pose. "Very nice," he said. "Sort of Twiggy meets Jackie Kennedy."

"Why are you dressed like James Dean?" I asked. "Isn't that the wrong decade?"

"James Dean is timeless." Marco flipped up his collar and held up his wrist. "Look what else I got."

A watch on a leather wristband encircled his left wrist.

"It's a watch."

"It's not just any watch. It's a Patek." He admired the face of the watch.

"It looks like my uncle's Timex."

"It's worth about fifty grand in our time. Do you know what this means?"

"We're running out of time?" I asked but smiled at Marco's joy over the watch.

"We have something to barter if we need it, although I would hate to sell it." He glanced down at it lovingly and then held out his watch-adorned arm to escort me out of the woods.

"We've got about six hours," he said, walking toward the biergarten. "I want to chat with the locals and get some intel on our night club."

I tightened my grip on his arm. "Marco, we don't have enough money to blow on booze."

"What do you think I have you for?"

We entered the area, and Marco asked me to sit at the end of one of the long wooden tables. A group of German students seated at the far end of the table eyed me as I took a seat. Marco left me to go speak to a man standing behind a makeshift bar. It was less than a minute before I had a dark German beer in my hands, compliments of a group of men at a nearby table. I smiled and gave a thank-you wave. Marco joined me and took a sip of my beer.

"I told you it wouldn't take long to get a pint. The Germans got a bad rap, thanks to Hitler and the Nazi regime. They are normally very hospitable people."

We shared the beer and listened to the three-piece band. One of the men squeezed an accordion while the crowd sang along to German beer hall songs. I thought that at another time, this might be a fun place to hang out.

Marco was staring down into the beer.

"When are you going to tell me about the Sleigh key?" I asked.

"You know all about it." He cut his eyes at me as he took another sip of my beer. "I love German beer—so much strength in the brew."

"Don't try and change the subject. Who is the owner of the Sleigh key?"

"Isla," he said, taking a much larger sip.

"You know I am asking about the current owner, and you don't have to tell me, because I already know the answer."

"You do?"

"Yes, I know the Sleigh key belongs to your sister."

Marco sighed and finished off the beer.

"It's Evangeline's key." I touched the hollow of my neck and felt the warm tingle of my key hidden safely under my shirt. "She doesn't know about the gift, does she?"

"No, and I'd like to keep it that way. My grandfather always wanted us to travel. I was almost relieved when he died before she showed any signs of the gift."

"Giorgio wanted you to travel together? Evangeline is your transporter?"

"Yes."

"Don't you think she has a right to know?"

"How do you feel now that you know Eli has the gift and could die any time the moon is full?" Marco slid down the table to have a conversation with the students. I wasn't sure I'd had time to process the idea of Eli traveling or what could happen to him if he did join the WTF. A few minutes later, Marco nudged me out of my reverie.

"Let's get out of here," Marco said, leaving the empty beer stein on the table. He interlaced his fingers with mine. We walked toward the exit, and to the casual observer, we looked like a couple strolling through the park. "Those guys I spoke with were students at the university. They told me the Eden club is owned by some rich guy, and they couldn't afford to get in."

"Great. How are *we* going to get in?"

"I've got you." He smiled and kissed my fingers. Heat shot up my arm, and I was about to pull away when the Berlin Wall came into view.

A few rows of cinder blocks topped off with barbed wire greeted us. It wasn't as tall as I'd imagined, and I'd expected it to be covered with amazing murals painted by political protesters.

"What's wrong?" Marco asked.

"I thought it would be covered with art," I said, pointing to a well-lit section of the wall.

"The wall was rebuilt in the eighties. The graffiti art became popular after the rebuild."

There was a big trench between the wall and the walkway. We proceeded along a deserted, tree-lined street, and I questioned how I would feel if I didn't know about my gift.

"What are you thinking about?" Marco asked, pointing at my free hand. "You're twisting your hair, so it must be serious."

A strand of hair was wound around my index finger. I let it go, and the hair corkscrewed down my shoulder. "I think we should have the right to choose our own path." I pointed toward the barbed wire, and Marco picked up on my meaning.

"You're right, but I'm not ready to show my sister the world of time travel, and Jake has agreed to respect my wishes."

Marco's gift was too valuable to refuse. Jake was sacrificing the Sleigh key in order to keep Marco on the team. *Postponing* was probably a better word. Eventually, Jake would find a way to recruit the owner of the Sleigh key to the WTF.

Marco stopped and put his hands on my shoulders. "If things don't go as planned, I might need to lateral travel to East Berlin and get that painting."

"Jake told us not to go to East Berlin," I said, standing firm.

"Jake said not to *land* in East Berlin. I could lateral travel to Strausberg and take a taxi to Berlin."

"It's not safe to lateral travel in the past."

"I know it's risky, but even if Isla remembers us, I don't see how she is going to identify my grandfather. I'm not sure *I* would recognize him if I saw him."

I didn't have any answers for Marco. Caiyan and I had lateral traveled in the past on a prior travel, and we hadn't encountered any problems. But Jake had warned me about travelers getting lost in time. Marco could call his vessel and do as he pleased, regardless.

"Let's find Isla first. We don't know if the painting is still hidden in the Märchenbrunnen."

"If Isla doesn't meet my grandfather and marry Henri, I won't be here when the moon cycle closes."

I ran my hand on the side of Marco's cheek. "We'll find Isla, and we will stay until your grandfather comes to the bakery."

Marco nodded and then leaned in and kissed me. The passion his kiss held was epic. We both knew the consequences of revealing ourselves to people in the past. Anna's bright face flashed in my vision as Marco hailed a taxi.

*O*ur cab pulled up at Eden. The club was attached to a hotel, and a long line of people stood against an adjacent wall, waiting for the giant bouncer to grant them entrance through the velvet ropes. Prostitutes strutted up and down the boulevard, displaying their goods for sale and bending into car windows to speak to interested clients.

As we exited the cab, a thin brunette in a sequined dress brushed up against Marco, licked her lips, and said something to him in German. He smiled and replied, shaking his head. The girl frowned and moved on.

"What did she say?" I asked.

"She told me what she would like to do to me."

"What does she want to do?"

"Let's just say she got my attention." A wide smile spread across his face.

Marco took his fifty deutsche mark and passed it to the bouncer. The guy removed the rope, granting us entrance, along with groans from the currently waiting guests. We pushed through a set of double doors, and I stopped short in the entranceway to give my eyes a second to adjust to the dim lighting.

The place was packed. Coughing from the thick cigarette smoke that hung in the air, Marco grabbed my hand, and we squeezed through the crowd. People were everywhere with a cigarette in one hand and a drink in the other. Girls were dancing in cages and gyrating around poles connected to various platforms scattered throughout the club. Marco and I shoved our way to the nearest bar. A guy on my left was snorting a line of cocaine off a dancer's breast, and the girl on my right was making eyes at Marco.

The music was loud, and scantily clad women walked around, carrying trays of drinks. A couple in the corner was getting busy, and I stood with my mouth hanging open as I watched them go at it. Marco pulled me in next to him.

"Stay close," he said in my ear. "The bars in Berlin are very different from American bars."

I was shocked. This was 1965. I'd expected Ward and June Cleaver to be foxtrotting on the dance floor. Marco was asking one of the bartenders if he knew Isla. Based on the head shaking and grim expression, it was a no.

"That's strange," I told Marco. "I read about the club, and one of its go-go girls was named Isla. I was certain it was her."

"The bartender normally knows everyone who works in the club."

"Maybe she is newly hired," I said hopefully.

"Maybe." Marco shrugged but didn't look as hopeful.

"I need to use the bathroom," I said, and Marco pointed me to a restroom. I passed by well-dressed couples sitting at small, round tables. Most of the men were wearing suits and ties, and all the women had on dresses. It was a bygone era, one that demanded paying respect to your elders, washing behind your ears, and saying a prayer each night at bedtime.

On my way to the restroom, a man resembling one of the Beatles came out of the men's restroom. My inner voice, who had been unusually quiet, was standing on her tiptoes to get a better look.

The bathroom was floor-to-ceiling black-marble tile with sinks attached to the wall on my left and a row of toilet stalls on the right. A few women were at the mirrors, patting their noses with makeup. I ducked quickly into a stall—no need for conversation, since I didn't speak the language.

As I stood at the sink washing my hands, I felt a presence breathing down my neck. I glanced in the mirror and jumped about three feet when I saw Toches staring back at me. His nose had a bandage across it and traces of bruising blackened the areas under his eyes.

I spun around. "Toecheese, what are you doing here?"

"We came for the key," he spat. "I stole it, and it should be mine."

He pulled at the crotch of his suit, as if maybe the high-waisted material didn't allow enough room for his manhood. His scrawny neck was minus a tie and a key, and that only meant one thing. Mahlia was here with him. She was the only transporter dumb enough to bring him after us.

"Where is Mahlia?"

An evil grin snaked across his face. "She's taking care of the blond god. Good choice for a partner. He's much easier to take out of commission than the Scot."

He was wrong. Marco could handle himself. Toches was blocking my exit. For such a crowded nightclub, the restroom was eerily empty. He caught me glancing at the door and moved in closer. His foul breath had me turning my head to the side.

"Sorry, there's an out-of-order sign on this one."

"How did you find us?"

"Do you think the WTF is the only one with a travel tracker? We might not be able to see you in the present, but once you make the jump, you're free game."

That was a relief. At least they didn't know about Gitmo.

"Now where did you hide my Sleigh key?" He reached a bony finger toward my jacket, and I batted it away, knocking my hat off in the process.

"Toecheese, I don't have the key," I lied.

"Quit calling me that," he snarled. "It's not how you say my name."

I thought about running. He noticed me checking for an escape route and pinned me to the sink.

"I'm going to strip you naked, check all the hiding places, knock you unconscious, and strap you to the toilet with electrical wire I found in the janitor's closet. You and lover boy will miss your return. Oh, they will probably send a rescue party the next moon cycle, but we will be long gone with the Sleigh key by then." He gave a cackle that would have made the Wicked Witch proud.

A spool of electrical wire was on the floor by the door. Toches *had* raided the janitor's closet. Where was my knight in shining armor? My inner voice began singing my mantra. She was right; it was up to me.

Toches pinned my shoulders with his hands, so I rammed my knee as hard as possible into his groin. His face contorted. He made a high-pitched squeal and grabbed his nuts. As he leaned forward, I karate chopped him with my palm to his nose. He flew backward with one hand on his crotch and the other on his nose. As he hit the floor, his head smacked against the marble tile, and he lay lifeless, blood oozing between his fingers. I bent down and felt the pulse at his neck. Good, he was still alive. If I killed a brigand by accident, did I die as well? I should probably get an answer to that for future reference.

I pulled the square knot tight to secure Toches to the toilet base. Then I bent over and picked up my hat from the floor, placing it neatly on my head. *Now let's see who gets left behind.*

Chapter 15

The confrontation with Toches, combined with the loud music and stale air, had me hustling back to Marco. After fighting my way through the masses, I finally reached the bar…only there was no Marco.

I stood on the barstool, searching the throngs of people gyrating like Elvis Presley for any sign of him. No Marco and no Mahlia. A few guys started waving bills at me, so I got down.

I was alone in Germany, and my inner voice was pushing the button for English is my first language. I secured my feet in the rungs of the stool and leaned into the bar, waving my hands to get the attention of one of the bartenders. What were the German words for *man* and *blond*? My inner voice was thumbing through her German dictionary but dropped it in her lap when one of the bartenders came over. He was tall, with dark hair slicked back like Keanu Reeves in *John Wick*. His white oxford was open a few buttons, revealing a patch of sexy chest hair. Standing in front of me and drying a glass, he looked me up and down and asked, "Wilst du hast ein Bier?"

"Nein, ein heir, um…man, blond?" I stuttered the words, held my hands up high to indicate a tall man, and pointed to my hair.

The man cocked an eyebrow at me. I sighed and tried again. "Tall, blond man…*schwarze Jacke?*"

"Your friend left here with a woman with long legs and long hair."

"You speak English?" I sat down on the barstool.

"Yes," he said. His accent was thick and rich. Any other time, I would have sat at the bar and listened to the purr of his sentence structure.

"Where did they go?"

"The lady put something in his drink and then helped him outside." He nodded in the direction of the exit.

"And you just let her dump drugs in his drink?" I was astonished.

"Hey, none of my business. Kinky things go on here." He paused for a second. "I get off in half an hour—you interested?" My inner voice was bobbing her head up and down and yelling, "Ja! Ja!"

A commotion broke out in the direction of the restrooms. I was saved by the distraction—the bartender focused on the ruckus—and I disappeared. The red exit sign was the navigational beacon in my sea of cigarette smoke and sweat. I cut through the mass of people with only a few minor ass grabs. As I exited, the cold wind whipped at my warm face. I grabbed at my hat, holding it on with one hand, and frantically searched for Marco.

A group of prostitutes were gathered around something lying on the sidewalk adjacent to the club. I approached the women, hoping one of them might have seen Marco or Mahlia. Peering around the group of spectators, I saw Marco out cold on the pavement. His pockets were turned out, and his jacket was crumpled up next to him. A large woman with hair styled like Diana Ross's in her Supremes era, fishnets, and a micro miniskirt about three sizes too small was kneeling next to him, checking his pulse. People were stepping over his legs on the way inside the club.

I shooed the onlookers away and bent down until I was face-to-face with the woman.

"Go away," I said, speaking loudly and motioning to her.

She sat back on her haunches. "Sugar, you don't tell Denise what to do. Nobody tells Denise what to do—except Denise."

"You speak English?" I said more than asked.

"Yes, honey, I'm from Jersey. Your friend here," she said, pointing at Marco. "He's been given one of them night crawlers."

"What's that?"

"It's a drug men put in the drinks of women they want to get friendly with. Looks like the tables got turned on this one. He walked out leaning on a skinny woman, and then he went down, and she couldn't get him up. That's what happens when you got no meat on your bones. You ain't got no muscle to do the heavy lifting."

"Is he going to be OK?" I asked, keeping an eye out for the brigands.

"Oh, sure. It don't last long."

"How long is he going to be unconscious?"

"Hard to tell." She put a finger to her chin and tapped as if she was doing a complicated mathematical equation. "He's pretty big, so the drug won't last as long on him. He might wake up real soon."

"I need to get him off the street." I wasn't sure whether I could move him by myself or where to move him to.

"Leave that to Denise." She grabbed Marco under one arm, and I did the same, except she lifted him off the ground as though he was a rag doll. Denise was tall and broad. If women could play in the NFL, Denise would be a first-round draft pick. We managed to walk/drag him through a side door of the Hollywood Hotel. Framed photos of Hollywood's Rat Pack graced the walls. An antique phone booth held court in the side lobby, and my heartstrings strummed a note for Caiyan. He had traveled in a bright red British-style phone booth before he gave it away for me. Reminding myself I was in 1965, I decided it probably wasn't so much an antique as I'd first thought. Giant artificial ferns and red velvet-upholstered chairs were the décor of choice as we shuffled through the foyer.

Hiding behind a tall statue of a polar bear, we waited until the desk clerk found something more interesting in the back office. We pulled Marco through a door off the main foyer. I turned to find myself in a huge media room. Rows of movie-theater chairs sat facing a large movie screen. The screen was framed by heavy red-velvet curtains, and small lights lined the center aisle, providing a runway for moviegoers to locate their seats. The lights also illuminated the room with a comforting glow, hiding the inhabitants in shadows from a casual observer.

"This room is used for the movie screenings, but at this hour, no-body uses it but me and my business partners," Denise said, casually fanning her arm out as if she were a tour guide.

I cocked an eyebrow at her.

"Sometimes we get a john who can't afford the hotel room, so we come in here for a—"

"All right then," I said, cutting her off before I had to listen to the details of her job duties.

"A girl's got to make a living." She said matter-of-factly.

We stretched Marco out on the floor, and I sat down and cradled his head in my lap.

"Do you speak German?" I asked Denise.

"Yes, my pops was German. We moved back to Berlin after my mom died a few years ago. He died last year, and I don't have nobody else here."

"I'm sorry," I said to her.

She slumped down into a nearby chair, pulled off her high-heel shoes, and rubbed her stocking foot. "Feels good to be out of those heels."

"Have you ever thought about another line of work?" I asked.

She looked off in the distance. "I'm saving my money to go to nurs-ing school. My cousin lives back in Jersey. She said I could come stay with her if I could pay some rent."

"I bet it costs a lot of money to travel to America and go to school."

"Sure does, and it's hard to get into nursing school when you're a black woman and the only thing you can put on your application un-der employment is prostitute." She sighed, and Marco made a groan-ing noise.

"He's a nice-looking man. You two married?"

"No, just friends." I ran my fingers through his blond hair, and he smiled. "We're looking for a friend named Isla who works at the Eden club."

Denise adjusted the gold bangles on her arms. "I know everyone who works on the inside, and I don't know an Isla."

Something was wrong with our intel. Isla should have been at this club. I explained about the two people chasing us, skipping the twenty-first-century details.

"You two gonna be all right? I got to get back to work." She put her shoes back on and started toward the door.

"Denise," I said, removing Marco's watch and holding it up at her. "For your nursing school."

"I can't accept this," she said, her voice squeaking up a few octaves. She leaned down to get a better look at the watch. "It's a Patek."

"It's OK. He can't take it where we're going. Thanks for your help."

Denise took the watch and admired it as she buckled it to her wrist. "If you're going to East Berlin, you should rethink that idea. It's not safe. I've had friends go visit their families and never return. And don't even think about sneaking over that wall. You'll get shot."

"Don't worry; we're traveling out of the country." *Hopefully.*

Marco started coming to as I ran the backs of my fingers across his cheek.

"Looks like your boyfriend is waking up. Good luck." She put her hand on the doorknob and then paused. "I think I'll knock off early tonight. I've got some packing to do."

We smiled at each other, and she closed the door gently behind her.

"What happened?" Marco asked, trying to focus on me in the dimly lit room.

"Mahlia and Toecheese have come to collect the Sleigh key."

He jerked upright.

"Don't worry; they didn't get it." I reached into my jacket pocket to show him it was safe and sound.

He let out a long breath and rubbed his eyes.

"I should have known better. I didn't see her. The bartender gave me a scotch straight up and told me it was from a beautiful woman."

"So you drank it, Alice?"

"Yes, and I have a headache from falling down the rabbit hole."

"At least I saved you before you could eat the cake."

"You're funny. I'm going to miss your sense of humor when I evaporate."

"Don't say that." A pinch of frantic caused my voice to waver.

"How did you get me in here?"

"I had help from one of the girls, um…doing business outside the club."

"You mean one of the hookers?"

"Yes, her name's Denise, and she's from Jersey, so we got along great."

He chuckled and shook his head. "Only you, Jennifer Cloud, would find a hooker from Jersey in the middle of Berlin in 1965. Help me stand." He put an arm around my neck and pushed up from the ground. I pulled, and he came in close to me. It was the first time we didn't send up smoke signals when we touched. His machismo was numbed by the fear of losing his lifeline, and I was beginning to worry we would never find Isla. My hat had fallen cockeyed on my head, and he reached up to straighten it.

"Jen, where is my watch?" he asked, showing me his naked wrist.

"I gave it to Denise for helping us."

"Do you realize that particular Patek Philippe watch was one of only four in the world and sold for millions at an auction house last year?"

"Gosh, look at the time. We need to get going."

"I'd look at the time, but I don't have my watch," Marco grumbled.

I leaned Marco against the wall for balance and then stuck my head out the door to see if the coast was clear. There was no sign of Mahlia or her evil henchman. I led Marco into the hall and out of the hotel. He was almost walking by himself, but his feet were slightly rubbery. He pointed to a taxi.

"What about Isla?"

"She's not here," Marco said. He had a look of desperation in his eyes. "No one has ever heard of her. I asked the club's manager."

"Yeah, Denise hasn't heard of her either. What are we going to do?"

"We don't have much time. The sun's coming up. Let's go to the bakery. You can wait for my grandfather while I go find that damn painting."

I couldn't take him back to Gitmo without finding Isla. There must be another way. My inner voice put on her thinking cap, and I helped Marco to the taxi stand. Denise was having an argument with a man outside the club. I assumed this was her pimp, but it looked like she had things under control. She gave me a thumbs-up, and Marco frowned at her watch-adorned wrist.

Behind her, I saw Mahlia exit the club with a wounded Toches holding an ice pack to his nose.

"There they are!" Toches shouted as Marco and I got into a cab. They hurried toward the taxi, and Denise stuck out a long leg. Toches fell flat on his face, halting their forward progress and taking the pimp down with him. Mahlia missed us by a split second. I shot her the finger out the back window of the cab as we pulled away from the curb.

〜

"What are we going to do now?" I asked Marco after he paid the driver. We stood staring at the bakery. It was the corner shop of a four-story building. The American checkpoint into East Berlin was to our left. Two guards were patrolling the tollbooth-like secured crossing area into the Communist half of Berlin.

There was a closed sign on the bakery, though the appearance of a few early risers sitting outside in the warm glow of the morning sun had me guessing it would open soon. Berlin was coming to life, and Marco's life was in the final countdown if we didn't find Isla. We sat down on a park bench that backed up to the bakery wall.

"I don't have much time left," Marco said, staring down at his hands as if they might start disappearing at any moment. "This is the last day of the moon cycle. I need to go get that painting."

"Jake said not—"

"I don't give a damn what Jake said," Marco interrupted. "You lateral traveled in the past and lived to tell about it." He ran a hand through his hair.

"I also had Caiyan riding with me." I bit my bottom lip. Jake *had* told us not to lateral travel, but Marco was right. We didn't have Isla, and without her, Marco wouldn't be born. We needed to get the painting and show it to every man who entered the bakery today. We weren't supposed to make contact with Marco's grandfather, but I didn't see how we had much choice.

"OK, we both go," I said.

"No way. I'm not putting you in danger." He stood with his hands on his hips and feet spread apart as though we were about to have a gunslinging showdown.

I stood too, staring straight into his blue eyes with determination. A man sitting at a table nearby stopped reading his morning paper to watch the spectacle we were making.

"I can't let you go," Marco said.

"Why not?" I asked. "You have a better chance of recognizing your own grandfather. If he shows up, you can simply give him the key, and he can help you find Isla."

"You're not going, and that's final." He crossed his arms over his chest.

I raised my finger and pointed it at his face. I was about to list all the reasons I was going when I caught a familiar figure out of the corner of my eye. My mouth gaped, and I slowly placed my hand on Marco's arm. He turned to see what had drawn my attention. Crossing the street was an elderly woman. Her head was wrapped in a wool scarf, and she walked with a cane. She kept her head down against the brisk morning breeze, and her eyes focused on each step she took as if she would lose her balance otherwise. We watched her walk up to the bakery door and turn the knob. After she entered, she flipped the closed sign to open.

"Was that who I think it was?" Marco asked, turning his back to the bakery.

"I think that was Anna," I said. The woman could have been anyone, but there was something distinctive about the way she moved.

"Come on," I said, grabbing his hand and pulling him behind me.

We walked into the bakery, and a small bell let out a tinkle, informing the owner of our arrival. The smell of freshly ground coffee and baked bread made my stomach rumble. The glass pastry case was filled with sweet treats ready to serve the early morning customers.

The elderly woman we thought was Anna was nowhere to be seen. I glanced at Marco, wondering if we had enough money to order a cinnamon roll. We should at least eat while we waited for the older woman to return.

A tall woman had her back to us, working dough on a marble counter. She shouted something in German that I assumed meant she would help us in a moment.

A few tables and chairs were spread neatly around the room. Checkered tablecloths set with tiny vases holding arrangements of spring flowers covered the tables, giving the bakery a pleasant atmosphere.

Black-and-white photos were framed on the wall to the right of the pastry case. The bakery's grand-opening photo was centered, showing two women standing out in front of the bakery. I squinted at the women, but I couldn't tell if either of them was Anna or Isla. There were a few pictures of patrons eating something yummy and a few photos of the war. I gasped when I came to one of the war photos. Marco leaned in behind me.

"I'll be damned! I can't believe it," Marco said, a wide grin spreading across his face. "That sneaky son of a bitch."

The photo showed a city destroyed by war. Piles of rubble surrounded partially standing buildings, and in the center of the photo was Caiyan carrying Anna from the remnants of the smoke-filled bakery she once had owned. Isla trailed behind her. My eyes filled up, and a few tears escaped down my cheeks.

"I wondered when you would come back," a voice said from behind us.

We turned to see a tall blond woman smiling at us.

"Isla?" I asked, wiping my face.

"Ya." She came forward, wrapping Marco and me in a deep embrace.

"It is so wonderful to see both of you again," Isla said.

"Your English has improved," Marco said, and we all laughed.

"Caiyan rescued both of you?" I asked.

She nodded. "The bomb dropped, and meine Oma was caught upstairs. The building fell down in flames around her. I got out through the basement window with the bakery staff, but I couldn't move the heavy debris to save her. I said a prayer, and like an angel, he appeared from nowhere. He moved the rubble and pulled her free from the wreckage."

A small tear leaked from my eye, and I wiped it away with my finger.

Isla reached up and touched the photo. "That pesky photographer was back snapping photos of the victims. I was angry at the time, but after the war, I hunted him down, and he gave me the photo of our hero."

"Only my leg was damaged." Anna was standing on the threshold of the adjoining room, holding a bouquet of flowers in one hand and balancing on her cane with the other.

I quickly crossed the room and hugged her tightly. Marco was on my heels.

"What brings you back?" Isla asked.

"My grandfather is going to visit your bakery, and I need you to give him the Sleigh key." As Marco said the words, I pulled the key from my jacket pocket.

Anna gasped. "You saved it from Hitler?"

"He wasn't the real Adolf Hitler," I said. "Only an impersonator to do Hitler's bidding at the end of the war."

Anna and Isla both stared in awe at the information.

"Yes, I don't know how you will recognize my grandfather." A crease formed between Marco's brows. "Before we traveled to 1945, he discovered the key, because you had the painting of your mother hanging in the bakery. And now the painting is buried in East Berlin."

Isla and Anna looked at each other, and Isla laughed. She put both hands on Marco's shoulders and spun him around. On the front wall of the bakery was an enormous rendition of the painting. Anyone leaving the building would see it on the way out.

"I do not think your grandfather will miss the painting," Anna said, chuckling. "Come—we should have tea, or would you Americans like coffee?"

We sat at one of the tables. Isla went behind the counter to help the guests, and Anna told us about life after the war. She explained how Caiyan had given her a priceless painting wrapped in an expensive tapestry along with the portrait of her mother.

"After the war, it took a while for Berlin to get back on her feet." Anna sighed. "My husband returned from war, but he was wounded and couldn't go back to his job. The money I made selling the tapestry paid for Isla's schooling, and I returned the painting to the museum. They gave me a stipend to open the two bakeries in Berlin. My husband, God rest his soul, insisted I buy this shop, because it was in the American sector of Berlin, and he knew the young American soldiers loved the sweet breads."

"Lucky for us, we were here when the wall went up," Isla said. She placed a plate of croissants in front of me and then returned to help a customer. I sipped my coffee and tried hard not to scarf down all the buttery pastries. They were delicious.

Anna asked about Caiyan, and I explained he was on another assignment. Technically, he was assigned to stay home, but from the looks of it, he wasn't obeying orders. Thank God.

I listened while Marco described his grandfather to Anna and explained how important it was for Isla to meet Henri. Anna put her hands together, clearly excited that Isla might finally meet a man and have children. I gave Marco a nudge, because he wasn't supposed to screw with destiny, but I guess even fate needs an occasional hip bump in the right direction.

We stood to go, and Anna kissed both of our cheeks. Isla came from around the pastry case and hugged both of us. "Just answer one question before you leave," she said, glancing out the window. "Does this horrible wall ever come down?"

"Yes," I said, "and Berlin turns into a beautiful united city."

Anna and Isla hugged each other as Marco and I left the bakery with smiles too big to contain.

Marco and I walked silently toward the Tiergarten. The morning light revealed that the city of Berlin was still struggling to recover from a war that had happened twenty years earlier. Most of the buildings were occupied but showed damage to the rooftops and sides, while others stood empty of the life that formerly filled them, waiting patiently for love and attention.

We passed a platform, and I took the stairs two at a time to see over the wall. East Berlin showed more signs of the war. The people moving about wore black and gray. It was almost like looking at a black-and-white photograph. The windows of the buildings were bricked up, as if looking over into West Berlin was a crime. A small child waved in my direction, and I waved back.

"It's sad the way families are separated," I said, climbing down from the platform.

We followed the wall back to the spot where we'd landed. The bier-garten was closed, and the happy, singing Germans were all at home sleeping off last night's consumption. I scouted the tree line for any sign of Mahlia or Toches.

"I think they gave up," Marco said, watching me canvass the area.

"I want to be sure before I call my vessel. There are so many trees—how can we be sure Toches isn't hiding behind one waiting to spring out and get a gander at my vessel?"

"Did you see the poor guy?" Marco smiled down at me. "He could barely walk. What did you hit him with?"

"Knee to the groin and palm to the nose." I mimicked my signature move for Marco.

"OK, SuperJen. Remind me not to make you mad." He interlocked his fingers with mine and drew me in close. The heat that had almost extinguished came in full force and sent flames sparking through my body. He tipped my chin up with his free hand. I looked up into his blue eyes, and I wondered if I could have the same kind of feelings for Marco that I did for Caiyan.

He brushed his lips across mine and deepened the kiss. His tongue lingered—warm, sweet, sensual, and perfect. This was different from the fire-inducing, temperature-raising kisses from Marco. This…was a good-bye kiss. My heart took a troubled skip as I drew away from the embrace.

"What was that for?" I asked, searching his eyes for an answer.

"I thought I should get that now, because when we return, I don't think it will be on the table."

"What do you mean?" I cocked an eyebrow his way. We'd found Isla. She would meet Henri, and Marco would be fine.

"Jen, the look on your face when you saw the photo of Caiyan saving Anna and Isla…" He shook his head. The blond curls fell across his forehead. "I can't compete with that."

He was right. I had already forgiven Caiyan. I just needed to tell him in person. But my head told me Marco might be the better choice, and I was missing an opportunity for happiness.

"Maybe we should try—"

"I don't like to finish second." He put both hands on my shoulders. "I'm scratching myself from this race until the track clears and gives me a more solid path."

"What about my debt?"

He smiled and dropped his hands from my shoulders. "Go find Caiyan and see if he turns into your Prince Charming. If he doesn't, I'll collect on what's due."

"Do you think he will be at Gitmo?" I asked.

"Only one way to find out." Marco put his hand to his key and called his vessel.

"You're not riding with me?" I asked as the red Indie race car appeared in the clearing in front of me.

"If I go directly to the WTF, Jake will expect me to follow orders all the time."

"You're supposed to return for debriefing when we complete a mission," I said, reminding him of the WTF rules.

"You can tell Jake I'll get around to it. First, I'm going to Italy to see my mother. She's at our house in Capri, and after this experience, I think a nice, long vacation is well earned."

"So…I'll see you next moon cycle?"

"Until then."

I called my outhouse, and we boarded at the same time. I was curious about the consequences of Caiyan stealing the Thunder key. Would the WTF allow him to keep it and regain his position as my defender? I gave Marco a small finger wave as my inner voice sat on the sofa, drowning her sorrows in a tub of Blue Bell ice cream over what might have been.

Chapter 16

*M*y outhouse landed smoothly with Marco's kiss lingering on my lips. My inner voice was holding up a sign that read *Team Marco*, but my heart yearned to replace Marco's gentle kiss with Caiyan's passionate one. I bounded from the platform, stumbling over my own feet. Jake caught me before I took a swan dive to the cement floor.

"Whoa," Jake said, pulling me to my feet. "What's the rush?"

"I need to find Caiyan," I said, breathless from my almost fall. I re-adjusted the strap on my sundress and found my balance. An account of the events of Berlin, round two, began spilling out of my mouth like water from a busted fire hydrant.

"We know," Jake said, interrupting my monologue.

"You know?"

"Yes, after you left, things started changing. Newspaper clippings about the bakeries owned by Isla and Anna appeared. I was worried you had disobeyed orders and gone to East Berlin. Caiyan stopped by and gave us the rundown."

"He did?" I couldn't help but smile, and Jake's face tightened.

"He did. He also tried to return the Thunder, but I told him to keep it."

"You did?"

"I did." Jake's strong jawline broke into a wide smile. "We need him. It took balls to go back and save Anna. There was a strong possibility he would cross over the fabric of time, and like the saying goes, you can't be in two places at once."

I nodded. If the bomb had dropped on Anna's bakery before we left Berlin, Caiyan would have died the moment he time traveled to 1945. I took a deep breath and let it out slowly, releasing all the pent-up frustration and worry I had been holding inside.

"I'm glad things worked out," Jake said. "I would hate to lose Marco."

Me too. But as the saying goes, you can't be in two places at once.

"Should I expect Marco anytime soon?" Jake stared at the empty landing pad, a glint of supposition in his eyes.

I shook my head. "He had an errand to run."

"I figured as much," Jake said. "I guess things will get back to normal now that Caiyan is back."

"Do you mean he can be my defender?"

Jake nodded. "I may not like it, but the brigands need someone who thinks like they do chasing their tail. We'll see if the two of you can work together."

"What about Marco?"

"I'm working on that one, and you might have to pull double duty until we find more recruits."

"Aye, aye, captain." I saluted Jake, and he frowned. I started to head toward the blue room.

"He's not here."

"Where is he?"

"I don't know, but you need to get back to Melissa Jo's wedding." Jake tapped his watch. "You've been gone about two hours. The reception should be going strong, and I need you back before people start wondering what happened to you."

The wedding—I had almost forgotten. I started toward my vessel. My heart would have to wait until after Melissa Jo rode off into the night with her Prince Charming—or in Melissa Jo's case, Emperor Charming.

I glanced back at Jake. He had his thumb hanging loosely from his pants pocket, watching me walk away with the same expression he'd had when we stopped being lovers and became "just friends."

"You know, I still need a plus-one. Do you want to come with me?"

"Mamma Bea does make a mean moonshine lemonade." He smiled, and his dimples winked back at me. "My paperwork can wait. Plus every guest was in possession of a concealed weapon, so someone with authority should probably be present."

"Absolutely." I laughed, and we boarded my vessel. I hoped the party was still going strong. After everything I had been through, a good stiff drink and a spin on the dance floor would be more beneficial than a week with a shrink.

The next sound I heard was Emperor KW Smooth Dog singing his karaoke rendition of the hip-hop song "Get Low."

"Holy shit!" I looked over at Jake, and he laughed a deep, gut-wrenching laugh I hadn't heard in a long time.

"You'd better get over there before your mom hears the word *fuck*. She'll ground the entire wedding party."

We cut through the woods and entered the barn through a side door. A bead of sweat threatened my upper lip as I envisioned my mom, mouth hanging open in horror at the crude lyrics of the offensive song. Instead, my mom and dad were bopping up and down on the dance floor.

I stopped dead in my tracks, and Jake almost ran into me. I glanced around the room. Gertie was dirty dancing with Brodie on the dance floor, and I was shocked at the way he moved. Not bad for a skinny white guy. Smooth Dog was up on stage with his new bride, rapping out the lyrics, and the entire family seemed to be having a good time.

Jake wrapped an arm around my shoulders. "Looks like you made it in time."

We stood on the edge of the dance floor watching the fun. The DJ commandeered the microphone, and "Boogie Fever" came over the speakers. Jake was hijacked by my aunt Mabel. She pulled him on the dance floor, and all three of her chins were flapping as they gyrated together.

Eli handed me a mason jar of moonshine lemonade with the happy couple's names hand painted on it in curly letters. We clinked glasses in a toast. "Crazy weekend, huh, Jen?"

"That pretty much sums it up," I said, taking a sip of the drink. The smooth liquid burned all the way down to my toes, and I put a hand to my chest. "Wow, that's a really good batch," I managed to squeak.

Eli put an arm around me. I rested my head on his shoulder and tried to forget the people I'd met in 1945 who lost their lives in World War II and the brigands we chased to these dangerous places.

"Where y'all been?" Gertie came up behind Eli, grabbed his moonshine, and took a long drink from the mason jar.

"We had a little WTF matter to clear up," I said. Eli cut his eyes at me.

"Gertie knows?" he asked, and both looked shocked the other knew about the WTF.

"I thought it was a secret?" Gertie asked, her bottom lip forming a pout.

I explained to Gertie how I'd had to tell Eli about the WTF, because the Mafusos had taken him hostage in exchange for a key. I left out the part about discovering his ability to time travel.

"Do you have the gift?" Eli asked Gertie.

"No," I answered for her. "She found out by accidentally jumping in my vessel and going back in time."

"Yeah, and let me tell you a thing, Eli Cloud." Gertie stood on her tiptoes and stared Eli right in the eyes. "You *do not* want to be part of that. If Jen ever asks you to go back in time, tell her to forget it. People shoot at you."

Eli downed the rest of his moonshine, and a few glasses later, I was feeling pretty good.

Melissa Jo was up on the stage, and the customary tossing of the bride's bouquet was announced. Beyoncé's song "Single Ladies" began to play. Gertie yanked my arm, and before I realized what had happened, I was standing in the center of the dance floor holding the bouquet.

"Dang, I thought I would catch that," Gertie said.

Brodie stood behind her, pretending to dodge a bullet and mouthing, "Thank you" in my direction.

I stood for a moment as the lights dimmed, and Brodie gathered Gertie in his arms for a slow dance. Brodie might not be ready for marriage, but I had a good feeling about the two of them. I felt a tap on my shoulder. "Ye cannae catch the bridal bouquet and naugh have a dance."

I turned to see Caiyan standing behind me in his black tuxedo jacket and black jeans, slightly torn. My heart rate tripled, and I think I nodded.

He held his hand out to me, and I placed my palm in his. He wrapped his arm around my waist, and we started to sway slightly. His green eyes cut deep into mine. "I missed ye, lassie."

I melted at his words. I could forgive Caiyan, but I wasn't sure I could forget so easily.

"You went back," I said as he pulled me in tight and nuzzled my neck.

"Aye, I had to go back. The *Tollatsch* was excellent."

I stopped dancing and tipped my eyes to meet his. "You could have died."

"But I didnae." He started moving again, and I was lost in the music and the comfort of Caiyan's arms.

"You lied to me," I said.

"Aye, I'm sorry."

I was divided like Berlin. Part of me wanted to trust Caiyan again, and the other part felt safe behind the wall. My life wouldn't be as exciting, and I would miss the sex, but could I risk my life and my heart doing this job? If Caiyan was back at the WTF, we would be traveling together. Me in my outhouse and him in—I had no clue. *What was he traveling in?*

"How did you get Toches to reveal his vessel to you?"

"I have run into Toches more than once in my lifetime, and I know what he drives, but I dinnae know his key was the Thunder. It would have saved us a lot of time if we'd known."

"What will happen now that Toches doesn't have a key?"

"He will most likely join the Mafusos and continue to cause problems for the WTF."

Another brigand on the loose. Jake's words rang in my head. *We need him.*

"It seems I have a new defender."

"Indeed." He paused, and his eyes twinkled under the rotating disco ball. "I heard he's more refined than the last guy."

"How will I know if I can trust him?" I asked as we coasted around the dance floor to a Miranda Lambert favorite. It was a song she'd written about her life and the end of her marriage.

The song felt bruised—slow and sensuous—not unlike the way my heart felt at the moment.

"Ye will need to have faith."

"Maybe he should take a vow of trust."

"Vows—now there's something scary."

"Why, Mr. McGregor, I had no idea you were afraid of those two little words the bride and groom exchange, committing them to a lifetime with each other."

"I dinnae say that. Maybe if the right girl were to forgive me for telling a small tale, I might consider the option of spending eternity with her."

"I don't know. My trust-o-meter is sort of screwed up at the moment. I'm not sure I could commit to those two little words either. Maybe if the right guy continued to show me he was trustworthy."

"How aboot something to seal the deal? Like a treaty."

"Signed in blood?" I asked as he dipped me in rhythm with the music.

He brought me in close again and slipped something on my finger. It was the ruby ring he'd taken from the Flaktürme. The ring sparkled on my right hand, and I raised a questioning eyebrow in his direction.

"A ring of trust, because ye look stunning in red. And it's a ruby, so ye can always find yer way home."

The *Wizard of Oz* reference had me holding back tears. "You took the ring for me?"

"I did." He moved me around the dance floor, and I felt like Ginger Rogers on the arm of Fred Astaire. "Do ye forgive me for not being entirely truthful?"

"I do."

Epilogue

I stepped out of my vessel into the warm May sunshine. Spring was blowing good-bye kisses in the form of dandelion seedpods floating through the air.

As I walked to Aint Elma's house, I bent down and pulled a dandelion puff from the ground, blowing its cottony wisps from the stem as I had as a child. I wondered if we were always going to call the little white house tucked back in the woods of Mount Vernon Aint Elma's house.

Mamma Bea had sent an invitation to come see her—no excuses. When Mamma Bea sent a handwritten invitation via snail mail, you went.

I entered the backyard through the gate and glanced at the barn, where only a few weeks ago, Melissa Jo had been married and Caiyan had slipped a ring on my finger. It hadn't been an engagement ring but a promise to be truthful. No more secrets. It was a step in the right direction.

Mamma Bea was sitting in a rocking chair on the back porch.

"Howdy, child. Come sit down with me," Mamma Bea said as she stood and wrapped her arms around me. The scent of White Shoulders perfume added to the smell of flowering buds, and the fresh breeze had me sitting back and relaxing. I was about to ask why she'd sent for me when Eli came out of the house.

"Good. Now you're both here," she said. She hugged Eli and insisted on getting us some refreshments.

"Did she send for you too?" I asked after the screen door had closed behind Mamma Bea.

"Handwritten." Eli smiled and turned to let out a loud *achoo.* "Sorry—allergies," he said, wiping his nose with a tissue. "Do you know what this is about?"

"No," I answered truthfully, but I had an idea. Our gun-toting grandma had been hiding secrets for years, and I was guessing she had one she couldn't keep any longer.

Mamma Bea returned with a tray containing a jug of sweet tea and three glasses filled with ice. She poured Eli and me each a glass, filled her own, and sat down. She took a small sip and cleared her throat. "Both of you have the gift of time travel."

"Yeah, and so far, it's gotten me seduced, kidnapped, pestered by the WTF to become a secret agent, and brought down here on my day off." Eli shook his head as if he needed to pinch himself to know it was all real.

The WTF had sent Jake to try and recruit Eli. Jake needed more travelers, but he wasn't too keen on enlisting another of his childhood friends, and Eli didn't make it any easier. His gift revolved around healing, and he enjoyed his work as a chiropractor. He didn't think chasing bad guys around during the full moon went with his code of ethics. It would take him away from his patients, and that was a deal breaker.

"I just don't get what all this is about," Eli said.

"It's in your blood." Mamma Bea put her glass down and gathered Eli's hand in her own.

"All this time, and I didn't know you knew," I said.

"It's a long story, dawrlin'. One day I'll tell you everything, but for right now, you only need to know your pawpaw John was a traveler and did a lot of good. He helped keep the world safe, but he didn't want his grandchildren to travel."

Eli looked as surprised as I felt. I hadn't known my grandfather was a traveler until Mamma Bea let the cat out of the bag at the wedding.

"The problem was…it also got him killed."

"Maybe we could go back and save him," Eli said, holding tight to Mamma Bea's hand.

"No, honey. You can't go back and change what was."

"Tell me about it," I said. "Every time we go back in the past, something gets screwed up, and Jake has to pick up the pieces."

"Jennifer's right," Mamma Bea said. "It's the main reason the WTF exists. Those asshole brigands think they can go and do as they please."

"We try to stop them," I added for good measure. Mamma Bea looked over at me, and a crease formed between her brows.

"I don't like that my grandchildren are involved, and I tried to keep Elma from giving you the key. In fact, I might have told your parents a few tall tales to keep you from seeing her."

"You lied to our parents?"

"Everything was going smoothly. None of your cousins showed any signs of the gift, and Eli didn't even spark when Elma went near him."

"What do you mean 'spark'?" Eli asked.

"Elma was what they called a reader." Mamma Bea took a sip of her sweet tea.

"It means when Elma touched someone with the gift, she felt the person's emotions," I said.

"Yes, that's right." Mamma Bea seemed surprised I knew.

"I'm a reader too," I said.

"Oh, Jen." Mamma Bea teared up, and Eli handed her a pack of tissues from his pocket. "When you were nine, Elma felt the gift in you, and I knew it was going to be difficult keeping our secret. I was lucky Elma loved to travel and wasn't ready to give up her key." She sniffed and dabbed at her eyes with the tissue. "Until it was too late, and she lost her life."

"These people died *because of* the gift of time travel?" Eli asked.

"That's right, and I'm asking both of you not to do it. Don't travel. Don't chase the brigands."

I was torn. I wanted to do what Mamma Bea asked, but I couldn't. Even though my time traveling skills could use a little work, I didn't want to go back to my dull, ordinary life. I wanted adventure, I wanted to be Caiyan's transporter, and I wanted to make a difference.

"I can't," I finally said. "It's my destiny."

"I was afraid you would say that." Mamma Bea hugged me tightly.

"I know I want to help sick people get well, and I want to keep them well. I don't think I'm cut out to chase bad guys." Eli frowned. "Even if I could travel, I don't have the equipment."

Eli didn't have a vessel or a key. The WTF had Mitchell's key, but we didn't have the vessel.

"That's not entirely true," Mamma Bea said, and she stood and went into the house. Eli and I looked at each other and shrugged, not sure if we should follow her.

We met her in the small den. The scent of vanilla wafted over from a candle burning on her breakfront. She returned with a Macy's shopping bag that looked like it contained a shoe box.

"Shoes?" I asked. I could feel my inner voice getting excited over our favorite word.

"No, dawrlin'," she said and pulled a mahogany box from the wrappings. "I've been keeping this for Eli. Elma thought he might have the gift, but I couldn't let her drag him into that world. The wounds were too fresh." She opened the box and took out a key. The moonstone glowed like water reflected off a calm pool. A snowcapped mountain was engraved on the stone, with blue diamonds forming a waterfall that cascaded down the face of the mountain. Mamma Bea leaned forward and handed the key to Eli.

"It's the necklace Elma kept trying to get me to wear when I was a boy."

"Yes," Mamma Bea said. "It can be a good part of you, or it can turn you into a greedy, backstabbing son of a bitch."

I thought about the two faces of Caiyan. Sometimes he was a ruthless defender and destroyed anything in the path to his goal, and other times he was my knight in shining armor.

"I know Mahlia used her motorcycle to cart me around. How do you travel?" he asked, his blue eyes full of questions.

"Remember that outhouse Aint Elma sent me for my sixteenth birthday?"

He laughed. "You've got to be kidding."

"Well, not everyone gets a Harley. And speaking of that"—I turned to Mamma Bea—"do you know the vessel that goes with this key?"

"As a matter of fact…" She walked over to her curio cabinet, opened the glass, and produced a miniature tepee.

"It's cute, but I don't think Eli is going to fit inside," I said, peering at the tiny tepee.

"Let's go outside, and we'll just see about that." She handed the teepee to me, and a smooth flow of energy transferred from the small object into my palm. The painted wolves howling at the moon on the canvas of the tepee suddenly became familiar to me.

A recollection of Caiyan and me rescuing my key from Pancho Villa and returning it to my great-grandma Mahala Jane flashed across my mind. Her husband, my great-grandfather Jeramiah Cloud, had traveled in a tepee very much like this one.

Mamma Bea looked around as we entered the backyard, as if a brigand might jump from the shadows at any second. We followed her to the old red barn tucked back in the knotty pines—the same barn Mamma Bea had cleared out for Melissa Jo's wedding.

Mamma Bea walked to the center of the barn and stood in the huge open space that the month before had held a dance floor and fifty wedding guests. She took the tepee back from me and set it down in the center of the wood floor. She turned to Eli.

Eli secured the key around his neck, and it glowed, creating an aura around him. Mamma Bea backed away from the tepee, grabbing my arm and pulling me to the side of the room with her.

Eli didn't need any direction. He brought his hands up in the air, and a whirlwind began churning around the barn. A tiny tornado formed at the tip of the tepee, stirring up dust and glittering remnants from the wedding. The tepee began to rotate and distort until, with a loud roar not unlike a wolf's howl, it transformed into a full-size vessel right before our eyes.

"How did you do that?" I asked him.

"I don't know. I just felt a pull toward the tepee."

"So this is the Tribal key?" I asked Mamma Bea.

"Yes, it was your great-grandpa's and his grandpa's before that."

I could feel the magnificent power emanating from the vessel. It was much more potent than it had been in its small form. "It has strong power," I told them.

"I kept it hidden all these years." Mamma Bea wiped at her eyes with the tissue. I wasn't sure if it was sadness or dust that made her eyes tear. "I couldn't live with myself if Eli was killed over something he didn't know about."

"How does it work?" Eli asked, amazed at his new power.

I reached out and ran my hand over the smooth buffalo hide that formed the walls of the tepee. We entered the vessel, and I showed him the word etched on the inside of the teepee, hidden in the Ancalites' ancient script. "Normally, the defenders track and capture a brigand who has traveled to the past. I'm a transporter, so the defender will summon me to bring the bad guy, or what we call a brigand, to our headquarters to keep him from screwing up the past. Lately, I have been working as a team with my defender and traveling with him."

"Dang, I knew you were looking more buff, but I didn't know the reason behind it." He frowned. "I don't know if I want to give up my life to travel."

"It's your decision. I won't divulge that we have the Tribal key. If they find out, they will take it from you, most likely. If you decide not to travel, it's yours, but anyone with the gift can use it, and I don't want to see it used for no good."

"I'm not sure how much longer I can protect it," Mamma Bea said. "Somehow the Mafusos figured out it was here."

"That's why they wanted to meet here." I stomped my foot.

We stepped out of the tepee, and Eli made it small again. He bent down and picked it up. "I remember playing with this when I was a kid."

"Elma was always trying to sneak it to you to see if you showed any signs of having the gift."

"I remember," I said. "The time I cut off my eyelashes. Mom and Dad were so mad they wouldn't let me stay with Elma after that."

"You didn't see her again until you were nine and not again after that meeting. I'm afraid that was my fault. I was trying to protect you."

Mamma Bea pulled me into an embrace. The scent of her White Shoulders perfume made me feel safe, protected. There was no doubt if it wasn't for her I would have been traveling much earlier, and I knew I wouldn't have been ready.

"I don't know if I want to travel, but I don't want Mamma Bea to be in danger," Eli said holding the tepee out in the palm of his hand. "I'll keep them safe."

Mamma Bea and I agreed. The best place for the key was with Eli. If a brigand came after the key, he had the power to keep them at bay.

The key around his neck twinkled slightly, and I knew everything was as it should be.

Eli smiled, and his blue eyes danced as he touched his key. "Looks like I'm going to wear a necklace after all."

—The end—

About the Author

*J*anet Leigh, a B.R.A.G. Medallion Honoree, was born in Garland, Texas, and has remained a loyal Texas native her entire life. She decided to take her love of storytelling and her archive of crazy family stories and write her own novel. She published her literary debut *The Shoes Come First* in 2014. Today, she is a full-time chiropractor and acupuncturist who splits her time between seeing patients and working on her next Jennifer Cloud novel.

Leigh lives in Dallas, Texas, with her husband, three children, one mean cat, and a dog with allergies. After working all day, chauffeuring kids around, and writing at every opportunity, she enjoys relaxing with a funny romance or mystery novel. Her favorite authors are Nora Roberts, Janet Evanovich, Leigh Michaels, Diana Gabaldon, John Grisham, and for those times when she needs a good cry, Nicholas Sparks.

JOIN JANET ON FACEBOOK FACEBOOK.COM/JANETLEIGH BOOKS

Janet Leigh

FOLLOW JANET ON TWITTER   @JANETLEIGHBOOKS

VISIT JANETLEIGHBOOKS.COM
FOR UPDATES, EXCERPTS, AND ALL THAT EXTRA STUFF

In case you missed it–Other books by Janet Leigh

The Shoes Come First

Jennifer Cloud leads a fairly normal life in Sunnyside, Texas, until a birthday present from her aunt sends her to Scotland. In the year 1568.

There she meets a charming Scottish rogue who introduces her to a world of time-traveling, mysterious keys and the top-secret association that makes the rules.

But when villains who will stop at nothing to acquire every last time-traveling key for themselves abduct Jennifer, she finds herself in a race against time to retrieve her key and save herself as well as her family.

Dress 2 Impress

Newly inducted into the World Travel Federation and defender of the keys to the time-travel vessels that have helped shape history, she's assisting Caiyan McGregor in his mission to stop a Brigand from stealing the key that would allow Bonnie Prince Charlie to cross the ocean to freedom.

Thanks to lust and hormones, the pair returns to the secret WTF headquarters empty-handed, to be written up by Jake, Jennifer's boss, and former romantic partner.

Upon discovering that her rakish Scot has become stuck in 1985 Hollywood while chasing a mystery traveler, Jennifer and her cousin Gertie secure the help of sexy racecar driver Marco.

But on her madcap rescue mission, will a nasty Brigand, a famous rock star or a serial killer prevent Jennifer from figuring out which gorgeous man to let into her life?